A Thread of Life

A Thread of Life

Anoop Verma

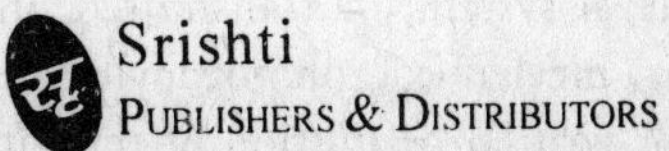

Srishti Publishers & Distributors
64-A, Adhchini
Sri Aurobindo Marg
New Delhi 110 017
srishtipublishers@yahoo.com

First published by Srishti Publishers & Distributors in 2005

ISBN 81-88575-50-X

Printed and bound in India

Typeset in AGaramond 11pt. by Suresh Kumar Sharma at Srishti

Cover design: Sandip Sinha

Printed and bound in India

to
Bombay

One

It was two o'clock when the taxi driver brought the old lady to a bungalow at Peddar Road in his black and yellow taxi. She had turned out to be one of those talkative types of passengers that he ferried every now and then. All the time she kept ranting about the taxi being hot, as if it were the taxi driver's fault that the sun was shining brightly and there was not a whiff of wind. She had a small plastic fan that she worked tirelessly in her hand. When she got down she walked unhurriedly to her house, murmuring to herself, swinging the fan lethargically. Little ahead of the house there was a dense tree, under the shade of which the taxi driver parked the taxi and began awaiting the next passenger. He switched on the two-in-one fitted on the taxi's console and a film song started.

A few meters away, under the shade of a pipal tree, a hawker was selling lemon juice from a temporary stall. When the song was over and the raucous beat of an advertisement started, the taxi driver switched off the radio and stepped out of the taxi. He sauntered to the stall and demanded a glass. A couple with three children, ages varying between four and eight, arrived at the stall at the same time. The family looked exhausted, having trekked on foot for sometime. Though dressed as Bombayites, the man in a cotton shirt and denim pant, the woman in a sari and the children in colorful dresses, they didn't appear to be locals. Their awkwardness betrayed them as small-town dwellers. From their accent the taxi driver placed them in the Hindi belt of north India. The man ordered five glasses. His children huddled close to the stall and waited in anticipation.

Presence of many customers charged up the stall-owner. He arranged six glasses and, with the dexterity of a performer, crushed a lemon in each. He added sugar, water and small chunks of ice, which he broke from an ice slab kept under a jute bag. Each glass was stirred vigorously and the beverage was ready for drinking. The taxi driver picked up one glass; the family took the other five.

'Is that your taxi?' the husband asked, looking at the taxi driver.

'Yes.'

'How far is Mahalaxmi Temple from here?'

'Not far! About one kilometer.'

'One kilometer?' the wife gasped.

'Yes,' the taxi driver nodded.

'We boarded a bus for Mahalaxmi Temple from Sion, but we missed the temple.'

'You must be new to this city?'

'We have been here for a month. It is such a hassle walking in the sun with three small kids.' He paused to wipe beads of perspiration from his forehead. 'How much will you charge to drop us outside Mahalaxmi Temple?'

'Whatever the meter says.'

'How much will that be?'

'Twenty rupees.'

The husband looked at his wife. 'He is asking too much,' she announced with a knowing air. 'I would rather walk.'

'I am not sure if the children can walk in this heat. I don't have the energy to carry them,' the husband said.

'Papa, I want to sit in a taxi,' a tot whimpered, running his tongue over a lump of ice.

'Me, too,' the second echoed.

'I will sit next to the driver,' the third declared with glee.

'You should be reasonable,' their father said to the taxi driver. 'A distance of one kilometer shouldn't cost twenty rupees. Give us some discount.'

'Petrol is costly these days. I can't afford to charge less than what the meter says.'

The man looked at his wife again and she whispered an amount. He turned back to the taxi driver. 'You should accept ten rupees from us.'.

'I usually get what the meter says. But I will accept fifteen rupees from you.'

'This city is too pricey,' the wife said irately.

'If we go on foot the kids may suffer sunstroke,' the husband sighed.

'We will have to throw money on a taxi, no other option I can see,' she said, with the look of a woman who has made up her mind about what to do, but still hates to do it.

'I will take the taxi,' her husband said.

'Okay,' the taxi driver went to his vehicle and sat behind the steering wheel. The children, swallowing whatever was left of their drink, accompanied their parents to the taxi. All three clamored to sit next to the driver and for a minute it seemed as if a quarrel was about to break out. The taxi driver solved the hitch by making all three jostle into the passenger seat beside him. The parents sat at the back.

'Uncle, start the radio,' a kid demanded.

The taxi driver turned a knob and a film song started. The kids clapped. He drove towards the Mahalaxmi Temple and reached the place in five or six minutes.

The family paid the fare and stepped out of the taxi. The lawn outside the brick-colored temple had shady trees under which there were wooden benches. Tempted by the benches, which seemed comfier than the hot taxi, the taxi driver locked his vehicle and entered the temple premises. He sat on the bench closest to the road, from where he could keep an eye on the taxi.

‡

Someone came from behind and said, 'You found a nice place to rest.'

The taxi driver turned around to find the same man whom he had brought to the temple. 'Your family is still inside the temple?'

Lowering himself on the bench, the man said, 'Yes. My wife's communions with God are a lengthy affair. She is still praying. Kids are with her. I will wait for them here.'

'Women tend to be more devout.'

'That is a fact,' the man nodded his head in agreement. 'You don't seem like a Marathi? What is your name?'

'Anirudh Shukla,' the taxi driver said.

'Are you from UP or Bihar?'

'Bihar.'

'How long have you been in Bombay?'

'About fifteen years! What about you? Are you also from Bihar?'

'No, from UP.'

'You are here as tourist?'

'I wish I could afford that luxury,' the man chuckled self-deprecatingly. 'I am here because I had a job in a textile mill.'

'You are working in a textile mill?'

'Not any longer.'

There was nothing in the man's voice to suggest that he was dejected at the loss of his job, rather, he seemed relaxed as if he didn't care whether he had a job or not. 'How did you lose your job?' he asked.

'I resigned. My wife and I are fed up of city life. We wish to return to our hometown.'

'Why?'

'People here are too selfish. They pursue their own goals without any thought for others. Everyone is in a hurry. No one has the time to bother about others or to pause and reflect,' the man said apparently giving expression to thoughts that had been gone over in the mind many times. 'Don't you get dazed by this fast life around you?'

'I am too busy driving taxi to be dazed about anything.'

'For me the town where my ancestral home is located is a better place. In two days I will board the train for UP along with my family.'

'What will you do there?'

'I will start a small business.'

Anirudh saw a fat man, clutching a briefcase, pause next to the taxi and look around impatiently. 'I have a passenger,' he said getting up.

'Okay,' his companion replied.

‡

Anirudh asked the fat man, 'Do you need a taxi?'

'Take me to Kalbadevi market.'

Anirudh sat behind the steering wheel and the passenger ensconced his portly spread on the backseat. 'I am in a hurry; drive fast,' the passenger said.

The demand made Anirudh remember what his last passenger had said. '...Everyone is in a frantic hurry. No one has the time to bother about anyone else or to pause and reflect...'

'I will do my best,' Anirudh started the taxi.

The passenger fished a mobile phone from his shirt pocket and dialed a number. 'Hello Vemichandji,' he spoke into the phone. 'How are you? I have got ten trucks of onions... onions are of the best quality... You can be assured about that... I have always valued my relationship with you. Doing business with you is a pleasure... I want to give you the first chance to bid for the onions... I am on my way to Kalbadevi...'

Listening to the phone conversation Anirudh guessed that

the passenger was a middleman. Kalbadevi was a Mecca for middlemen, who bought from one party at a low price and sold to second at a higher price. In the process they cornered tidy commissions. Buying and selling went on at Kalbadevi day in and day out. He had heard of a rice trader, who had bought and sold the same consignment of rice nine times in a single day. It was all a game of nerves. One had to know when to buy and when to sell.

After the conversation with the onion merchant was over, the passenger dialed another number. This time he spoke of a consignment of jute bags. The businessmen of Kalbadevi Market would deal in anything that could be bought and sold. They had an uncanny ability to gauge the market. They traded in goods as brokers at stock exchange traded in shares.

At Marine Drive the taxi driver took the left turn, and the taxi passed through narrow streets, hemmed by small shops, bustling with people, handcarts and vehicles. This was Kalbadevi; a place in complete contrast to the spaciousness, orderliness, modernity of neighboring Marine Drive.

Anirudh hated to drive through these crowded labyrinthine streets where vehicles inched forward at 10 to 15 kms per hour. Handcarts were a big nuisance, constantly on the move, jutting in from here and there, transporting goods from one shop to another. At Kalbadevi, traffic moved at the speed of a handcart. A handcart bumped against his taxi. Anirudh glared at the handcart man but kept driving ahead. It was useless to squabble over a minor bump. Bumps and shoves were common at Kalbadevi. He parked the taxi where the passenger had to alight.

'How much do I pay?' the passenger asked.

Taking a look at the meter Anirudh said, 'One hundred and twenty rupees.'

The passenger paid in silence and stepped out of the taxi. Anirudh remained parked at the same spot, gazing disinterestedly at the hustle and bustle going on around him.

‡

He didn't have to wait for long before a passenger appeared. A young man peered into the taxi's window and named the place where he had to go, 'Linking Road?'

'Yes,' Anirudh nodded.

'Park the taxi in front of the shoe shop over there,' the young man said pointing to the fifth shop on the right side of the road. 'I have to load some luggage.'

Anirudh maneuvered the taxi to the entrance of the shop. The luggage turned out to be two large cartons. 'You will have to pay extra for loading these,' Anirudh said.

'The cartons are not heavy,' the young man maintained.

'I will charge 30 rupees above the usual fare,' Anirudh retorted obstinately.

'I will pay twenty,' the young man countered.

'Okay,' Anirudh said. They loaded the two cartons on the roof. The young man sat on the passenger seat beside him. Anirudh revved up the engine and began navigating through the dense crowd. A handcart overloaded with bales of cotton was plodding forward at a wretched speed. Anirudh honked several times to make the handcart move aside but the handcart man took no cognizance. The passenger, sitting beside Anirudh, hung out his head and shouted, 'Oie Chachu, did your father take contract for the whole road? Won't you spare any space for other vehicles?'

This time the handcart man yielded space. The taxi surged ahead.

'Driving in and out of Kalbadevi is a nightmare. I don't know how you taxiwallahs manage it?' the young man said.

'If some passenger wants to come here, I can't afford to turn down the business.'

'Yeah, that's true. No one can turn down a business,' the young man mused.

'Do you work at Kalbadevi?'

'I work at the shoe store, from where we picked up the cartons.

The taxi emerged from the bottleneck of Kalbadevi Market. The road widened and the traffic picked up speed. 'At last I can go at normal speed,' said Anirudh pressing his feet to the accelerator.

'Do you have any audiocassette?' the passenger asked.

'In the glove compartment.'

The passenger opened the glove compartment and after rummaging through many cassettes, he selected one containing songs of Mukesh. He inserted the cassette into the tape recorder and a song started. Mukesh was singing about the wiles of beautiful women. The passenger closed his eyes. Anirudh was not sure whether he was awake or asleep. When the last song was over, the passenger opened his eyes and changed the cassette to side B. Another round of songs started.

'We have reached Dadar,' the passenger said gazing out of the window.

'Yes. We will be in Linking Road in about 20 minutes.'

'Tell me when we are at Bandra Talkies,' the passenger said, closing his eyes again.

The taxi passed Mahim Masjid. As usual, hordes of beggars were squatting outside the Masjid. At Bandra Creek, koli fishermen had stretched long lines of fishing nets between bamboo posts. Salted fish and prawns were being dried on the black sand of the creek. The air hung heavy with the tangy smell of fish. A koli woman with her sari tucked firmly at her waist, dividing her ample buttocks into two equal halves, stood on the roadside with a basket of fish, waiting for a taxi to take her to the market. Anirudh loathed having fishmongers as passengers; water dripping from their baskets would mess up the seats, making the vehicle smell of fishes.

Three tall buildings, with offices of many companies, had come up in the area where Bandra Talkies once stood. But the place was still famous as Bandra Talkies. 'We are at Bandra Talkies,' Anirudh said.

The passenger opened his eyes. 'Keep going. The shop where I get down is not far from here.'

They entered the Linking Road market, popular shopping place for the city's upper strata. The wide road lined with glitzy showrooms selling designer apparels, jewelry, footwear, artifacts, souvenirs, furniture, here and there beauty parlors for men and women, fashionable restaurants serving cuisine from around the world, made a flamboyant statement in consumerism. The curbsides were full of enthusiastic shoppers, walking to and fro, coming in or out of shops, or just standing by.

'This is what I call a real market,' the passenger said. 'The shops at Kalbadevi probably make as much money as the shops here. But that place looks like a garbage dump compared to this place.'

'It takes all kinds of markets to make a city,' Anirudh retorted. 'All of Bombay cannot look like Linking Road.'

'Take the right turn from here. That shop with the hoarding 'Kings Shoes', stop there.'

Anirudh took the right turn and parked the taxi in front of Kings Shoes. When the taxi was unloaded, he received his payment and made a u-turn for the main road. He decided to wait beside Mcdonald's for his next passenger.

‡

A woman looked, stopped beside the taxi, and asked, 'Will you go to Pali Hill?'

'Yes.' Anirudh stretched his hand to open the rear door. The woman sat down on the backseat with a ten-year-old boy, who had a packet of Mcdonald's french-fries in one hand and a can of coke in the other. He nibbled French fries and sipped coke at the same time.

'Finish french-fries first and after that you can have your coke,' the mother admonished.

'Why? They will mingle anyway inside my stomach.'

'It is not the proper way to eat, you idiot,' the mother said irately and snatched the coke from the boy's hands. 'Finish the french-fries first, then I will give you the coke.'

'You are always pestering me,' the boy said glumly and continued to eat french-fries.

'I will stop bringing you to Mcdonald's if you behave like this.'

'I am sorry,' the boy was sulking. 'Now will you please let me eat in peace. It is bad to talk while eating, and you are making me talk.'

The mother started to say something, thought otherwise and began gazing out of the window, a frown on her face.

The hot exchange between the mother and the son amused Anirudh. He looked at them through the rearview mirror. The woman had short pomaded hair, painted lips and wore a trendy blue dress. The boy had on expensive denims. When the boy finished the last french-fry, he crumpled the wrapper and chucked it out of the window. 'My coke?' he demanded from his mother. She passed him the can. He took a sip and said, 'I will play video games on the computer when we get home.'

'Have you done your homework?' the mother asked.

'I will do it later.'

'Make sure you do.'

They reached Pali Hill and the woman told the taxi driver, 'Take left turn from the signal and stop at the third building.'

Few minutes later the taxi parked in front of a posh high-rise building, the woman asked as she got off, 'What is the fare?'

'Forty rupees.'

Fishing out a fifty-rupee note from her purse she said, 'Keep the change.' She followed her boy inside the building.

‡

Anirudh remained positioned on the road as he waited for his next passenger. It was 6 PM and the sun was slowly going down. At a food stall across the road, some boys and girls were sipping soft drink. Cars with stereos blasting and bratty youngsters at the steering wheels were streaking past at regular intervals. Anirudh spent thirty or forty minutes waiting for a passenger. But no one approached. Deciding to try his luck elsewhere, he drove leisurely through the streets of Pali Hill and reached Turner Road, where a couple in early twenties hailed him.

'Take us to Juhu,' the man said.

Anirudh opened the rear door to let the new passengers in.

The moment the taxi was on its way, the young man began cozying up with his female companion and pulled her into an embrace. She laughed and tried to push him away. But he continued to hold her and planted kisses all over her face. Anirudh looked at their antics through the rearview mirror with rising anger. Bloody exhibitionists, hissed to himself.

The woman saw him staring through the rearview mirror. 'Let me go,' she whispered to her companion. 'The driver is watching.'

Releasing her reluctantly the man shouted at Anirudh, 'Hey you! Keep your eyes on the road.'

The taxi driver's temper soared. But, keen to avoid trouble inside the taxi, he removed his eyes from the mirror. Satisfied that he had taught the errant taxi driver a lesson, the man turned his attention to his female companion once again; hugging and kissing resumed on the backseat.

'Be patient. We are on the road,' the woman moaned.

In answer her partner pulled her even closer.

Anirudh stepped on the accelerator. He wanted these loonies out of his taxi, quickly. There was a red light near Lido Cinema and he was forced to apply the brake.

Eunuchs roaming among waiting vehicles were importuning passengers for small amounts of money. Two of them noticed the young couple in the taxi, and they hurried towards them to collect the tax on love. While the government taxes everything else, the prerogative of collecting the love-tax has been left to the eunuchs. One of the eunuchs stood beside the window facing the young man, while the other stood confronting the woman.

'Give me something to remember you by,' the eunuch on the side of the young man said, sticking out a dirty callused palm.

'Go to hell,' the young man said, drawing back.

'Your rudeness breaks my heart.'

Anirudh amused at the predicament of his passengers sat in silence, as if he was not noticing anything unusual.

The eunuch on the woman's side said, 'Honey, why don't you tell him to spare something.'

'Oh, hand them over some loose change, or they will go on pestering us,' the female passenger said.

'Damn!' the young man muttered as he pulled out a fifty paise coin from his pocket and dropped it into the eunuchs palm. 'Now, both of you, be off.'

The eunuchs stayed put. 'Just 50 paise! I expect at least 10 rupees from a man such as you,' the eunuch, who had got the money, said.

'Tell him not to be such a miser,' the other eunuch said to the woman.

'Ten rupees, my foot!' the man said. He pulled out a two-rupee coin from his pocket and placed it on the eunuch's hand. 'That's all you will get.'

The eunuchs realized that they could not extort any more money from this couple and moved ahead to target other vehicles.

'They were funny,' the woman said.

'Not to me,' the man said. 'Why is this signal taking so long?'

'Maybe the traffic authorities, in league with the eunuchs, want to give them enough time to carry out their trade.'

'I won't be surprised if you are right. The constables are perhaps getting a cut. I feel disgusted.'

The signal went green and the taxi surged ahead with other vehicles. 'Thank God, we are out of this place,' the man said. The encounter with the eunuchs had dimmed his ardor and he left his female companion at peace, for the rest of the journey. Soon they were at Juhu Beach.

‡

The passengers paid and walked off. Anirudh stood leaning against the taxi and gaped at the carnival atmosphere of Juhu Beach. Long rows of colorfully decorated stalls, lit brightly by neon lamps, did brisk business selling bhelpuri, cold drinks, burgers and ice creams. A snake charmer was displaying his snakes to a group of cheering children and merry adults. Merry-go-rounds, of different shapes and sizes all festooned with bright lights, were operating here and there. The taxi driver tried to be as happy as everyone around him was, but his face remained a grim mask.

'You seem to be having a lot on your mind?' Anirudh heard someone say and turned to see Wahab Mia, another taxi driver, smiling through his thin white beard. At fifty, Wahab Mia was twice as old as Anirudh but they were fast friends. They lived in the same area and met often.

'It's good to see you,' said Anirudh. 'What are you doing here?'

'Same thing as you – waiting for my next passenger,' Wahab Mia said, pointing to his taxi parked few meters away. 'What were you thinking?'

'Nothing important, I was watching those people on the beach. I wonder if they are as happy as they appear.'

'Most of them only pretend to be happy.'

'Why?'

'They don't want to reflect on their long list of miseries. They delude themselves by pretending to be happy. This laughter, wild shouts of joy, is a charade. These people have no idea what it takes to be happy.'

'Do you know what it takes to be happy?'

'I think I do. To be happy one needs intelligence. Anyone who uses his brain will never be unhappy. But brain is something humans avoid using.'

'Most of these beach revelers are much more educated than us.'

'Education has nothing to do with intelligence. I have been a taxi driver for more than thirty years. Everyday I ferry all kinds of people, some educated, some not. In my experience the educated are as dumb-witted as the uneducated.'

'You are right,' Anirudh said, relishing the idea that the educated were no better than he was.

After a moment's pause, Wahab Mia said, 'There is another way of looking at it. Since both of us are not as happy as those people on the beach, we are trying to sneer at their happiness out of jealousy.'

This new line of reasoning incensed Anirudh. He said passionately, 'You see the filth that is strewn on the beach, the plastic bags, food packets, cold drink cans, beer bottles and other kinds of rubbish. The littering has been done by the educated, the well-to-do. For their few minutes of pleasure they have turned the whole beach into a garbage dump. The ugliness is not confined only to the beach. There is filth wherever you go and the higher strata of society is primarily responsible for that.'

'You should not harbor in your mind such strong feelings.'

'What is the harm if I do.'

‡

A husband and wife, each with a four or five year old child in arm, walked to Anirudh's taxi. The children wore similar conical caps and had plastic whistles, which they blew often to create small bursts of shrill sound.

'Where is the driver?' the husband asked.

'Where do you have to go?' Anirudh asked.

'Dadar.'

Anirudh looked at Wahab Mia and asked, 'You wish to go?'

'No. You take them,' said Wahab Mia, walking off.

Anirudh opened his taxi's door and took his seat behind the steering wheel.

Once inside the taxi, the children huddled at the window and blew their whistles at passing vehicles.

'The kids had a jolly good time,' the man said to his wife.

'Yes. It was a good thing that we brought them to the beach,' the wife said.

'We should plan such an outing every Sunday.'

'That would be the right thing to do. I have read somewhere that outings are good for a child's development.'

'Of course outings, sports, such activities play a vital role.'

'Did I tell you about Mrs. Mehta's daughter?' the wife suddenly asked, lowering her voice to a whisper.

'You didn't. What happened to her?'

'She had an abortion last week,' the wife tried to sound somber, but could not hide the fact that she was gloating.

'Is that true?' the husband exclaimed.

'I learnt from Mrs. Bhatia. She swore me to secrecy before giving me the news.' The wife said slyly, now gloating openly. 'Her husband did the abortion. It is well known that Mr. Bhatia does abortions, as a lucrative side business.'

'But the Mehta's girl is unmarried?'

'Of course, she is unmarried. She is only fifteen.'

'Then how did she get pregnant?'

'In the normal fashion, I presume,' the wife said mockingly.

'I mean, by whom.'

'According to Mrs. Bhatia's grapevine, she was having an affair with her father's driver.'

'My God! What a downfall! She gave herself to a menial driver. If she was so eager to beat the gong, at least she should have enlisted someone from her own class.'

'When a bitch is in heat, a dog of any breed is good enough. The driver for that matter is young and quite good looking. I have not seen him but Mrs. Bhatia has. She says he looks like a film star.'

'Is that driver still working with the Mehta's?'

'They got rid of him last week.'

'And the girl? How is she?'

'She has not been seen outside her house for the past few days. The Mehta's are keeping her locked inside the house. Only God knows, how they are able to tolerate their wayward daughter.

She deserves to be thrown into the streets. I am planning to visit them tomorrow, to find out what the situation in their house is.'

'While you are in their house,'don't let them suspect that you already know all this. Otherwise they will get the feeling that you have come to insult them.'

'Don't you worry about that. I am not going to insinuate anything. I just want to look in the face of the uppity Mrs. Mehta. Just because her husband is a senior civil servant, she used to behave superciliously with everyone in the neighborhood. Her daughter's shameful conduct must have brought her down to earth. How humiliated she must be feeling?' the wife said with glee.

Finally, the taxi reached Dadar. The passengers got down outside a building at Dadar's Shivaji Park area. Anirudh checked his watch. It was 9.30 PM. Thanks to the heavy traffic, it had taken him twice the usual time in reaching Dadar. The long day of heat and dust had left him exhausted. He decided to call it a day and started driving towards the slum in Santacruz, where he lived.

Thirty minutes later, he was at Jai Ganesh Wadi. Many other taxis and autos, belonging to other drivers were parked along the road, running parallel to the wadi. Anirudh parked his taxi at the usual place and, after locking it, marched to his one, room-tenement.

‡

Jai Ganesh Wadi, one of the major slums of Bombay, had more than ten thousand shanties, cheek by jowl. Only few of them had concrete walls. Most were jerrybuilt, with corrugated sheets of iron held in place by rusted nails stuck into bamboo or iron frame. Living conditions for the fifty thousand odd inhabitants were cramped and unhygienic. Narrow lanes and alleys, wide enough for only one person to pass at a time, crisscrossed the slum and led to different shanties. Overflowing gutters and open drains were a norm, rather than an exception.

Anirudh walked through the lane that led to his room. A small boy, the son of Anirudh's neighbor, was urinating in the open drain flowing parallel to the lane. While still passing water, the boy said, 'Namaste, Anirudh chacha.'

'Namaste, Raju,' Anirudh said. 'Has your father returned from work?'

'Yes. He is inside the house. You want to see him?'

'No. I asked just like that,' Anirudh said. He opened the door to his room and went inside. It was a small eight-feet by ten-feet room, one corner of which served as a washing place. A foot wide granite slab fixed into the wall was the kitchen. Rest of the room was free to be used for sleeping or for sitting down. Anirudh took off his shirt and hung it on a nail. He washed his face with few mugs of water from a plastic bucket and after drying himself with a dusty towel, lay down on the mattress spread on the floor. The room felt stuffy. There was a ceiling fan whirring from a beam slung along the roof but it made more noise than air.

The sound of a fracas going on next door permeated the walls. Ismail Bhai was calling his wife a prostitute, a witch. She retaliated by saying he was a good-for-nothing drunkard. Almost ritualistically, every night Ismail Bhai and his wife would be at hammer and tongs. The husband would come home drunk as a lord and start cursing and berating his wife. But the fault was not all his. The wife gave back as well as she got. She screamed and swore like a regular harridan. After quarreling for an hour or two, their vocal chords tired, they would go to bed.

Anirudh hissed to himself, 'The fools don't even have the sense to keep their voices down. Night after night, the whole neighborhood is forced to be a witness to their altercations. If they hate each other so much, why don't they kill each other and be done with it? ' He pressed the pillow to his ear to muffle the sounds. But the pillow could not turn him deaf and he continued to listen. Only when he fell asleep that the ravings of his neighbors ceased to bother him.

‡

Hunger gnawing his stomach shook him out of slumber. He sat up on the mattress and remembered that he had not had his dinner. It was 1 AM, his watch said. He had slept for more than three hours. Ismail Bhai and his wife had ceased their feud; no sound came from their house. They had probably fallen asleep. From somewhere came the faint melody of a popular film song. Someone was playing a radio. The song and the sound of the drain flowing outside the room broke the monotony of the night.

He got up and rummaged the shelf that served as his kitchen to find something to eat. All he could find was a mildewed loaf of bread and some sour milk. He chucked the bread and the milk into the drain flowing outside. The hotels were closed, but there was a roadside stall nearby, which opened till late in the night. Hoping to get something to eat from there, he put on his shirt and left the room, putting the bolt on the door.

Few paces away the door of one room was open and two women sat on the steps, chatting in muted tones. He recognized Jyotsna and her mother.

'Still awake at this hour?' he said.

'Our electricity went off an hour ago,' said Jyotsna. 'Without fan the house feels like an oven.'

'But there is electricity in my room,' Anirudh said.

'I think there is a problem with our fuse,' Jyotsna's mother said. 'Everybody, but us, has electricity. I don't know how we will get through the night.'

'I will check the fuse,' Anirudh offered. 'Show me where the fuse box is.'

'I will show you,' Jyotsna said with alacrity.

She got up and went inside the room. Anirudh followed her. In the light of a small kerosene lamp, she pointed out the rectangular fuse box fixed to the wall. Anirudh pulled out the fuse and found the fuse wire damaged. 'As I suspected,' he said triumphantly, 'it is the fuse that is causing the problem. Do you have a piece of wire?'

'I don't think so.'

'I keep a bundle in my house. I will get it in a minute.'

He went to his room and returned moments later with two or three inches of copper wire. Jyotsna and her mother watched with anticipation as he mended the fuse with the copper wire and then plugged it into the socket. The tube light and fan began to work.

'God bless you!' Jyotsna's mother exclaimed. 'You saved us from a hot and sleepless night.'

'It was only a minute's work for me,' said Anirudh. 'I will leave now.'

'But where are you going so late in the night?' Jyotsna asked. 'Are you doing nightshift on your taxi?'

'I am going to have my dinner.'

'Your dinner! But I saw you returning to your room at 10. What were you doing since then?'

'Oh, I fell asleep on empty stomach.'

'Where will you find dinner so late? All the hotels will be closed.'

'The roadside Chinese food stall is usually open even at this time. I hope to get something there.'

'Why not have something here,' Jyotsna asked. 'We can serve you rice and vegetables.'

'Well…'

'I insist that you have your dinner here,' Jyotsna's mother interrupted.

Jyotsna arranged a mat on the floor and said, 'Sit here. We will serve you in a minute.' She and her mother served Anirudh from pots and pans. Anirudh began to eat.

'So, how do you find this food?' Jyotsna smiled. 'It isn't as spicy as the Chinese food.'

'This isn't the first time that I am eating at your place,' said Anirudh through a mouthful of rice and vegetables, 'I have always liked eating here.' It was his habit to eat quickly and in no time he was swallowing the last morsel.

'Here, have some more,' Jyotsna started to serve from a pot.

But he pulled his plate away, saying. 'I have had my fill.' She didn't try to force him and placed the pot down. 'I will leave now,' he said.

'My God! It is 2 o'clock!' Jyotsna exclaimed. 'When are we going to sleep?'

‡

In his room the taxi driver lay down on the mattress. Sleep kept away from him and his thoughts veered around Jyotsna. He had known her since he moved to this slum, five years ago. He found her attractive. She had sharp features and a fair complexion. In spite of living in a crowded slum there was always an aura of aloofness about her. At times she came out as opinionated about various things. It surprised him that someone so delicate as her should be capable of holding strong views. When her father died four years ago, Jyotsna didn't allow herself to be swamped by grief. Instead she found a job as a nurse, at a local hospital, and with her earnings she and her mother lived comfortably.

He didn't know what her feelings were about him. She was always polite and friendly. Was it because she liked him? Or was it because it was her nature to be polite and friendly with all her neighbors? He had never tried to gauge her feelings, though many times he had thought of doing so. If he invited her to a restaurant or a movie what would her reaction be? He had no idea. Maybe she was only waiting for him to make a move and was prepared to accept him. Life would be good with her. He was so lost in thinking about her that he didn't even realize when the train of his thoughts broke and he fell asleep.

Two

Mohanti Singh, another resident of Jai Ganesh Wadi, worked as attendant for a company involved in renting movie cameras to film producers. On most days he was Anirudh's first passenger.

At 7 AM next day Anirudh was washing his taxi, when Mohanti Singh came. 'How much time you need to leave?' Mohanti asked.

'Ten minutes,' Anirudh said quickly, 'I am almost finished. Where are you going today?'

'Shooting is at Filmalaya Studio.'

When the taxi was washed, they left for Venus Towers, in Lokhandwala complex, where the camera was stored. They loaded the various boxes that contained fittings of the Arriflex movie camera and then were on their way to Filmalaya Studio.

The watchman opened the heavy green gate of the Studio and the taxi passed into the world of make-believe. In an open ground, set-designers were applying finishing touches to the set of a mansion's exterior. A group of junior artists, looking atrocious in colorful tribal costumes, were standing in front of the studio office, chatting with each other. Workers were unloading heavy art material from one tempo and heavy shooting lights from another tempo. Anirudh parked the taxi in front of the floor No. 2, where the camera was required and helped Mohanti in unloading the camera.

A row of air-conditioned makeup rooms, meant for senior artists, stood opposite the shooting floor. The door of one room opened and out came Raj Bhanot, the leading man of many successful films.

'Good morning,' Mohanti said, glancing obsequiously at the matinee idol.

'Morning,' Raj Bhanot said in his inimitable drawl, which had won him many fans throughout the country. 'Can I take this taxi?'

This question was of prime interest to Anirudh and he hastened to answer, 'I will take you wherever you wish to go. Give us a minute to unload the camera.'

'Take your time,' Raj Bhanot said with a patronizing air. 'By the way,' he added, 'I have to go to Juhu.'

'What happened to your car?' Mohanti asked.

'I sent it back to my house thinking that I won't be leaving before evening. But now the director tells me that I am needed on the set only after 1 PM. I'd rather spend those hours at home, than cooped up inside a makeup room.'

'That is the right thing to do,' Mohanti said.

'Yeah.'

The camera unloaded, Raj Bhanot slipped into the backseat, while Anirudh took the steering wheel.

'What is your name?' Raj Bhanot asked.

'Anirudh Shukla.'

'Do you smoke?'

'I don't.'

'Oh, it's my hard luck, you don't,' Raj Bhanot uttered, 'I was hoping to borrow a cigarette or a beedi from you. I feel like pulling a few puffs.'

'There is a stall outside.'

'Stop there.'

They were out of the studio and Anirudh stopped the taxi beside the stall.

'Get me a packet of Nandi beedi,' Raj Bhanot said.

'I have loose change on me. Don't bother about money,' Anirudh said confidently. He was feeling thrilled that a superstar was sitting in his taxi.

'Fine,' Raj Bhanot chuckled.

Anirudh stepped out of the taxi and purchased a beedi bundle of two rupees. A motley group of people standing in the vicinity of the stall noticed the superstar inside the taxi and gawked at him with silly smiles on their faces. Raj Bhanot laughed and waved at them. Some demanded autographs. He obliged everyone. Graciously, Anirudh gave him the beedi bundle. Raj Bhanot lit a beedi and exhaled a loud cloud of smoke. They were on their way to Juhu. Anirudh hated it when anyone lit a cigarette in his taxi. But this time he didn't mind the beedi smoke, as it was Raj Bhanot who was smoking. Fifteen minutes later the taxi was at Raj Bhanot's palatial bungalow.

Anirudh was about to park outside the gate, but the film star said, 'Take the taxi inside the gate.'

The watchman saw who was in the taxi and promptly opened the gate. The taxi cruised to the portico and parked there. Anirudh got down to open the door for his esteemed passenger.

Raj Bhanot wriggled out and asked jauntily, 'How much do I owe you?'

'How can I demand money from you?' Anirudh said reverently. 'You pay me anything you like.'

Raj Bhanot laughed, 'Yeah, yeah, I will pay you the proper fare. I have some idea how much it costs to get from Filmalaya to this place.' Anirudh licked his lips with anticipation as Raj Bhanot took out a thick bundle of currency notes from his trouser pocket. He felt sure that Raj Bhanot was going to pay him more than the usual 50 rupees. He expected to get hundred or even two hundred. 'Today is my lucky day,' he told himself, eyeing the bundle with covetous eyes.

Raj Bhanot pulled out two, ten rupee notes, from the bundle and handed them over to Anirudh. 'Will that be fine?'

The taxi driver was crestfallen. What he had received was less than half the actual fare. Instead of getting extra tip, he was forfeiting thirty rupees. Yet he could not bring himself to ask for more. How could he, when he had already offered to accept whatever he was given? He looked at the superstar's gleaming face and said, 'That'll be enough.'

'I look forward to traveling in your taxi again.' Smiling brightly, Raj Bhanot went inside the house.

‡

Anirudh drove outside the gate and parked on the roadside to wait for his next passenger. The loss of thirty rupees gnawed his mind, making him seethe with anger. A feeling started getting hold of him that Raj Bhanot knew what the actual fare was, and had duped him intentionally.

'The worthless miser!' he hissed to himself, 'What kind of superstar is he, who goes about cheating taxi drivers! He spouts moralistic lines in his movies, but in real life dupes honest people of their hard-earned labor.' He contemplated going back to the bungalow and demanding what was due to him. Failing to muster the courage, he cursed himself for his cowardice.

Suddenly he recollected that he had paid two rupees from his own pocket for the beedi bundle. He had, in actual terms, got only eighteen rupees. This realization of additional loss added fuel to the fire inside him. He felt as if he was about to explode.

'Excuse me,' someone said. He turned to see a wizened looking man, obviously in the wrong side of 50, standing beside the taxi, peering at him through round-rimmed glasses.

Another passenger, Anirudh thought. 'Where do you have to go?'

'Is that film star Raj Bhanot's house?' the man said, pointing towards the bungalow.

'What if it is?' Anirudh asked peevishly.

'You brought him to that house few minutes ago. Didn't you? I saw him sitting in the backseat of your taxi.'

'Look man, if you want to go anywhere, say so. But if you don't then get lost this minute. I am in no mood for chitchat.'

'I wish to meet Raj Bhanot.'

'What?' Anirudh exclaimed. 'Don't you think you are too old to be a drooling fan of Raj Bhanot?'

'I am not his fan. I want to see him for a very important reason.'

'They all say that.'

'I am Govind Shastri. I have come from Lucknow to find my daughter. She disappeared a month ago. I learned from her friends that she had gone to Bombay to become a film star. Raj Bhanot is her favorite actor. She used to watch all his movies. She could have met him since coming to this city. I want to ask him if he has seen my daughter. Maybe he can help me trace her.'

Anirudh realized how trivial his own loss of few rupees was compared to what this man had undergone. 'I am sorry,' he said hastily. 'I hope you are able to find her.'

Govind Shastri took out a photograph from a bag he was carrying and showed it to Anirudh. 'This is the photo of my daughter, Rachna. You travel around the city and meet many people. You may have encountered her somewhere.'

Anirudh took the photo and looked at the picture of an eighteen or nineteen years old girl. 'I haven't seen her,' he said returning the photograph.

Govind Shastri let out a sigh and replaced the photograph inside his bag.

'Why don't you meet Raj Bhanot?' said Anirudh. 'Who knows he may be able to shed some light on your daughter's whereabouts.'

'The watchman is not permitting me to go inside the bungalow.'

'That is the way it is with film stars. They are unapproachable.'

Suddenly Govind Shastri exclaimed, 'There he is! He has come out on the balcony.'

Anirudh glanced up and saw Raj Bhanot on the balcony. 'Let us go to the bungalow's gate. It will be easier to draw his attention from there. Hopefully, he will agree to speak to you.'

They walked towards the gate with brisk steps.

'Raj Bhanot sahib,' Anirudh shouted, waving frantically.

The watchman marched towards them brandishing a short stick. 'What is the problem with both of you? Stop creating nuisance here.'

'We are not creating nuisance,' Anirudh retorted. 'This gentleman has come all the way from Lucknow to meet your boss.'

'So what if he has come from Lucknow?' the watchman countered spitefully, 'People come from London and Paris to see him and he doesn't even spit at them.'

Anirudh ignored the watchman and shouted again, 'Raj Bhanot sahib.'

This time Raj Bhanot noticed Anirudh. Taking him to be an awestruck fan he waved back.

'Don't you remember? I brought you from Filmalaya Studio.'

'Yeah, yeah, I remember,' Raj Bhanot said, finally recognizing the taxi driver. 'What do you want?'

'This man has come from Lucknow to see you for a very important reason.'

'Please allow me to have a few words with you. I won't take more than five minutes,' Govind Shastri pleaded.

'Should I clear the gate of these people?' the watchman asked looking up.

Raj Bhanot was in an obliging mood, he said, 'Let them come in and wait in the front garden. I will come down and speak with them.'

'My boss has deigned to grant an audience. But if both of you create trouble I will be around to throw you out,' the watchman said.

'Okay, now open the gate,' Anirudh said crankily.

The watchman opened the gate and escorted Govind Shastri and Anirudh to the small garden in front of the bungalow. Few minutes later Raj Bhanot joined them. 'So, why do you want to see me?' he asked.

Govind Shastri told him about his daughter and showed him the photograph. Raj Bhanot gave the photograph a disinterested glance. 'Nope, I haven't seen her,' he said.

'I was hoping that she may have met you,' uttered Govind Shastri.

'She didn't. I am sorry to disappoint you. Why don't you visit the studios around the city? You might find her somewhere or meet someone who has seen her.'

'I have been in this city for only two days. I don't know where the studios are.'

'Your friend can take you to the studios,' Raj Bhanot said looking pointedly at the taxi driver.

‡

When Anirudh came out of the bungalow with Govind Shastri, he said, 'I want to help you, but you must understand, I can't afford to take you around without payment. You will have to pay me the regular fare.'

'Don't worry about the payment. I will pay what the meter says,' Govind Shastri said.

'Filmalaya is nearby. We shall begin our search from there,' Anirudh said. They sat in the taxi and Anirudh drove towards the studio.

Shootings for three different films were going on simultaneously in different shooting floors and there was considerable hustle and bustle inside the studio. Anirudh parked the taxi in front of floor No. 2 and got down with Govind Shastri. Govind Shastri looked around hoping to catch a glimpse of his daughter.

'My friend Mohanti Singh works as an attendant here. He might be able to help us,' Anirudh said.

They went inside. The loudspeaker was blaring a raunchy dance number and on a stage, brightly lit by powerful arc lights, popular film actress Savitri, clad in a skimpy costume, was dancing along with few other actresses. Anirudh noticed Mohanti Singh standing next to the camera. When the director yelled Cut, the music stopped, he ambled up to Mohanti Singh.

Mohanti said, 'I thought you had gone to Juhu with Raj Bhanot.'

'I had gone with Raj Bhanot, but I came back with him,' Anirudh said, pointing towards Govind Shastri, standing few feet away.

'Does he want to watch the shooting?' asked Mohanti Singh.

'No,' Anirudh said. 'If you can spare a few minutes I will tell you about him.'

'You go outside with him. I will join you after giving charge of the camera to someone else.'

Anirudh left the shooting floor with Govind Shastri. They waited beside the taxi. In a few minutes Mohanti Singh was with them. 'He has come from Lucknow to trace his daughter,' Anirudh explained. 'She came here a month ago aspiring to become an actress.'

Govind Shastri showed the girl's photograph to Mohanti Singh and said, 'Her name is Rachna. I will be grateful if you can help me locate her.'

'I don't think I have seen her,' Mohanti Singh said, after taking a look at the photo. 'Why don't you meet the studio management? Aspiring artists often contact them.'

'Take us to the office,' Anirudh said.

They went to the studio office. But none of the staffers could recognize the girl in the photograph. When they came out of the office, Mohanti Singh showed the photograph to members of different shooting units. More than two hours they spent making inquiries, but no clue to the girl's whereabouts emerged.

'Why don't you try Filmistan Studio?' Mohanti Singh suggested. 'Many shooting units are working there. Maybe someone there will be able to recognize her.'

'Yes. We should visit Filmistan,' said Anirudh, looking at Govind Shastri.

'Okay,' Govind Shastri nodded sadly.

‡

Five film units were working in the sprawling Filmistan studio complex. They met members of different shooting units, showed them Rachna's photograph. Govind Shastri pleaded with everyone, who would listen, to help him find his daughter. But despite their efforts they left Filmistan Studio empty handed after three hours. They headed for the Natraj Studio. One shooting unit was filming its sequences here. They met the studio management and also many people from the shooting unit, all without any success. By the time they finished their inquiries, it was 7 PM and dusk had started setting in.

'We will have to postpone visiting the other studios till tomorrow,' said the taxi driver.

'Why? I was so hopeful of finding her today.'

'It is 7 PM. The shooting units pack up for the day around this time,' Anirudh explained. 'I will drop you wherever you are putting up for the night and tomorrow at 9, I will pick you up.'

'That seems to be the only thing we can do,' said Govind Shastri.

'Where are you staying?'

'At Vrindavan Lodge, next to Santacruz Railway Station.'

Anirudh started the taxi and drove towards Santacruz. Govind Shastri sat in silence, lost in thoughts, his face a picture of despair.

Anirudh wanted to say something to console him, but he knew that whatever he said would sound platitudinous and would not suffice to assuage the feelings of the grieving father. He kept quiet.

They had reached halfway to Santacruz when Govind Shastri broke the silence saying, 'I was thinking...'

'What?'

'Will you take me to the red light area?'

It took one or two moments for Anirudh to realize the import of what he had heard. Govind Shastri feared his daughter might have been lured into prostitution. The fear was not groundless. Anirudh had heard of girls who flocked to Bombay hoping to get launched in the tinsel world but ended up as prostitutes.

'There is no need to torture yourself,' Anirudh said.

'Do as I say. Take me there,' Govind Shastri snapped.

Anirudh could read the tension on his passenger's face and he did not argue further.

It was 9 PM when they reached Kamatipura, Bombay's red light area. Long lines of decaying chawls, all of one or two storey, festooned with red, green and yellow lights, hemmed the narrow street that was littered with filth. Colorfully attired girls, their faces encrusted in cheap makeup, stood on the doorsteps and the balconies, displaying themselves for potential clients. Beggars afflicted with all sorts of wounds and deformities sat on the pavements or roamed about soliciting alms. The area was littered with beer bars, taverns, and pubs out of which emerged a steady stream of drunks. The scores of people in the street, leering at the girls on display were a quaint amalgam of the poor and the rich, the educated and the uneducated, the sophisticated and the lumpen.

Anirudh drove slowly through the crowded street to avoid bumping into any drunkard coming in or out of some tavern or brothel. Pimps of many brothels ran along the taxi, offering first-rate merchandise to Govind Shastri, whom they took to be a client. Govind Shastri ignored the pimps and kept staring at the women standing on the doorsteps and the balconies of the chawls.

Fearing that Govind Shastri may want to step out of the taxi and make inquiries, Anirudh said, 'It won't be a good idea to stop here.'

'Just drive through and take me to my lodge. She cannot be in a place like this. She would rather kill herself.'

In a few minutes the taxi exited the red light area. They reached Vrindavan Lodge and Govind Shastri got down. 'How much do I pay?'

Looking at the meter Anirudh said, 'Four hundred fifty.'

Govind Shastri counted the money silently and handed it to Anirudh. 'I expect you will be here tomorrow morning at 9?'

'I will pick you up at 9,' the taxi driver said. 'I hope we find your daughter tomorrow.'

'If God bestows mercy on me…' Govind Shastri let the sentence linger in the air and plodded inside the lodge with his head hung low.

The time was 10.30 PM and Anirudh decided to call it a day. A medley of emotions racked his mind as he drove to Jai Ganesh Wadi. The daylong fruitless search for Govind Shastri's daughter had left a deep impression on him. The feeling had caught hold of him that somehow he was personally involved and that it was his business to restore Rachna to her father.

After parking the taxi along the road opposite Jai Ganesh Wadi he made his way to a nearby beer bar for a tryst with alcohol. The dimly lit interior of the beer bar reeked of alcohol fumes and cigarette smoke. The gramophone was singing a song, whose lyrics proclaimed that the only remedy for a broken heart was a bottle of rum. Many tipplers, in various stages of inebriation, some gay and boisterous, others grim and silent, sat around the tables. Anirudh sat at a table and ordered beer. He drank two bottles of beer and had mutton biryani for dinner.

‡

Next day he was outside Vrindavan Lodge at 8.40 AM. In spite of being early by twenty minutes, he found Govind Shastri waiting for him outside the lodge. Govind Shastri's eyes were swollen. Anirudh knew that he had spent a sleepless night. 'I am glad you came early,' Govind Shastri said as he sat on the front seat.

'I will drive you to Film City,' the taxi driver said.

'Okay.'

Film City, the largest studio in Bombay, sprawls across almost 15 square kilometers of area. On any normal working day, it is routine for more than a dozen shooting units to be filming their scenes here. Anirudh and Govind Shastri traveled from one part of the studio to another, showing Rachna's photograph to members of different shooting units. During the four hours that they spent in the studio, they inquired from hundreds of people.

Everyone was sympathetic, but that was of little consolation to the distraught father, as none of them recognized the girl in the photograph.

Now Crown Studio and Famous Cine studio were the only two studios left for them to visit. They went to the Crown first and then to the Famous Cine. In these studios also they failed to make any breakthrough. Govind Shastri was overcome with grief and appeared only a step away from breaking down.

'Why don't you lodge a police complaint?' Anirudh suggested, when nothing else came to his mind. 'They may be able to find your daughter.'

'Policemen are not going to waste their time helping an ordinary person like me. Take me to a temple. I want to pray.'

‡

Anirudh brought Govind Shastri to Bombay's very popular, Siddhivinayaka Temple, dedicated to the elephant headed God Ganesh. The road running along the temple was lined with stalls selling flowers, coconuts, incense sticks, sweets and much else. Anirudh parked the taxi at the temple and said, 'You can purchase offerings from those stalls and then go inside the temple to pray. I will wait for you.'

Govind Shastri opened the taxi's door and stepped out. A young woman was handling a nearby stall. Instead of making a purchase Govind Shastri stood in front of the stall, with his eyes fixed on the woman's face. She, too, seemed transfixed by him and stared back at him as if in a daze. Anirudh, watching from the windshield, wondered what could be the reason behind their strange behavior. Suddenly the woman cried, 'Father.' The cry awakened Anirudh to the fact to which he had remained oblivious till now. He noticed the uncanny resemblance between the woman at the stall and the photograph that he had been showing in different studios. Govind Shastri had found his daughter.

The girl jumped down from the stall and hugged her father. An impulse to watch this happy scene from close quarters made Anirudh step out of the taxi and walk towards the father-daughter duo.

'At last I have found you!' Govind Shastri said.

'I was so miserable,' the girl cried.

'Since the day you disappeared I have not eaten a complete meal. How happy your mother will be when she learns that I have found you?'

'I am sorry for the pain I caused.'

Govind Shastri noticed the taxi driver watching them with a beatific smile on his face. 'For the past two days I have been traveling in his taxi,' he said, introducing Anirudh to his daughter, 'scouring for you in various studios. It is his efforts more than anything else that united you and me.'

Many people had collected around the joyous father and daughter, and were wondering what the fuss was about. They soon learnt that the father, who had been searching his daughter for many days, had found her outside the temple. Everybody called it a miracle. Govind Shastri and Rachna went inside the temple to offer prayers. When the father and daughter were out of the temple and seated on the backseat of the taxi, Govind Shastri asked, 'Tell me now, how you happened to be at that stall?'

'I visited many studios during my first few days in the city. But I could not find any work. The money I had brought with me ran out and I didn't know what to do. The old woman, at whose stall I was working, moonlights as a junior artist in film shootings. I chanced to meet her in one studio. In course of conversation I let her know about my precarious financial situation. She had pity on me and offered me a job at her stall. I accepted.'

'All is well that ends well,' Govind Shastri said. 'I am glad that Anirudh brought me to this temple, otherwise I may not have found you.'

When they reached Vrindavan Lodge, Govind Shastri asked, 'What is my fare for today Anirudh?'

'You don't have to pay me anything,' Anirudh said with a smile.

'Why?'

'The contentment I got, from seeing your daughter restored, is sufficient payment.'

'You have been a great help. I will be indebted to you for as long as I live. I can't let you go empty-handed. Accept this 500 rupees.'

'There is no need, really.'

'This money is a token of my gratitude.'

'But the fare is only 300 rupees. You are paying me 200 rupees extra.'

'I am not paying you the fare. Didn't I say that this money is a token of my gratitude?'

The taxi driver accepted the money. After the passengers were out of the taxi he started the taxi. He felt giddy with happiness. The world, in which sorrows yielded so abruptly to gaiety, could not be such a bad place after all. The wonderful ending to the saga of Govind Shastri and his daughter was like a personal achievement for him. He thought that he had never been so happy before.

He felt the craving to share his happiness with someone who was close to him. Jyotsna came to his mind automatically. It was 6 PM now. He knew that Jyotsna's duty at the hospital ended at 6.30 PM. He turned the taxi towards the hospital.

‡

The time was 6.25 when he reached outside the hospital. He parked the taxi close to the hospital's gate and waited for Jyotsna to emerge. Fifteen minutes ticked away before she came out, clutching a jerkin bag in her hand, ambling leisurely towards the nearby bus stop.

Anirudh put his head out of the taxi's window and called, 'Jyotsna.'

She heard him and looked back and saw him sitting inside the taxi. He stepped out of the taxi. 'What are you doing here?' she asked.

'A passenger brought me here. I was about to drive away, when I saw you,' he surprised himself with the glibness with which he lied. 'Come with me. I will drop you home.'

'I can't afford the taxi fare. I would rather take the bus.'

'I am not going to demand money.'

'I still prefer the bus. This is your business hour, I don't want you to waste time driving me home.'

'I won't lose anything, since I am going home, too. I have decided to close the taxi early today.'

'Well, in that case I don't mind coming with you.' They sat inside the taxi. 'Why are you closing early today?' she asked. 'Normally you work till sunset.'

'I had a pleasant experience, which encouraged me to take the rest of the day off.'

'Why don't you tell me about it?'

'It is a long story.'

'Don't keep me waiting,' Jyotsna said enthusiastically.

'I know of a fine restaurant, not far from here. We can stop there for a few minutes, have some snacks and talk in leisure.'

'Well.'

He thought that she was about to refuse his invitation. 'Oh, don't say no to me. I want to talk to you. Should I stop at the restaurant?'

'It was not by chance that you met me outside the hospital. You were waiting for me. Isn't that the case?' she asked looking at him sideways.

'Yeah. That is right,' he answered, meeting her eye squarely.

'I will come to the restaurant,' finally she said what he wanted to hear. 'I want to know what you have to say.'

Anirudh parked the taxi outside the restaurant. Only a few customers were inside and most of the tables were empty. A family of four, a couple and their two children, was sharing a large pizza at one table. Around another table three college students were sipping cold drinks. Anirudh and Jyotsna occupied seats at the far end of the restaurant, away from other customers. Both were tense – Anirudh, for what he was going to say to her and Jyotsna, for what she might hear from him. They had a vague feeling that this conversation in a restaurant was somehow going to make a difference to their lives.

'What will you have?' Anirudh asked.

'Anything light,' she uttered breathlessly.

Anirudh ordered idli sambar followed by cold drinks. Moments later their orders arrived and they dipped their spoons into steaming idlis.

'You were going to tell me about your pleasant experience,' said Jyotsna, eager to learn about his purpose in getting her here.

'Yeah,' Anirudh began. 'Yesterday, in the morning I was parked outside Raj Bhanot's bungalow in Juhu, waiting for a passenger, when a middle-aged man approached me. He gave his name as Govind Shastri...' By the time he finished speaking Jyotsna was in throes of amazement.

'My God!' she exclaimed, searching Anirudh's eyes to see if he was speaking the truth. 'Did all that really happen?'

'That is the way it happened.'

'It cannot be attributed to mere chance. It was a miracle that brought the father and daughter together.'

'It made my day when I saw Govind Shastri reunited with his daughter.'

'You have made my day, by telling me this story.'

'Will you marry me?' he asked abruptly. He had not brought her to this restaurant with the intention of proposing to her. The words had tumbled out of his mouth without any conscious effort and he had no idea what her response would be, but now that he had made clear his intentions, he felt that the most intricate part was over and he stopped and gazed at her.

Jyotsna looked at him with surprise.

'I make sufficient money,' the taxi driver said eagerly, like a persistent salesman delivering sales pitch to a reluctant customer. 'I will keep you well provided. Will you be my wife?'

'You have taken me by surprise!' she whispered in pretty mock confusion, while rosy blushes crossed her neck and shoulders and smiles of embarrassment played about her lips.

'You have not answered my question.'

'I have been expecting you to ask me this question since the day I first saw you five years ago. Why did you make me wait for five long years?'

'You have not answered my question,' Anirudh repeated.

'I will, damn you,' she laughed. 'You will be my husband.'

He smiled and took her hand and pressed it. Whatever had to be said, had been said and there was nothing to be done now except to feel happy. They finished their food in silence. He paid the waiter and they got up. He and Jyotsna! They came out of the restaurant. For a brief moment they stood and looked at the vista that spread before them. The sun had started to go down, streetlights were brightening up the evening's twilight, cars and buses were going, pedestrians hurrying... The world was on the move. They sat down in the taxi and the taxi joined the crowd of vehicles on the road.

‡

It was past 10 PM and Anirudh sat on the mattress in his room, reflecting on the day's events. Returning to Jai Ganesh Wadi, he had accompanied Jyotsna to her room. Jyotsna's mother was surprised when they told her about their decision to marry. She displayed anger and said something about young people taking decisions behind their parents' back. All that was just pretence, as it became obvious she was more than pleased that they were marrying.

How fortunate Govind Shastri had been for him, Anirudh wondered. It was the miraculous reunion of the father and daughter that had provided him with the impulse to speak to Jyotsna. A chance encounter with Govind Shastri had changed his life. The thought entered his mind that if he had not been waiting outside Raj Bhanot's bungalow that day, and Govind Shastri had not approached him then this sequence of events, which led to his proposing to Jyotsna, might not have happened. He thanked his lucky stars that contrived to place him at the right place at the right time. To think of it he had been furious with Raj Bhanot because he paid him few rupees less than what the taxi fare was. But now he didn't mind that loss at all. After all, it was Raj Bhanot who brought him to Juhu where he met Govind Shastri. If Raj Bhanot had not hired his taxi none of this would have happened. In retrospect, seemingly unconnected events seem so intricately interwoven.

When he got up to have a glass of water his eyes fell on the idol of Shiva that lay gathering dust in one corner of the shelf. The idol made him remember Jungali Baba, the Naga sadhu with whom he had spent so many years of his life. Jungali Baba had given him this idol at the time of their parting. During his chaotic days in Bombay, he had managed not to lose this sole reminder of Jungali Baba. He gazed at the statue and wondered where Jungali Baba could be now. Was he meditating in a snow-covered mountain, or was he praying beside a flowing river?

Questions about Jungali Baba's whereabouts kept rising in his mind from time to time. But he had no means of finding an answer to those questions. He remembered what Jungali Baba had said at the time of parting: If Lord Shiva wills, then we will come together again. Anirudh drank water from the tumbler and lay down on the mattress.

‡

Two days later it was a Sunday, Jyotsna's weekly holiday at the hospital. The taxi driver decided to make it his holiday, as well, and they went to Juhu beach. 'I am not going to bring my wife to a filthy slum room,' he said as they sat on the sand at a secluded spot.

'What are your plans?' Jyotsna asked, searching her future husband's eye.

'I make enough to rent a small flat. You would like to live in a flat, won't you?'

'Of course, I am dying to get out of Jai Ganesh Wadi. In fact, I was about to make a similar suggestion, but you preempted me.'

'That goes to show how alike our views are.'

'I hope we don't differ much after we are married.'

'Are you contemplating having differences with me after you become my wife?'

'Every normal husband and wife are bound to have some differences from time to time and there is no reason why we shouldn't.'

'You may not believe me,' said Anirudh with emphasis, 'but I am sure we are not going to be like any so-called normal couple. No difference of opinion will ever arise between us.'

'But we already are differing,' Jyotsna laughed.

'How?'

'I am of the opinion that we will have differences while you are sticking to the stand that we won't.'

'We are having this little difference only to spice up the conversation. You shouldn't take it seriously.'

'I am not taking it seriously.'

'It felt as if you were.'

'Is this another attempt to spice up the conversation,' Jyotsna laughed again.

'You bet it is. There is something else I want to tell you.'

'What?'

'I want you to quit your nursing job after we get married.'

A shadow of a frown came on Jyotsna's face. 'And what will I do after leaving my nursing job?' she asked.

'You will have much work at home to keep you busy. You

will cook food for us, do the laundry, clean up the house, take care of babies we will eventually have.'

'Don't make me nervous,' Jyotsna shuddered.

'A wife is expected to do all this. Didn't your mother tell you?'

Jyotsna looked into Anirudh's eyes and said firmly, 'Let me make myself clear, Mr. Future Husband. I am not going to be a plodding housewife. I will keep my job.'

'Hey, but what about the housework! Who is going to do the stuff that a housewife is supposed to do?'

'Both of us will pitch in for the house work.'

'But why do you wish to continue your job? You think my earnings won't be sufficient? You are shattering my fragile male ego.'

'I know that you are capable of providing for your family. But when you talk about sufficient earnings, you have to keep in mind the quality of life you aspire for. I want us to live in a respectable neighborhood, have modern amenities in the house, send our children to good schools, maintain a decent bank balance, enjoy the good things that make life worth living. We will not be able to achieve all this, if only one of us is working. To maintain a decent lifestyle we need two incomes.'

'I will work for twenty hours and make sufficient money,' the taxi driver said obstinately.

'And make me a widow within five years of marriage,' Jyotsna retorted. 'I will not allow you to work for more than eight hours. I know why you are so adamant on my giving up the nursing job. You think that being husband, it is your prerogative to be the breadwinner of the family and by keeping my job I am encroaching on your turf. That I tell you is a very old-fashioned view. Such male chauvinism is uncalled for.'

'Oh yeah!' Anirudh ejaculated peevishly.

'There is nothing wrong if women work and bring some additional income. Moreover I enjoy working as a nurse. I like caring for patients.'

Anirudh realized that Jyotsna was determined about continuing with her job. Instead of dragging the issue he decided to let her have her way. 'Well in that case it is a completely different matter. If you enjoy being a nurse you can continue to be one.'

'Thank you for your graciousness,' Jyotsna said sarcastically.

A hawker carrying green coconuts in wicker basket on his head passed them. 'Hey, want to have some coconut water,' said Jyotsna. Anirudh hailed the hawker and asked him to prepare two coconuts. The hawker placed the wicker basket on the ground. 'Give us the best coconuts, the sweetest ones,' Anirudh said.

'All my coconuts are sweet,' the hawker said, fetching two coconuts from his basket.

'No, no I don't want those,' Jyotsna said quickly, 'Give me the bigger ones.'

'Believe me I have selected the best coconuts,' the hawker intoned.

'I don't care,' Jyotsna countered, 'Just give me the bigger ones, those two,' she pointed out the coconuts she wanted.

'This lady knows all about coconuts,' Anirudh chuckled.

'You bet, I do,' Jyotsna nodded.

The hawker replaced the two coconuts into the wicker basket and brought out the ones that were Jyotsna's choice. With a long knife he deftly pierced them and inserting a straw, he handed them over. Jyotsna's lips puckered around the straw as she sipped.

'You like it' Anirudh asked.

'Of course? I do,' Jyotsna said, 'These coconuts have to taste nice. Don't forget I selected them.'

'You always choose the best, don't you? Maybe that is why you have selected me to be your husband,' the taxi driver winked mischievously.

'Now, that is carrying an argument too far.'

The taxi driver looked at her with warm eyes. 'You know what I am thinking,' he said.

'What?'

'I am thinking how delighted my mother would have been to see you had she been alive.'

'You have not told me about your mother and other family members. Why don't you tell me about them now? I would like to know about the rest of your family.'

'I was born in a village in north Bihar called Sarita,' the taxi driver began. 'A sprawling brick house surrounded by a sea of rice fields had once been my home. From dawn to dusk the house bustled with activity of family members and their children. Silence fell only in the night when everyone fell asleep. The house was so big that at least a hundred rooms of our slum could have fitted into it. It had many rooms, two kitchens, a large courtyard, an orchard with different varieties of fruit trees, a front verandah where menfolk sat and discussed village issues with other villagers, a shed where cows and goats were kept and a muddy front lawn where the children played. Had my mother not died when I was seven, I might still be living there…'

Three

'Anirudh...Anirudh, Where are you?' Anirudh heard his mother calling him. He was crouching behind a guava tree in the orchard, hoping that mother won't find him. He thought that if she failed to find him for some more time, then it would be too late for him to go to school and he could spend the day playing at home. But he knew that his luck had failed when he heard her footsteps drawing closer to the guava tree.

'So you are hiding behind the guava tree this time?'

'How do you always manage to find my hiding places?' he asked with frustration.

'I know magic.'

He believed her. It had to be magic, which led her to his hiding places. In the past he had tried to avoid school by hiding under the bed, in the kitchen, behind the barn, and inside the cattle shed but without any success. She always managed to ferret him out.

'What are you thinking? Get up. You have to get ready for school.'

'I don't want to go to school. Please let me stay at home. I won't make any mischief, I promise.'

'Get up, get up,' mother said clutching his hand and pulling him to his feet.

He tried to wriggle out of her grasp but couldn't. 'I know that you send me to school because you don't want me around the house,' he complained sullenly.

'I am sending you to school to study and become an officer.' She dragged him to the hand pump in the courtyard, where his cousin Jhankana was brushing her teeth with a mango twig. At nine, she was three years elder. She laughed with glee when she saw him being dragged by his mother.

'See, Jhankana is getting ready for school,' mother said. 'You should be as sensible.'

Jhankana brought the mango twig out of her mouth and said pompously, 'Stop being a nuisance, Anirudh. All good children go to school, don't you know that.'

'Where is Hari? I am not going to school, if Hari isn't,' Anirudh whined. Hari was Jhankana's brother and Anirudh's cousin.

'Hari is not like you. He is brushing his teeth in the verandah,' Jhankana announced with satisfaction.

'I, too, will brush my teeth in the verandah,' Anirudh declared sullenly.

Mother gave Anirudh a mango twig and led him to the verandah. Eight-year-old Hari was squatting on the verandah with grandfather. Both had mango twigs in their mouths.

'Where were you Anirudh?' grandfather asked with mirth. 'We searched you all over the house.'

'In the orchard,' Anirudh said, sitting down beside grandfather. Mother went inside the house. 'Grandpa, can I stay at home?' he pleaded.

'If you don't go to school, how will you become an officer?'

'But I don't want to become officer.'

'When you, Hari and Jhankana are back from school, we shall go to the snake charmer's,' grandfather said.

'Yeah, grandfather is taking us to see snakes when we are back from school,' Hari said gleefully.

Anirudh brightened at the news. 'Really!' he exclaimed.

A hen with a large brood of small chicks strolled into the open ground in front of the verandah, foraging for food.

'Our hen has given so many chicks,' Hari shouted happily.

'Where is the hen taking her chicks grandpa?' Anirudh asked.

'They are looking for food.'

'After they are fed they will lay eggs for me,' Hari said.

'For me, too,' said Anirudh.

'Let us go inside the house,' grandfather said.

They threw their well-chewed mango twigs on the ground and went to the courtyard. The kids took turns in operating the hand pump to fill the bucket. But the pump was quite heavy and they managed only seven or eight pulls between them. Grandfather took charge of filling the bucket. They squatted around the hand pump to have their bath. The kids laughed as they scrubbed themselves with a red bar of Lifebuoy soap. When the bucket was empty, grandfather filled it for the second and, then, the third time. A sliver of foam entered Hari's eyes and he groaned with agony, but he became fine after grandfather rinsed his eyes with water. When the bathing was over, grandfather dried himself and the two kids with a towel.

‡

Hari's mother, Gautami, emerged from the kitchen and took charge of the two boys. She made them wear indigo half pants and white shirts, the dress that all school children of the village wore, and led them to the kitchen for breakfast. Jhankana, dressed in an indigo skirt and white shirt, sat on a mat, having her breakfast. The boys huddled down beside her.

'After we return from school grandfather will take us to see snakes,' Anirudh boasted.

'I will also come,' Jhankana declared.

Anirudh's mother placed a frying pan over the smoking wood fire, at the earthen fireplace and broke two eggs into it, to prepare omelet for the boys. 'Have your breakfast quickly,' she said, serving the omelets to the two boys.

Few minutes later grandfather came into the kitchen. He was in his trademark attire of dhoti-kurta. 'Have the kids finished their breakfast?' he asked. 'It is time to take them to the school.'

'I have finished,' Jhankana said.

'We will take one minute,' Hari said.

'I am waiting in the verandah. Come out when all of you finish eating,' grandfather said and left.

'I will have a darshan of bhagwanji,' Anirudh said after he finished his breakfast.

'I will come with you,' Hari said eagerly.

'We will get late for school, if you two fool around,' Jhankana shouted.

'Don't worry we will be back in a jiffy,' Hari said.

The boys scampered off to the staircase, which led to the roof. They panted for breath by the time they finished climbing the steps. The roof was a large open area, in one corner of which stood a small temple, packed with vivid images of Hindu Gods and Goddesses. Grandmother sat outside the temple, her eyes closed, telling her prayer beads. Hari and Anirudh crept stealthily towards the temple. They grabbed a handful of sweets from a brass plate in front of photo's of the Gods and retreated. When they were halfway down the stairs they laughed and gobbled up the succulent sweets. It was a daily ritual for them to steal a portion of the sweets that grandmother placed as offering. Grandmother often asked them if they knew who stole sweets from the temple. Her inquiries used to amuse them and they told her that the culprit must be some giant monkey. It amused them even more when she pretended to believe them.

‡

Gautami gave them their schoolbags, which had few tattered schoolbooks, and they came out of the house. Jhankana and grandfather were waiting in the verandah. The boys went running down the narrow mud path that cut through the rice fields. Jhankana and grandfather came walking. The rice crop had acquired the golden yellow hue and in another few days, it would be time to harvest the crop.

After walking for about twenty minutes, they reached the main residential area of the village. A dusty lane ran through groves of tall mango, pipal, guava and banyan trees. There were many houses along the lane, most with thatched roofs and walls made out of brown clay, though some solid brick and concrete structures, with wooden doors and iron grills at windows, stood here and there in stark contrast to the general landscape.

At the center of the village there was the large pond, with buffalos wallowing in the murky water, drinking and bathing. Colorful lotuses, blooming in sheer abundance, were a sight to behold. Amidst the lotuses ducks waded placidly foraging for food. Here and there in the water stood snow-white egrets on one leg, patiently waiting for fishes to come their way. A bevy of women laughed and shouted as they washed their clothes, by beating them on flat slabs of stone, sending up huge clouds of spray.

The school was located beyond the pond. It was a one-room school. All the school- going children of the village, between the ages of five and ten, were taught here by the same teacher. The ground outside the school was chock-a-block with boys and girls in indigo and white dress, all of them shouting, laughing and playing. Hari, Anirudh and Jhankana hurried to join their friends.

'I will come to take you home at noon,' grandfather said after them.

'Don't forget that we are going to see snakes today,' Hari shouted back.

'I won't,' grandfather said.

The teacher arrived few minutes later and struck the brass gong, hanging on a nail on the school's wall, few times. The happiness dried up from the faces of the students and they quietly shuffled inside the classroom and in random disorder squatted on the straw mat spread on the floor. The teacher entered shortly after them.

All students droned in unison, 'Namaste, masterji.'

'Namaste, namaste,' the teacher said. 'Take out your notebooks and copy what I write on the board.'

‡

At noon, when the teacher declared the class was over, students cheered wildly and rushed out. Jhankana, Hari and Anirudh stood on the ground and looked around for their grandfather.

'Where is grandpa?' Anirudh asked.

'Maybe he forgot to come,' Hari ventured.

'He never forgets,' Jhankana said and pointing towards a mango tree down the path exclaimed triumphantly, 'There he is.' Grandfather was standing under the shade of the tree, chatting with some villagers. The kids ran towards him, swinging their worn-out school bags and entwined themselves against his legs.

'Easy...Easy,' he chuckled and pulled them away from his legs.

'Take us to see the snakes,' Anirudh gasped.

'We shall have lunch at home and then we go to see the snakes,' grandfather said.

'Oh no!' Hari groaned. 'Why can't we go now and have lunch later?'

'We are not hungry right now,' Jhankana spoke for all three of them.

The villagers standing under the tree laughed at the children's enthusiasm for snakes. 'What if the snakes bite you?' one of them asked.

'Grandfather will be with us,' Jhankana said, 'He won't allow the snakes to bite.'

'My kids are very smart,' grandfather declared with pride.

'Let us go home grandpa,' Anirudh said. He was eager to finish his lunch and then start for the snake charmers place.

'Okay, lets go,' grandfather said.

They walked back to their home by the same path, which had brought them to school in the morning. A group of black and white goats had strayed into someone's rice field. The farmer was creating a rumpus to scare them away. The children stopped for a few moments to watch him run after the goats.

‡

Anirudh's mother was grinding wheat in the courtyard. Her hands pushed and pulled the heavy grinding wheel, moving it round and round in circles. From time to time she added fistfuls of wheat in a hole at the center of the wheel. Flour trickling from the edges of the wheel had piled up on the floor and a thin film of flour covered her hands and clothes. Grandmother sat on a mat chatting with few village women.

Anirudh ran to mother shouting enthusiastically, 'Give me lunch quickly mother.'

'My brat has returned from school,' mother simpered. 'What did masterji teach today?'

'I will tell you about all that later,' Anirudh said urgently. 'Give me my lunch first.'

Hari and Jhankana arrived.

'We have to go with grandpa to see the snakes after we finish our lunch,' Hari panted.

'Where is my mother?' Jhankana asked.

'Gautami is in the kitchen. She will serve lunch to all of you,' mother said.

'Hari-Anirudh, do you have any idea who stole the sweets while I was praying?' grandmother asked.

'I don't know,' Anirudh said sheepishly.

'It could be a monkey,' Hari said in a smart-alecky manner.

'A really big monkey,' Anirudh said, spreading his hands wide apart to show how big the monkey, who stole sweets, could be.

Grandmother and the village women started laughing. The children ran off to the kitchen. Gautami served their lunch and they ate squatting on the kitchen floor. When they came out of the kitchen, they found grandfather was in his room still having his lunch.

'Eat quickly, grandpa,' Anirudh said impatiently.

'Hush,' grandmother said, 'Let grandpa eat in peace. Wait in the courtyard.'

The kids shuffled out and waited in the courtyard for their grandfather to emerge.

'Don't get close to the snakes while watching them,' Anirudh's mother said.

'I will watch them from distance,' Anirudh promised quickly out of fear that mother won't let him go if he didn't.

Grandfather came out of the room wiping his face with a small towel and said, 'Let us go children.'

‡

The children raced each other out of the house. The sun was shining fiercely, but it did not feel very hot because of the light breeze that was fanning the landscape. The rice crop swayed gently in the breeze. The air carried the sweet fragrance of the ripening rice crop.

'We shall go to our rice field first before going to the snake charmer's place,' grandfather said. 'I have to meet my sons, Shambhu and Sadashiv.' Shambhu was the father of Jhankana and Hari, while Sadashiv was Anirudh's father.

'Why can't we go there after we see the snakes?' Hari asked petulantly.

'We will stay at the field for a few minutes only.'

'I hope father does not hold us for too long,' Jhankana said.

'He won't. Don't worry,' grandfather said.

They walked through narrow mud paths that formed the border between different rice fields. All the fields had scarecrows of various shapes and sizes to frighten away the birds. The children pointed out the different scarecrows to each other with amusement.

‡

Thirty minutes of walking brought them to their own rice field. Hari's father and Anirudh's father were working in the swampy rice field with their dhotis tucked up to their thighs. Their legs, below their knees were caked with mud.

'Father,' Hari shouted.

Shambhu and Sadashiv looked in their direction.

'We are going to see the snakes,' Jhankana said gaily.

'We are going to see the snakes,' Hari echoed merrily.

Shambhu and Sadashiv waded out of the swampy rice field.

'Rice crop looks very good,' grandfather said, fingering a blade of rice crop.

'Yes, our village is going to have a bumper harvest this year,' Shambhu said.

'In another fortnight we will be able to harvest the crop,' Sadashiv said.

'Pray to God that he blesses us with such a crop every year,' grandfather said, looking up at the clear blue sky, where God is supposed to reside in his heavenly abode.

'Father, we are going to see the snakes with grandpa,' Anirudh said.

Sadashiv laughed and said, 'Make sure that the snakes don't follow you back home.'

'Can they do that?' Jhankana asked fearfully.

'We will have to make sure that they don't,' grandfather said.

The elders discussed the crop while the children stood and looked around. Jhankana noticed a praying mantis that was clinging to a rice stalk. 'Look, a praying mantis,' she exclaimed.

The three children stared at the insect curiously.

'Is it eating our rice?' Hari asked.

'Let it eat,' Jhankana said, 'It will make no difference to us if it eats a few grains.'

'When will it fly away?' Anirudh asked.

'After it is finished eating?' Jhankana said.

Hari threw a pebble at the insect. The pebble missed its target and struck the stalk to which the praying mantis was clinging. The insect fluttered away in a jiffy.

'Why did you do that, you monkey?' Jhankana asked angrily.

'I wanted to see the praying mantis fly,' Hari chuckled.

Anirudh went to grandfather and asked edgily, 'When will we leave?'

'We will go now,' grandfather said.

'He is eager to see the snakes,' Sadashiv said.

'We all are,' Jhankana said.

'When will both of you return home?' grandfather asked.

'By sunset,' Shambhu said.

‡

Grandfather and the three children resumed their march to the snake charmer's place. They came out of the rice fields and reached the railway tracks, which divided the village into two halves.

Hari picked up a few small stones from those strewn around the tracks. 'If any snake dares to follow us home,' he swaggered, 'I will throw stones at it.'

'Yeah, we are going to hit the snakes,' Anirudh said, gathering a few stones for himself.

'How far do these railway tracks go, grandpa?' Jhankana asked.

'They go very far,' grandfather said, 'Right up to the Himalayan Mountains.'

The swaying greenery of sugarcane plants and banana plantations lay beyond the railway tracks. Further ahead, few peasants were sitting on wooden cots, in the shaded arbor of a mango grove, chatting and smoking chillums. They greeted grandfather and invited him to smoke chillum with them.

To dissuade her grandfather from accepting their invitation, Jhankana quickly said, 'We don't have the time to sit, grandpa.'

'We will stay for a few minutes only,' said grandfather, settling down on the charpoy.

'I don't want to spend few minutes here,' Hari whimpered. 'I want to see the snakes.'

'While I take a few pulls at the chillum all of you can munch sugarcane,' grandfather said. 'Don't you want to eat sugarcane?'

The prospect of having sweet sugarcane seemed enticing enough to the kids. 'Okay,' Jhankana and Hari said.

'I will eat the biggest sugarcane,' Anirudh declared.

'I am allowed to sit with you people only if my kids get sugarcane,' grandfather intoned to his peasant friends.

A peasant went to the field and returned with a long stick of sugarcane. With a sharp scythe he divided it into three parts and, after cleaning the skin from the pieces, he gave them to the children. Jhankana, Hari and Anirudh huddled in one corner of the charpoy and engrossed themselves in munching sugarcane. Grandfather shared the chillum with the peasants and discussed the affairs of the village.

‡

The dwellings of the snake charmers and other low caste inhabitants of the village lay beyond the sugarcane fields and the banana plantations, at the very edge of the village. Their frugal huts, made out of mud and bamboo sticks, had thatched roofs and clustered around an open area. The earthen walls of many of the huts were crumbling and the windows gaped without shutters. Women were drawing water from the well with an iron bucket tied to a long rope. Pot-bellied children scurried about naked with dust caked to their bodies. Few peasants sat under a pipul tree. They got up and greeted grandfather.

'Where is Gobar?' grandfather asked. Gobar was the snake charmer of the area.

'I will call him,' a peasant said and went off in one direction. Few minutes later he returned with Gobar. The children had been here on many occasions and Gobar's bearded face was familiar to them. They cheered him enthusiastically as he approached.

'Gobar, show us your snakes,' Hari said happily.

'Gobar, Gobar, Gobar,' Anirudh shouted, jumping up and down with joy.

'My little masters are eager to see the snakes,' Gobar chuckled

'Have you caught any new snake?' grandfather asked.

'I caught a big King Cobra two days ago,' Gobar said with pride.

'Grandpa, is a King Cobra very poisonous?' Jhankana asked. Fear and thrill was palpable in her voice.

'Much so,' grandfather said.

'I will bring the snakes,' Gobar said. He went inside his hut and returned with few spherical straw baskets, which he piled up on the ground, one on top of the other. Picking up the first basket said, 'This basket contains a very angry viper.'

The children huddled close to grandfather and stared at the basket with anticipation. A sizable crowd of urchins and peasants had collected to watch the snakes.

Gobar removed the cover from the basket and a mottled gray snake slithered out. It moved with amazing swiftness on the dusty ground. Gobar allowed it to travel for a few feet and then pulled it back by its tail. 'Does anybody in the crowd dare to hold this snake?' he asked, looking around him.

'My God! No,' Jhankana screamed.

Hari and Anirudh hugged grandfather's legs fearing that Gobar may make them actually touch the snake.

Gobar returned the viper inside the basket and from another basket pulled out a python. The python was not as swift as the viper, but it was much larger and thicker. It had rectangular black markings on its body. 'Now I will show you the King Cobra,' Gobar said. With a small amount of histrionics, he opened the basket that contained the snake. The serpent rose into the air and dilated its neck in the form of a hood. It looked around angrily and tasted the air with its forked tongue.

'This is the most poisonous snake in the world. A drop of its poison is enough to kill an elephant,' Gobar announced dramatically.

'Grandpa, is it the Lord Shiva's snake?' Hari asked.

'Yes, it is,' grandpa nodded.

'I hope this snake does not follow us home,' Anirudh whispered.

'See how angry this snake is,' Gobar said and brought his hand close to the snake's hood. The King Cobra bent forward quickly, thirsting to sink its fangs into the hand. But at the last moment Gobar moved his hand away and eluded the fangs. The audience gasped with fear and wonder.

Gobar fished out a long flute from his bag and said, 'The king cobra will now dance to the tunes of my music.' The serpent swayed its hood from side to side as Gobar played the flute.

After they had seen few more snakes, grandfather gave Gobar a one-rupee coin and then left with the children. Hari and Anirudh kept turning back to check if any snakes were following them.

‡

'Are you feeling tired children?' grandfather asked when they were at the railway tracks.

'No, we are not tired,' Jhankana answered for all three of them.

'I have to purchase some medicines for grandmother. We shall go to the market first and then return home.'

'Yeah, let us go to the market,' Hari said enthusiastically.

'I will eat sweets at the market,' Anirudh proclaimed.

The small market of the village was situated behind the railway station. As they walked, the boys threw stones into the thick grass and bushes of wild flowers that were abundant on both sides of the railway tracks. Butterflies with colorful wings and small birds rose as the stones fell. Sweet voiced koels sang from the trees. A pair of eagles floated in the sky, searching for prey.

Many people were waiting for the train at the railway station.

'Grandpa, is the train about to come?' Hari asked.

'It is time for the evening train to arrive,' grandfather said.

'I want to see the train,' Jhankana said.

'Yeah, I want to see it, too,' said Anirudh.

'Let me inquire how much time the train will take to arrive,' grandfather said. He asked the pointsman, who was standing at the platform.

'It will be here in 8 to 10 minutes,' the pointsman said. 'It has already reached the outer signal.'

The ground shook when the train thudded into the railway station. Its engine belched a dense cloud of black smoke and the myriad wheels screeched hysterically as it grounded to a halt. The station was filled with clamor and shouting. There was pandemonium as people with many pieces of luggage started clambering up and down the train. Men shouted, women yelled and children cried. Hawkers with trays laden with samosas and sweets ran up and down the platform. The air smelled of carbolic acid and steam.

Within two or three minutes, the engine sounded a piercing whistle and the train started sliding forward. The wheels moved slowly at first, but accelerated in speed quickly, until they became a continuous blur of motion. Soon the train vanished leaving a gaping hole in the air. Jhankana, Anirudh and Hari laughed and cheered.

'Grandpa, when will we ride the train?' Anirudh asked.

'We will go to Patna by train some day soon,' said grandfather.

'Last time when we went to Patna, I sat beside the train's window and looked at all the villages, fields and towns that went past. It was so nice,' Jhankana said with glee.

'Yeah. We saw so many places on the way,' Hari laughed.

'When we go to Patna again, I will sit at the window seat,' Anirudh declared.

'Let us go to the market,' grandfather said.

‡

Sarita's market ran along the road behind the railway station. Most of the shops were shacks built out of wood, bamboo and tarpaulin sheets. However some brick structures were also there. Fruit and vegetable vendors squatted along the roadside with their wares in wicker baskets.

There was a small crowd of evening shoppers in the market. Rewa was sitting behind the counter in his sweet shop. As usual, his gramophone was blaring a bhojpuri folksong at full volume. From the road the children looked at the mouthwatering sweets on display inside the shop.

'Grandpa, jalebi,' Anirudh said pointing towards the sweet shop.

Grandfather said nothing and continued to walk towards the medicine shop. 'Grandpa, buy us some jalebi,' Jhankana and Hari chanted, 'Buy us some jalebi.'

'Okay,' grandfather said gruffly, 'I will buy jalebi, but only after I finish my work at the medical shop.'

Krishna sold medicines along with rice, wheat, sugar and kerosene in his shop. The medicines were kept in a dusty wooden shelf fixed along one of the walls while the floor of the shop was heaped with wicker baskets containing various varieties of grain. The shop was stuffy and dark, and smelled of a gunnysack. Jhankana, Hari and Anirudh absolutely abhorred Krishna. In their mind he was associated with all the foul tasting medicines they were made to swallow from time to time.

Krishna greeted grandfather with folded hands and gave him a stool to sit down. The children waited impatiently as he searched the shelf for medicine. Finally he found it and, wiping the dust from the small bottle with a napkin, gave it to grandfather.

When they came out of the shop Hari asked, 'Grandpa, are we now going to Rewa's shop to eat jalebi?'

'Okay, let's go there.'

The kids marched happily towards Rewa's shop. Rewa gave a wide smile, displaying all his tobacco stained teeth, when grandfather and the children entered the shop.

'Because of you I lose two rupees every time I come to the market,' grandfather said with mock anger.

'That is a small price to pay for the affection of your grandchildren,' Rewa chuckled.

'It is very easy for you to say that,' grandfather said. He sat at a table along with the children. 'Get some fresh jalebis for my kids.'

'My jalebis are always fresh, the reason why people from neighboring villages flock to my shop.'

'We all know that,' grandfather said sarcastically.

Rewa served jalebis in four small plates. The children started gobbling the jalebis in a hurry.

'Eat slowly,' grandfather remonstrated, 'The jalebis are not going to run away.'

'Even if they do, I have more jalebis in my shop,' Rewa said.

‡

Finishing their jalebis, they walked back home. Mahto, the servant who looked after the cattle, had just returned after grazing the two cows and five goats. He sat on the verandah smoking his hookah.

'Where are the cows and the goats, Mahto?' grandfather asked.

'I tethered them inside the shed, sahib,' Mahto said.

'Did the cattle graze well today?'

'Yes. I took them to the Hanuman Tekdi.'

Grandmother came out of the house looking infuriated and demanded, 'What took all of you so long?'

'Ask your grandchildren,' said grandfather placidly.

'Grandmother, we had a jolly good time today,' Hari said.

'We ate sugarcane, saw the snakes and the train, and ate jalebis at Rewa's shop,' Jhankana said blissfully.

'We also saw a praying mantis at the rice field,' Anirudh added.

'So, all of you are returning home after making an excursion of the whole village,' said grandmother irately.

'The children insisted on having it that way,' grandfather said. 'Have Shambhu and Sadashiv returned from the field?'

'They haven't. Like their father they, too, lack a sense of time. It is already 6 PM and we still don't have firewood for cooking dinner. Don't blame me if dinner is served at midnight.'

'Why didn't you ask Mahto to chop some wood?'

'Ask him to chop wood?' said grandmother spitefully. 'As if you don't know any better than that! This old chicken has hardly any strength to wield an axe. He is fit only to loiter behind cattle and smoke his hookah.'

Mahto grinned sheepishly.

'Okay, I will chop the wood,' grandfather said.

After venting her anger on grandfather, grandmother now turned on the children. 'Jhankana, it is time you started behaving like a girl of your age. When I was of your age, my mother had given me so many responsibilities. Go to the kitchen and start chopping vegetables.'

'Yes, grandma,' Jhankana mumbled morosely and went inside the house.

'Both of you have been eating sugarcane, jalebis and who knows what else,' grandmother glared at the boys. 'If I hear either of you say at dinner that you are not hungry, then you will get a thorough spanking from me.'

The boys crouched behind their grandfather with fear that grandmother might begin spanking them now instead of waiting till dinner.

'You should not be so hard on children,' grandfather said.

'If I am being hard it is for their own good,' grandmother said and went inside the house in a huff.

'Is she angry because we did not bring jalebis for her?' Anirudh asked.

'Yes, that is why she is angry,' grandfather said. 'Let us go to the shed and chop some wood for her. You can go home now, Mahto.'

'I will, sahib, after I have taken some more puffs at my hookah,' said Mahto.

‡

Behind the house was the shed where cows, goats, cattle-feed, logs of wood and much else were housed. The shed's interior always carried the not-too-unpleasant smell of cowdung and dried grass.

The two cows, having fanciful names of Lakshmi and Saraswati, sat on the floor chewing cud from a trough containing a mixture of finely chopped dried grass and water. Five goats, all of them bleating intermittently, shared another trough containing similar gruel.

Grandfather patted the two cows lovingly on their necks and head. Hari and Anirudh climbed on the backs of the two bovines. The cows, used to antics of the boys, made no attempt to throw them off, but grandfather intervened on their behalf and told the boys to stop pestering the animals. The boys slithered off to the ground.

At the other end of the shed, a 30-inch log of wood had been turned on end to make a chopping block. Stuck in place on the block was an axe. A high pile of logs lay close to the block. Grandfather placed a large log on the chopping block and started splitting it into many pieces with the axe. Hari and Anirudh squatted out of the range of the falling axe and sharp slivers that sprang from the slab, and watched their grandfather's wood chopping chore. The fresh smell of wood pitch filled the air as kindling popped off the chopping block and for a time drove the cow dung smell away. After the chopping was done, Hari and Anirudh gathered the sticks in a sack and dragged it inside the house.

‡

The sun had started setting and it was getting dark. Shambhu and Sadashiv were back from the field. They sat in the courtyard chatting with grandmother. A wicker lamp was flickering in the kitchen, where Jhankana and her mother were chopping vegetables and Anirudh's mother was engaged in grinding spices on a stone slab.

The boys dragged the kindling up to the kitchen door.

'Mother, we brought the kindling,' Hari panted.

'Let it remain there,' Gautami said.

Anirudh went inside the kitchen and asked his mother, 'When will dinner be ready?'

'Are you feeling hungry?' mother asked.

'Yes.'

'It will be ready soon.'

After she finished grinding the spices, she brought the kindling inside the kitchen and arranged it in the earthen stove. The wood sizzled and bubbled as it caught fire.

'Mother, why is the wood making noise?' Anirudh asked.

'It is green and not fully dry.'

When the fire was hot enough she placed an aluminum utensil containing rice on the stove. Anirudh was drowsy by the time dinner was ready. He whimpered that he wished to go to bed and refused to eat his food. Mother made him sit in her lap and fed him with her hands.

‡

Hanuman Tekdi, a large swath of open area situated in the southern edge of the village, was abundant with leafy shrubs, tall oak, pipal, neem, mango and casuarina trees, and carpeted by a dense undergrowth of green grass. Many villagers brought their cattle to feast on the greenery here. At the center of Hanuman Tekdi was a small hillock, on top of which there was a temple dedicated to Hanuman, the monkey God. It was from this temple that this area got its name. An elderly white-haired priest, with menacing brow and blazing eyes was the caretaker of the temple. Though mild mannered by nature, his stern visage made him seem ferocious to the village children, who thought that he used to commune with ghouls and demons and, in all probability, was either of the two things himself.

But, despite the fear of the priest, boys and girls flocked to Hanuman Tekdi. They came here primarily to play, but the sense of danger and suspense associated with this area was for them an added attraction. Hide-and-seek was the most popular sport. The trees and shrubs around Hanuman Tekdi provided ample places for the children to hide. Lame was another game, they played. One of them hopped on one leg and tried to catch the others who ran in a square, marked by pebbles. However the children always kept a safe distance from the hillock housing the temple where the priest lived.

When tired of their games they would huddle together in groups under the shade of some tree and talk about different things. The proximity to the Hanuman temple naturally made the old priest a favorite topic of discussion. The older children used to terrify the younger ones by narrating bizarre stories about him. One boy claimed that he had seen the priest walking alongside a headless corpse. Another vouched that he had seen him flying through the air.

It was a Sunday and many boys and girls were playing hide-

and-seek at Hanuman Tekdi. Anirudh was hiding behind a thick shrub. He heard footsteps behind him and turned to see who it was. The old priest was walking towards him. With a wail of terror, Anirudh ran, but his feet collided against a rock and he fell.

The old priest was with him in a moment. 'Are you hurt, boy?' he asked.

Anirudh's bruised knees ached badly but, struck dumb with terror of the old priest, he could not utter a word. He sobbed quietly.

The priest noticed his wounded knees and picked up Anirudh in his arms. Paralyzed with fear, the boy could not protest. Other kids, hiding behind bushes and trees, did not notice the priest carry Anirudh to the temple. The priest seated Anirudh on the temple floor and washed his bruised knees with water. Anirudh continued to sob from fear and pain.

'There is no need to cry,' the priest said with a toothy smile, 'The wound is superficial. You will be alright within minutes.' He applied some ointments on Anirudh's knees and bandaged them with a clean cloth. 'There you are,' he said, 'Don't you feel better now?'

'Yes,' Anirudh mumbled faintly.

'Then, why don't you stop crying?'

'I am afraid of you.'

'Of me! Why?'

'You are a friend of the headless corpse, you fly through the air.'

'Who told you that?' the priest chuckled.

'Chandu and Hari and Jhankana and all the other children.'

'I am a friend of Hanumanji. The headless corpse dare not come

near me. As for flying through the air, I wish I could.' The priest picked up sweets from a tray lying in front of the idol and gave some to the boy saying, 'Here, take that. You like sweets, don't you?'

'I do,' Anirudh mumbled and accepted the sweets.

'Now, go out and play with your friends,' the priest said and led Anirudh out of the temple.

The other children were still searching for Anirudh among the bushes and trees. When they saw him emerge from the temple with the priest, they were filled with apprehension. Jhankana mustered courage and shouted, 'Anirudh, what are you doing there. Run away quickly.'

Heeding their advice Anirudh ran down the hillock. The priest laughed and went inside the temple. The kids surrounded Anirudh when he reached the base of the hillock and bombarded him with questions.

'Did the priest fly you to the temple?' Chandu asked.

'No, we walked,' Anirudh said.

'Did he perform some magical rite on you?' Sonu asked.

Anirudh wasn't sure if bandaging his knees could be considered a magical rite. 'I don't know,' he said doubtfully.

'What happened to your knees?' Jhankana asked. 'Who applied those bandages?'

'I fell down and hurt my knees. The priest bandaged them.'

'Did you see any ghouls, demons, witches or headless corpse at the temple?' Mina asked.

'I didn't.'

'Where did you get those sweets?' Hari asked.

'The priest gave them to me.'

'There must be some magic in those sweets. We should not eat them,' Jhankana warned.

'They look fine to me,' Chandu said. He snatched a sweet from Anirudh's hand and quickly gobbled it.

Before anybody could deprive him of the second sweet, Anirudh placed it in his mouth and started eating it merrily.

‡

On every purnavasi, the day when there was a full moon in the sky, a prayer ceremony was held in courtyard of the house. Though the prayer commenced at sunset, after the full moon appeared in the sky, preparations for the ceremony would start from noon itself.

Jhankana, her mother and Anirudh's mother splashed the courtyard with many buckets of water and then scrubbed it with long-handled brooms. Hari and Anirudh felt excited by the splashing water and swishing brooms, and tried to join the water sport by filling buckets at the hand pump or by wielding the brooms. But they were too small to be of any real help and were often told that they were in the way.

When the cleaning was done, in one section of the courtyard, grandmother created a square fireplace of few bricks smeared with cow dung to make them stick together. The boys sat with her and helped her in any way they could. After the fireplace was completed, the boys scampered off to the shed to fetch kindling. Grandmother arranged the kindling at the fireplace in an intricate conical form.

A carpet was spread behind the fireplace for the family members and the villagers to sit during the puja.

In the evening the boys accompanied grandfather to the market for purchasing fruits, sweets and other prayer material. Jhankana would normally stay behind, as she had to help the women in their chores. When they returned tugging bags bulging with their shopping, the fruits were chopped in small pieces and arranged in a copper plate along with the sweets. Anirudh and Hari invariably tried to gobble a few sweets when no one was looking, and mostly succeeded in doing so.

The family priest arrived few minutes before sunset. He was a short corpulent man, with chubby cheeks and short-cropped hair, and always wore white kurta and pajama. On the back of his head there was a thin tuft of hair, longer than the rest. The boys found the tuft amusing and called it rat's tail, though not in the hearing range of adults. On one occasion when the priest was sipping tea in the courtyard, Anirudh came from behind and out of curiosity pulled at the tuft. The priest screamed with pain. Anirudh tried his best to flee the scene but was caught by his father and awarded with a slap.

When the family members and other villagers were seated on the carpet, the priest set alight the kindling and started chanting the mantras in a monotonous drone. He added ghee and grains to the fire from time to time. Soon the courtyard was filled with the sweet smell of burning ghee. When the chanting of the mantras was over, the priest blew his conch shell a few times. After that he gave sweets and fruits to everyone as prasad.

‡

Sarita was not graced with a movie theatre. Seeing a movie was a daylong business for the villagers, for the nearest theatre was in the town of Gomantak, about 20 kilometers away. Those determined to see a movie left for Gomantak early in the morning, usually in a bullock cart and managed to return only after evening.

A film called Sholay was running in Gomantak's Kohinoor theatre. All who had seen this film were full of praise for it. Anirudh felt jubilant when mother told him, one day, that they would go to Gomantak on the morrow, to see Sholay.

'Will this movie have action scenes like the last film we saw?' Anirudh asked happily.

'Yes, it will,' mother replied.

'And song and dance?'

'Yes, that, too.'

'I will wake up early in the morning tomorrow and wake up everyone else so that we are not late for the film,' Anirudh announced enthusiastically.

'If only you could be as enthusiastic about your school.'

Next day at 7 AM, Mahto hinged the two cows, Saraswati and Lakshmi, to the cart. A tarpaulin canopy was stretched at the back of the cart forming something akin to a mobile hut. All the family members ensconced themselves inside the canopy. The sitting conditions were a bit cramped, but discomfort was for the privilege of seeing a movie, so no one minded it. After all, they were going for a movie after more than six months. The atmosphere was festive and the men, women and children laughed and joked.

Mahto sat at the front end of the bullock cart and drove the cows with a switch. As the cows plodded forward, the bells around their neck rocked in merry tintinnabulation. Anirudh, Hari and Jhankana sat beside Mahto and waved at the villagers, as the bullock cart passed through the village.

'We are going for a movie,' they announced to every boy or girl they met.

By 9 AM, they had reached the banks of the Saryu River, which lay halfway between their village and Gomantak. Dense bamboo thickets and great trees of different varieties – teak, pipal, mango, banyan, neem – flourished on the banks of this river. Whenever they were on way to Gomantak it was customary for them to stop at the Saryu River for few minutes to have their breakfast and to rest their cows.

Mahto stopped the cart at a mango grove. A mat was spread in the shade of a tree and they sat down to have breakfast of puri-bhaji, which they had brought with them in a wicker basket. Saraswati and Lakshmi munched the green grass growing on the riverbank. Pairs of crested bulbuls sang from treetops. Green parrots hopped from tree to tree in gay abandon. A female monkey with two young ones attached to its shriveled teats wandered close to them and stared at the food. Anirudh, Hari and Jhankana were amused to see the monkey and its two young ones and threw them small bits of food.

‡

When the breakfast was over the journey to Gomantak was resumed. At around 11.30 the bullock cart was parked on the street outside Kohinoor Theater. The family emerged from the bullock cart and stared with awe at the marquee depicting the names of the stars and at the colorful posters depicting scenes from the film. The next show started at 12 PM. Shambhu and Sadashiv went to the booking counter to purchase tickets. They returned shortly with tickets for everyone. Grandmother checked the tickets and immediately a frown came on her face. 'Who told you to buy balcony tickets?' she asked.

Sadashiv and Shambhu looked at each other in bewilderment. 'We just asked the man at the counter for tickets and this is what he gave us,' Shambhu said.

'He took both of you to be stupid peasants. That is why he foisted balcony tickets, which are much costlier,' grandmother thundered.

'Well...' Sadashiv mumbled sheepishly.

'A balcony ticket costs two rupees more than a stall ticket,' grandmother continued, 'Don't you know that?'

Sadashiv and Shambhu remained silent.

'Such a waste! It is morons that I have begotten from my womb. They don't know how to save money. An ordinary booking clerk can make fools out of them.'

'Don't create a fuss,' grandfather said. 'Two rupees is no big deal.'

'Two rupees is no big deal,' grandmother echoed sarcastically. 'You talk as if you have Kuber's treasure at your disposal. You should have had the sense to go to the booking window yourself instead of relying on your good-for-nothing sons.'

'I will do that when we come here next time. But now for God's sake let us go inside the theatre,' grandfather said peevishly.

A Thread of Life

Anoop Verma

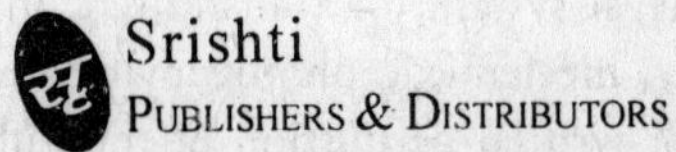

SRISHTI PUBLISHERS & DISTRIBUTORS
64-A, Adhchini
Sri Aurobindo Marg
New Delhi 110 017
srishtipublishers@yahoo.com

First published by Srishti Publishers & Distributors in 2005

ISBN 81-88575-50-X

Printed and bound in India

Typeset in AGaramond 11pt. by Suresh Kumar Sharma at Srishti

Cover design: Sandip Sinha

Printed and bound in India

'Mother, does all this mean that we can't see the movie?' Anirudh asked his mother.

'Hush, keep quiet,' mother said quickly, squeezing his arm.

'Ask the booking clerk to give us stall tickets in place of these tickets and get the balance refunded from him,' grandmother said.

Sadashiv and Shambhu went to the booking counter dutifully. They returned few minutes later looking crestfallen. The booking clerk had refused to take the tickets back.

'Why should he take them back? After all, he has earned two rupees extra for them,' grandmother grumbled, making a face. 'The cheat.'

'What do you wish us to do now?' grandfather asked with frustration.

'We can do nothing except watch the movie from balcony seats,' said grandmother. The family entered the theatre.

In order to save money, tickets for the three children had not been purchased. Jhankana sat on grandmother's lap, while Anirudh and Hari sat on the laps of their respective mothers. By the time the film began, the fiasco over the tickets was forgotten and they started enjoying the drama unfolding on the screen. Anirudh watched with interest even though most of the film was beyond his comprehension. He frequently asked his mother to explain what was happening on the screen. She answered his queries in hushed whispers. It was part of the cinema ritual to eat some snacks during the interval. Shambhu and Sadashiv brought hot samosas for everyone, at interval.

‡

On the full moon day, in the month of phalguna, came Holi. The villagers celebrated this festival with zest by throwing colored water, colored powder and sometimes, even cow dung and slush on each other. The revelry would start in the morning and carry on till evening. A grand procession of men soaked in color would march through the streets chanting the popular film song, 'Govinda alla re alla, jara matki sambhal brijbala' and applying colors on everyone they encountered. By the time the day ended, the whole village, even the cattle and the stray dogs would be drenched with the myriad colors of Holi that would take many days to wash off.

Holi was next day and the house carried a festive air. Colorful rangoli patterns were painted in the doorways and the courtyard. Smell of sweets and other delicious tidbits being fried in desi ghee wafted from the kitchen. Hari, Anirudh and Jhankana checked and rechecked their caches of colors many times and formulated diverse strategies for smearing their friends and relatives with colors when the next day dawned. They planned and conspired and laughed throughout the day.

At night when mother tucked Anirudh in the bed, he said, 'Why can't the hours pass quickly? I wish tomorrow could be here now. I want to begin playing Holi.'

'You will soon get the chance to play all the Holi that you want when the sun rises again in a few hours.'

'I am going to throw colors at everyone in this house and on all my friends. I will not spare anyone, not even you.'

'I don't plan to spare you, either,' mother replied. 'Now, close your eyes and go to sleep.'

'But I don't feel sleepy.'

'If you don't sleep on time, how will you wake up early in the morning to play Holi?'

That was all the prodding that the boy needed. He quickly closed his eyes.

‡

He woke up drowsily to the sound of his mother's voice and saw it was morning. Suddenly, he remembered that today was Holi and a bright smile appeared on his face and he exclaimed, 'Today is Holi, mother.'

'Yes, it is.'

He jumped down from the bed, saying, 'I will get my colors.'

The moment he was out of the bed, mother sprinkled colored water on him from a pichkari, which she was hiding behind her back and chuckled, 'Happy Holi!'

Anirudh snatched the pichkari from her and squirted rest of the colored water on her. 'Happy Holi,' he shouted with glee.

'Now, go and apply color on everyone else,' mother said.

'Okay,' Anirudh said conspiratorially. 'I will get my colors.'

Few sachets of colored powder were lying on the table. Anirudh snatched a sachet in one hand and ran out. Grandmother, grandfather, Shambhu and Sadashiv were sitting in the courtyard. He chucked colored powder on everyone, merrily chanting, 'Happy Holi! Happy Holi'. Jhankana and Hari emerged from their room, clutching their own pichkari's and colored powder. It was a free-for-all and within minutes the whole family was painted in vivid colors from head to toe.

A motley crowd of men, women, boys and girls arrived outside the house at around 10 AM. They made a great din in the verandah and ordered everyone in the house to come out. There was breathless excitement among the family members as everyone thought and planned how to tackle the mob waiting outside. Finally grandfather, Sadashiv and Shambhu picked up buckets of colored water and went out to meet the gang of Holi revelers. They shouted Holi slogans and splashed colored water on the crowd, but were soon caught by many hands and doused over and over again with colored water, cow dung, mud and slush, until they were barely recognizable. Hari, Anirudh, Jhankana and the two women threw colors at the crowd from the doorstep and from the window. They, too, were caught and splashed with colors and slush. The air was thick with screams of laughter and cries of jubilation. Sweets were served and everyone sang popular Holi songs.

The women went back inside the house while the men and the two boys became part of the rampaging Holi mob. The crowd roamed the village chanting Holi songs and applying colors ard muck on everyone they met. No soul, not even cattle and stray dogs were spared; they, too, were given the same colorful treatment. The animals, surprised at the sudden madness that had overtaken the generally peaceful villagers, scurried about in confusion.

By noon, when they started feeling exhausted, Anirudh and Hari, returned home with the adults. They sat under the hand pump in the courtyard, one after the other, to wash themselves.

But it never was possible to get rid of the hues of Holi by a single wash. They continued to appear colorful even after finishing the bath. Grandfather's white hair was now green on one side and red on the other. He jokingly cursed the revelers for not using black color on his head, as that would have made him look younger. All family members sat in the courtyard and chatted about the joyous events of the day.

‡

Evening was on its last legs when Anirudh's mother groaned, 'Ah! I feel pain in my chest.'

'But you were fine a few minutes ago?' Sadashiv said.

'The pain is very sharp,' mother cried out, pressing her chest with her hand. 'Feels like I am having a heart attack.'

'Nonsense,' grandmother said, 'You have caught cold due to all the Holi revelry. Few minutes of rest will make you feel fine. Go and lie down on the bed.'

Anirudh's mother got up and staggered to the bedroom.

'Is my mother feeling sick, grandmother?' Anirudh asked.

'She will be fine,' grandmother answered.

'I will go and talk to her,' Anirudh said, getting up.

'No, you must not disturb her now,' grandmother said. 'Why don't you play marbles with Hari and Jhankana?'

'Okay,' Anirudh said enthusiastically. The three children ran out and started playing in the verandah.

Two hours later grandmother came out and said, 'It is time to have dinner children.'

The kids rushed into the house. 'Where is my mother?' Anirudh asked.

'She is resting,' grandmother said. The children sat down in the kitchen and grandmother served them dinner. They were halfway through the dinner, when grandfather walked in. 'She is still suffering pain in the chest. Her condition worries me.'

'She played Holi with such zest during the day. I wonder what happened all of a sudden,' grandmother said.

'We don't even have a doctor in this village,' grandfather said with frustration.

'We shall take her to the town in the morning, if she isn't better by then.'

'That is the only thing that we can do.'

'Is Sadashiv with her?'

'Yes. Gautami is also there,' grandfather said and went out of the kitchen.

When Anirudh finished his dinner, he announced, 'I am going to my mother.'

'No, today you will sleep with grandfather,' grandmother said.

Grandfather carried him to his room and laid him down on the bed. The daylong activity had tired Anirudh and he fell asleep immediately.

‡

He woke up when he heard wailing in the courtyard. It was still dark and grandfather was not beside him on the bed. Wondering what the matter was, he got down from the bed and shuffled out of the room. The courtyard was full of villagers. Everyone was crying. Grandmother was sitting outside the door of mother's room. She was wailing loudly and beating her chest.

Anirudh noticed Jhankana crouching in one corner of the courtyard. He went to her and asked, 'Why are all of them crying?'

'Don't you know? Your mother is dead,' Jhankana replied.

' What is dead?'

'Even I don't know for sure,' Jhankana said secretly. 'But it is something very bad. That is why everyone is crying.'

Anirudh ran towards his mother's room. Grandmother caught him at the doorstep and cried, 'Poor child, his mother is no more.'

'Let me go,' Anirudh shouted and extricated himself from grandmother's grasp.

Mother was lying on the bed, her eyes were closed and there was a strange expression on her face. He had never seen her look like this. He thought something was wrong with her, but was too afraid to ask or to say anything. Sadashiv sat sobbing beside her. Gautami and Shambhu were trying to console him. Anirudh felt surprised that mother could remain asleep with all the crying going on around her.

Grandfather picked him up and carried him out of the room. He was relieved to be out of the room. He remained cooped up in grandfather's room along with Jhankana and Hari for rest of the night. In the morning when he was finally allowed to come out, he could not find mother anywhere in the house.

'Where is mother, grandmother?' he asked.

'She has gone to heaven.'

'When will she return?'

In answer, grandmother hugged him tightly and began sobbing.

‡

Four

Talking about the events from his past was a liberating experience for Anirudh. It was almost as if his memories had found new wings and were now soaring free. He looked at Jyotsna and in her eyes he found the understanding he craved for. His gaze turned towards the sea glowing under the bright noon sun, its shimmering waves glittering like silver when it is polished. Few people were sauntering along the water's edge, while others were lounging here and there on the sand. Colorfully attired children running along the shoreline made an eye-catching scene. Flocks of birds soaring in the sky produced soulful melody by their merry cackle. Far away, close to the horizon, could be seen the outline of a solitary fishing boat.

Anirudh reflected that the same sun brightened up his village as the sun here, the same air blew there as here. A longing swept over him to be among his own people, to walk on the land where he was born, to breathe the fragrance of rice plants that grew around his ancestral house. His mother was dead but other relatives would still be there. Hari and Jhankana would be grown up by now, as he was. Maybe they would be married and even have children of their own. Maybe his relatives in the village were looking for him although it was almost two decades since he fled from home.

'Don't worry. One day you will visit Sarita,' he heard Jyotsna say, and looked towards her, surprised to know that she had read his thoughts, that she knew he was pining for his village. 'We will go together,' she continued, 'You will introduce me to everyone in Sarita as your wife.'

'Yes, we will go together.'

'What happened after your mother's demise?' Jyotsna asked.

'I remained sad for many days. I cried for her. But with the passage of time, I got adjusted to life without her.'

'How did you reach Bombay?'

'Oh, my life took a sudden turn and I left my village. I will tell you about that some other time. I think I should return you to your home now.'

'Okay,' Jyotsna nodded. They got up and strolled out of the beach to the taxi parked on the road.

‡

A week later Anirudh and Jyotsna sat beside a square havan kund made on the floor of Jai Ganesh Wadi's Ganpati Temple. A gnarled old priest sat opposite them, chanting mantras, and from time to time chucking small quantities of grain into the tongues of flame that leapt from the kund. Anirudh was dressed in a white safari suit that he had ordered especially for this day and Jyotsna looked pretty in her new red bridal sari. Relatives and friends stood around them looking at the marriage ceremony with beatific smiles on their faces.

'Husband and wife will hold hands,' the priest droned.

Anirudh and Jyotsna took his words to be part of some meaningless mantra and did not react.

'The priest wants both of you to hold hands,' Jyotsna's mother whispered from behind.

They fumbled for few moments before they found each other's hand.

The priest chanted few more mantras, 'Husband and wife will circumambulate the holy fire seven times.'

They got up and went seven times round the fire. Suddenly, it was over. The priest pronounced the couple was now wedded for eternity. Jyotsna pressed Anirudh's hand softly, to show her happiness. They touched the priest's feet and prepared to leave. The priest looked upset. 'He is expecting something,' Jyotsna whispered in Anirudh's ear.

'Oh! I forgot,' Anirudh said. He pulled out a hundred-rupee note from his pocket and placed it on the tray. 'My gratitude Panditji and that of my wife,' he said.

The priest looked at the worn out note sourly. He had been expecting more. His disappointment communicated itself to Anirudh, who was about to pull out another note from his pocket, but Jyotsna whispered, 'Let us go. What you have given is just fine.'

They walked away from the scowling priest. Friends and relatives poured congratulations on them. Jyotsna's mother distributed sweets. The crowd escorted the couple to Anirudh's taxi, parked on the road. Anirudh was surprised to see Wahab Mia behind the steering wheel.

'What are you doing in my taxi?' Anirudh asked.

'Let me transport you to your home in style,' Wahab Mia said. 'Give me the keys.'

Anirudh would have preferred to have Jyotsna all to himself inside the taxi but Wahab Mia's kind offer could not be brushed away. He dropped the bunch of keys into Wahab Mia's lap. Turning towards Jyotsna, he said, 'How about it! We are going to be driven to our new home in style.'

'I remember a movie, in which the newlyweds were driven to their home in a six door limousine,' Jyotsna said with glee.

Anirudh opened the back door of the taxi and bowing magnificently, said with a flourish, 'Welcome to my limousine.'

The crowd behind them laughed and waved. Anirudh and Jyotsna waved from the taxi's window. Wahab Mia hit the road.

‡

Half an hour later, the taxi stopped outside a ramshackle three-storey building, with a small balcony on every floor. Anirudh had rented a flat on the second floor. Here and there on the building paint had washed away and patches of gray cement and muddy red bricks gaped vacantly. Jyotsna was not at all bothered by the building's poor condition. For someone who had lived in a slum all her life, even such a ramshackle building was a great blessing. She was satisfied with her new home. Most pleasing to her was the small balcony looking into the street. It was a typical one room flat with an attached bathroom and a cubicle that went for a kitchen. The day before, Anirudh had carried few things into the flat. There was a single bed, a wooden table with two iron chairs, a dresser with mirror and a steel cupboard. The kitchen had a primus stove and few utensils.

A tray of sweets lay on the table.

'You remembered to get sweets,' she gushed.

Without batting an eyelid Anirudh said, 'I know how much you like sweets.'

There was a knock on the door. 'Damn!' Anirudh said. 'I wonder who has come to pester us?'

'Sh-h, whoever is at the door may hear you,' Jyotsna whispered.

Anirudh opened the door. Their neighbor Janki was standing with a big smile on her face. 'Hello,' she chirped. 'I came to welcome the bride. I hope I am not intruding.'

Janki's unexpected arrival was a bother, especially to Anirudh, but he put on a diplomatic smile and said, 'Not at all, not at all' and then turning towards Jyotsna he said, 'She is Janki, our next-door neighbor.'

'I am pleased to meet you,' Jyotsna said demurely. 'Do come in.'

'All I came to say is that if you need anything, feel free to knock at my door.'

'It is nice of you to make that offer,' Jyotsna smiled.

'I hope you like the sweets I placed on your table?'

'Sweets? What sweets?' Jyotsna exclaimed.

'The tray is lying on the table,' Janki said, pointing with her finger towards the tray full of sweets.

Before Jyotsna could respond, Anirudh interjected, 'Of course, we liked the sweets. Thanks for sweetening our day.'

When Janki left and the door was shut, Jyotsna turned towards Anirudh and said, 'So you knew that I liked sweets? Liar!'

'Oh! Come on. Don't call me names on our wedding day.'

'What did you intend to achieve by lying?'

'How could I know that our fat neighbor was going to barge in and claim credit for the sweets?'

'My God! This is too much. You are not sorry for lying, instead you are blaming Janki for telling the truth.'

'Our first day of marriage and you have already started nagging,' he said, somewhat flustered by the way things were turning.

'Nagging?' she glared. 'Why don't you accept that you made a mistake by lying to me? Then I will quit nagging.'

'Okay, damn it!' he shouted. 'I made a mistake by claiming the credit for those lousy sweets.'

'Don't holler at me.'

He grabbed her roughly and pulled her into an embrace. He kissed her eyes, her nose, her mouth and the nape of her neck. His right hand pressed her breast.

'Stop,' she screamed. 'What are you doing?'

'Come on. You have no idea how I feel. Charged up since morning and waiting, and waiting. It is enough to make a man crazy.'

'Let me go. You are hurting me.'

He threw her down on the bed and pounced on her. She tried to push him away and failing to do that, she screamed. He placed his hand on her mouth and through clenched teeth, hissed, 'What the hell! Do you want to summon the whole building?'

She started to cry. Sobs burst from her throat, as tears ran down her cheeks. He moved away from her. She arranged her sari over her breasts with trembling fingers.

'Why are you crying?' he asked.

'I don't know.'

'What is the matter? Don't you love me anymore?'

'I need a glass of water,' she said, getting up from the bed.

'I will get it for you.'

'I will get it myself,' she said stubbornly.

He followed her into the kitchen and watched suspiciously as she poured water from a bottle and began to sip slowly. He waited impatiently.

They were in the bedroom again. He caught her long, plaited hair and pulling her head back, roughly placed a bruising kiss on her throat. With all her strength she pushed him away.

'What is the meaning of this nonsense, Jyotsna?' he demanded hotly.

'Don't try to force me.'

'I am your husband. It is my right to be with you.'

'I am a person first and then your wife. The person in me doesn't like being forced.'

'You are depriving me of my marital rights.'

'I am not going to sleep with you.'

'But why?'

'I am not prepared for that yet,' she said, looking away from him. 'You will have to give me time.'

'Okay, be easy. I won't force you.'

He walked out into the balcony and gazed at the street below. In no time he tired of watching the endless procession of people and vehicles passing by and returned inside the room. Her eyes were closed as she lay on the bed. He knew that she was awake and only pretending to be asleep. Quietly he made a bed for himself on the ground by spreading a coir mat and lay down. In few minutes they were both fast asleep, she on the bed and he on the ground.

‡

They would have liked to have a few days to themselves, days in which they didn't have to bother about the everyday routines of earning a living. But they had parted with a substantial amount of money for the marriage ceremony and for renting and furnishing the flat. Now their financial situation being quite precarious, they could not afford the luxury of holidays.

Anirudh was getting ready in the only room in the flat, when he heard Jyotsna say from the kitchen, 'There is nothing in the kitchen to cook breakfast from.'

'Don't bother about cooking. We will eat at a restaurant,' he said.

She emerged from the kitchen and said; 'This will not do. We have to stock the kitchen today itself.'

'Why bother about cooking? I don't mind hotel food. I have been eating in hotels all my life.'

'That was before you got married. Now onwards you are going to have your breakfast and dinner at home with me.'

'But how will you manage to cook coping with job pressures?'

'I will,' she said, adding with a wink, 'With your help, I will.'

'I am prepared to help,' Anirudh answered quickly, even though the thought of toiling in the kitchen filled him with dread.

'While returning from the hospital I will purchase the provisions we need.'

'You are going to do nothing of that sort,' he declared emphatically. 'I won't allow you to tug bags of provisions up the stairs of this building. It is a man's job to buy things for the family and I am going to do that.'

'You will purchase all the wrong stuff,' Jyotsna said skeptically.

'Are you kidding? Don't you consider me fit even for purchasing things like tea, sugar and grains?'

'Okay, lets not get into a debate on this issue. I will make a list of the things we require.'

'That is the way it should be done.'

Jyotsna tore off a page from a notebook and began to write. She made a list mentioning the precise quantity of each item.

'Don't change anything in this list,' she said, giving the paper to Anirudh. 'Buy as I have written.'

Anirudh placed the paper in his pocket and said, 'After I return home with the provisions, you will find what a fine purchaser of household goods I am. I have been buying things all my life.'

'I am sure you will do fine.'

‡

For breakfast he took her to the Rishi Restaurant, which was located near their building. It was rush hour and many people were sitting on the neat rows of chairs and tables in the well-lighted hall. All the places were occupied. Anirudh and Jyotsna stood in the center of the hall waiting for a couple of seats to be vacated. There was din and clanging of vessels as waiters scurried about serving the customers. The agreeable aroma of delicious foodstuff was in the air.

A waiter appeared. He was a resident of Jai Ganesh Wadi and knew Anirudh. 'Family rooms are upstairs,' he said, 'Follow me.'

Anirudh felt proud of his social contact with this waiter. 'Let's go upstairs,' he said to Jyotsna.

There were only a few customers in the hall upstairs and Anirudh and Jyotsna had a table all to themselves.

'It is a good thing that the waiter brought us here,' Jyotsna said. 'At least we will be able to eat in peace. Downstairs is so chaotic.'

'The waiter knew me,' Anirudh said self-importantly.

'Nothing extraordinary in that.'

'Why?'

'Anyone who has been eating in hotels all his life will be familiar to waiters.'

The waiter came carrying a tray of idli-sambhar. The couple had little to say after that, as both got busy eating. Anirudh ordered espresso coffee.

'Big spender,' Jyotsna raised her eyebrows.

'Espresso coffee does not cost much. Someday I will take you to dine at a five-star hotel.'

Jyotsna frowned. 'We will eat at a five-star hotel after you sell your taxi and all the furniture and utensils we have at home.'

'Don't be so practical. I know we can't afford to dine at a five-star. It was just a dream.'

'Start dreaming realistically.'

They finished the coffee and the waiter brought them the bill.

'Let me see how much the food has cost us,' Jyotsna said. Anirudh showed her the bill. 'Heavens!' she gulped. 'We could have had five meals at home at the price of this one meal.'

The waiter laughed at her words.

'Don't embarrass me,' Anirudh whispered.

She shrank back into her seat. Anirudh paid the bill and they came out of the restaurant.

'We will never come to this restaurant again,' she said. 'The rates are too high.'

'I used to eat here regularly before we got married,' Anirudh said.

'That is why you don't even own a bank account after driving a taxi for so many years.'

'You may have a point there.'

'You can bet I have a point,' she said and checking her watch exclaimed, 'I am going to be late for my hospital today. You go to your taxi. I will catch a bus.'

He took her hand and said, 'Come with me.'

'What?' she uttered with surprise, looking up at his face.

'I will drop you to your job.'

'But why! You may earn 20 or even 30 rupees in the time you will waste taking me to the hospital.'

'I want to be with you for a little longer.'

She opened her mouth as if to say something, but he interrupted, saying, 'Your hospital is not far from here. It will take me only a few minutes to take you there.'

Seeing that he was determined, she relented. 'Okay, Today I will come with you, but from tomorrow it will be the bus for me.'

'That will be fine.'

They sat in the taxi and he drove her to the hospital.

‡

It was 8 PM when Anirudh returned, tugging bags loaded with provisions. He rang the bell. Jyotsna opened the door. She looked drowsy.

'Oh! It is you,' she said stifling a yawn.

'Were you expecting the Pasha of Dubai?'

'I fell asleep after returning from the hospital. In my sleep I thought I was at home and my mother had come from somewhere.'

'When did you return from hospital?'

'About an hour ago. Did you get everything in my list?'

'Yeah. Everything,' Anirudh said placing the bags on the table. 'I had no idea that you had ordered so many items. It took the shopkeeper an hour to put things together. You sure we will consume all this?'

'What do you think?' Jyotsna smiled. 'These provisions will barely last us a month.'

'You probably know more about household economy than I do.'

'You bet I do. I will get water for you.'

Anirudh kicked off his shoes and lounged on the bed. Jyotsna fetched water from the kitchen.

'You told me I should not drive taxi till late, so I made sure I reached home by 8. Now I deserve a hug.'

'You will have all that after I finish arranging the provisions,' Jyotsna said. 'Give me the list and the shopkeeper's bill.'

'What for?'

Throwing her arms akimbo, Jyotsna said point-blank, 'I want to compare the list with the purchase.'

'Don't you believe me when I say that I have purchased everything?'

'I believe you, but the shopkeeper could have made a mistake,' she insisted.

'Now where did I keep those damned papers,' Anirudh said, checking his pockets. He pulled out two sheets and after giving them a cursory glance uttered, 'Found it.'

'15 kg of rice, 10 kg of atta, 5 kg of masur dal…' Jyotsna murmured with satisfaction, as she went through the bags lying on the table. Suddenly she exclaimed, 'You got 2.5 kg of maida?'

'Are you talking to me?' Anirudh asked disinterestedly.

'There is no one else in this room, so I must be talking to you.'

'I got what you wrote in the list.'

She brought the list to him and said triumphantly, 'Look here I have clearly written 250 grams of maida and the shopkeeper has billed you for 2.5 kg.'

'In that case, he must have given me 2.5 kg of maida by mistake.'

'I have checked the bag. It contains 250 grams of maida. The shopkeeper has cheated you.'

'Come on. I am sure he has not done this intentionally.'

'Where did you buy these things from?'

'From Dinesh stores, at Jai Ganesh Wadi.'

'From Dinesh stores,' she shuddered, 'Don't you know, how big a crook the Dinesh stores man is?'

'He is my friend. I have always purchased my provisions from him. He will never cheat me intentionally. I will get a refund from him for the extra maida that he has billed us for. Don't you worry about that.'

'The Dinesh stores man never gives correct measure to his customers. I am sure that everything you have bought weighs less than it is billed for. My mother never bought anything from there.' She played nervously with the papers she held in her hand and gave him the hard glance grownups give to erring children.

'You should learn to trust people,' Anirudh said philosophically. 'It is not good to suspect everyone.'

'Dinesh stores man is not everyone,' she said, getting red in the face.

He kept quiet to avoid further argument. She went back to checking other items. Few minutes later, she turned towards him again and said, 'I had asked for red rajma and he has given you white rajma.'

'He didn't have red rajma.'

'What kind of a shop has he, if he does not have red rajma?'

Anirudh did not respond.

'Heavens! He has given you lux soap instead of lifebuoy that I asked for.'

'That is not his fault. I asked him to give me lux.'

'Why?'

'Lux is a beauty soap. It is good for the skin.'

'It costs 2 rupees more than lifebuoy,' she retorted.

'I got lux for you. You will look beautiful if you use lux. Have you not seen the advertisements, in which film actresses proclaim that lux is the secret of their beauty?'

'There is nothing wrong with lifebuoy. My mother always bought lifebuoy.'

'I don't want you to look like your mother, that is why I bought lux.'

'Don't you criticize my mother,' Jyotsna snapped.

'There is no reason to shout.'

'You have wasted at least 20 rupees on this shopping,' she carried on in the same vein. 'We can't afford to be so profligate.'

'Well-well, I am sorry.'

'Just because the Dinesh store man happens to be your friend, you allow yourself to be cheated. He means more to you than your wife.'

'Hush! Otherwise neighbors will think that a couple of lunatics live in this house.'

'They won't be far from truth if they think like that.'

'I promise that I won't set foot inside Dinesh stores ever again in my life,' Anirudh pleaded.

'You must ask him to refund the extra amount he has billed us for the maida and replace lux with lifebuoy.'

'I will do that tomorrow,' he promised.

She began arranging the provisions in different containers. Anirudh could make out from her face that she was still angry. He remembered the gift that he had bought for her. He brought out the little box from his handbag and placed it on the bed. 'I bought something for you,' he said.

'What is it?' she said, looking up from many containers.

'Open the box and see for yourself,' he said pointing towards the box.

She came and picked up the box with her flour-covered hands. 'O My God!' she gasped.

'It is pure gold,' Anirudh said nonchalantly.

'No kidding,' she said, her eyes wide open.

'It is 20 carat gold. That is what the jeweler told me.'

'It must have cost a fortune,' she laughed. 'Why did you buy it?'

'This is my wedding present to you. I should have brought it yesterday but I forgot. I guess you won't mind the delay.'

'It is beautiful. But I didn't buy anything for you.'

'That makes me one up on you. Let me help you put these on.'

'I will wash my hands first. They are covered with flour.'

'Later. Gold does not spoil by contact with flour.' He led her in front of the dresser, removed old glass earrings from her ear and attached the new earrings in their place. 'See how beautiful you look with these new earrings.'

She handled the gold earrings gingerly, as if she was afraid of damaging them, 'This is a wonderful gift.'

'I am pleased that you are in a better mood now.'

'I should not have been so rude. After all, it was only 15 or 20 rupees that you wasted in the purchasing. That is no big deal.'

'You were not rude to me. You behaved exactly like a wife should. Put your head on my shoulders and relax.'

She snuggled close to him and they hugged.

‡

It was still dark when Jyotsna woke up in the morning. She wondered what the time was. Anirudh was lying on the bed beside her. She turned his hand slightly to look at his wristwatch.

'What time is it?' he asked.

'Sorry, I didn't mean to wake you. It is 5 AM.'

'That means I can sleep for another hour,' he mumbled drowsily and turned to the other side.

'Yeah, you can.'

Anirudh closed his eyes. She got up and tiptoed to the balcony. A faint orange glow had started to lighten up the sky, though the brightness was not strong enough to vanquish the moon's crescent in the sky. A light breeze, which carried the freshness of early morning, was blowing. Few fitness freaks could be seen in the street walking and jogging their way to good health.

A voice came from behind. 'What are you looking at?'

She was startled. 'Oh, it's you,' she said turning back. 'I thought you were sleeping.'

'Didn't you wake me up a minute ago?' he asked mischievously.

'I didn't. I was as silent as...'

'As what?'

'As anything that is silent,' she said simply.

'I don't think so. I heard all your movements loud and clear. When you got up and walked to the balcony I heard the rattling of your bones and the flexing of your muscles. I also heard the rustling of your clothes. You created quite a din. Really.'

'You forgot to say that you heard my eyes blink.'

'Yeah, that, too.'

'Now that both of us are up, why don't we engage in some morning walk like those people,' Jyotsna asked, pointing towards the street.

'Yawn. I am going back to bed.'

'Don't be such lazy bones. Come with me,' she said, pushing him to the bathroom. They got ready and came out of the flat.

‡

Soon they were walking in the street that ran in front of their building. There was a nip in the air. A group of schoolgirls, resplendent in red and blue school uniforms, were giggling under a tree, because some boys were pressing their attentions on them.

'How nice the morning air feels?' Jyotsna said, taking a deep breath.

'It sure does.'

After going for about hundred meters the street branched off in two directions. They took the right turn.

'Hey! I know that woman. She works as a nurse in my hospital,' Jyotsna said, pointing towards a woman walking with a four-year-old boy.

'So you have found an acquaintance in this area,' Anirudh said, 'I hope she isn't the chatty type. Or she will visit our house everyday to bore us with her drivel.'

'You are antisocial,' Jyotsna said accusingly.

Anirudh didn't get the chance for a repartee as they had reached close to the woman and the boy. Jyotsna said, 'Hello, Vimla.'

'Hello,' the woman said with a smile.

'Do you stay close by?'

'Yes, in the green building over there.'

'He is my husband, Anirudh Shukla,' Jyotsna said. Vimla and Anirudh greeted each other with folded hands. 'Is he your son?' Jyotsna asked.

'Yes, his name is Atul,' Vimla said, 'Say good morning, Atul.'

'Good morning,' the boy said obediently.

'He is cute,' Jyotsna said, patting the boy on his cheeks.

'Where do you stay?' Vimla asked.

'My home is a few buildings down that street.'

'We are almost neighbors.'

'I am glad we are.'

'Mummy let's go,' the boy said, tugging at his mother's dress.

'Your boy is eager to resume his walk,' Jyotsna chuckled.

'Yes. He is very active.'

'We should not rein in the young man any longer,' Jyotsna said. 'See you at the hospital.'

'It was a pleasure meeting you here,' Vimla said.

They walked off in opposite directions.

'How nice it feels when you bump into someone,' Jyotsna exulted.

'I wonder why her husband was not with her?' Anirudh said.

'He may not have heard his wife's bones rattling, muscles flexing and eyes blinking and could still be asleep.'

'You never miss making a point.'

When they returned to their building they met Janki, who was chatting at the gate with another middle-aged woman.

'Good morning,' Janki said cheerfully.

Anirudh and Jyotsna returned the greetings.

'I hope both of you know Shalini. She lives on the first floor of our building,' Janki said, pointing towards the middle-aged woman.

'We were not acquainted earlier, but we know her now,' Jyotsna said good-naturedly and introduced herself and Anirudh, to Shalini.

'Are you returning from a morning walk?' Shalini asked.

'Yes. Today my wife got inspired by the morning walkers she saw from the balcony,' Anirudh said.

'People say walking is good for health. I have not missed my morning walk for five years. But my husband rarely joins me. He prefers to sleep till 7,' Janki said.

'Given a chance most husbands would sleep till 7,' Jyotsna said looking at Anirudh.

'There she comes,' Janki said suddenly, her voice dropping to a conspiratorial whisper.

'Who?' Jyotsna asked.

'That wench,' Janki said spitefully, pointing towards the svelte young woman in early twenties, jogging towards the building in a figure-hugging nylon tracksuit. 'Look at the way she jogs, wriggling her hips from side to side, as if her waist were a pendulum!'

'She is flaunting her figure to the whole world. The shameless creature,' hissed Shalini, her face distorted by hatred.

'Who is she?' asked Jyotsna.

'She lives on the third floor. Though she claims to be working as a dancer in the film industry, her main profession is something else,' said Janki secretly.

'And what is that?' asked Jyotsna.

'Can't you make out by her appearance? She is a hooker.'

'Don't tell me,' Jyotsna gasped.

'Why should we bother about her?' said Anirudh with disgust.

'You don't understand,' Janki said. 'A bad woman like her gives a bad name to all the women of this building.'

'One bad fish sullies the whole pond,' Shalini spewed philosophically.

The young woman jogged past the four, standing at the gate and without making eye contact with anyone, went inside the building.

'Doesn't even have the decency to say good morning,' Janki snarled after her.

'But is there any proof that she indulges in those kinds of activities?' Jyotsna asked.

'I have seen her laughing and talking with different young men many times and so have other residents of this building. No woman with an honest bone in her body would flirt with young men so brazenly,' Janki declared.

'She should be thrown out of the building,' Shalini said.

'We will leave now. We have to get ready for work,' Jyotsna said and went inside the building with Anirudh.

When they were inside their flat, Jyotsna said, 'I don't like Janki.'

'Why?'

'She is always interfering in other peoples, business. Just because she saw her laughing and talking with young men, she calls her a harlot. Now that is ridiculous.'

'You have a point there. These are modern times. There is nothing wrong in laughing and talking with members of opposite sex.'

'As long as you don't sleep around.'

'Of course.'

'Shalini is also like Janki. Both of them are no good,' Jyotsna said.

'I disliked Janki from the moment I learned that she had placed those sweets on our table. She should have waited for us to arrive and then presented us the sweets in a decent fashion,' Anirudh said.

'Yes, she had no business slipping anything inside our house without our permission.'

'That's correct.'

'I can bet that the young woman is of decent character and Janki is calling her a harlot out of spite.'

'That may as well be the case.'

‡

Anirudh didn't take out his taxi on Sunday, which was Jyotsna's day off at the hospital and they went to a movie. At the theater, Anirudh would have purchased balcony tickets, but Jyotsna insisted on stall.

'What is wrong with balcony?' he asked.

'It is costlier,' she said flatly.

'You are just like my grandmother. She always insisted on stall.'

'I don't understand why people pay more for balcony tickets. After all, they show the same movie in stall or balcony.'

'Seats are more comfortable in balcony.'

Jyotsna was not convinced. She said, 'It is foolish to pay extra for comfortable seats. If comfort is what someone desires then he should stay in bed at home.'

'No man can ever win an argument with a woman.'

'Is that because women are generally smarter?' Jyotsna winked mischievously.

During interval Anirudh came out of the theatre and purchased popcorn, ice cream and cold drinks. Jyotsna accepted her portion of the eateries with alacrity, but said, 'You should not have got so many things.'

'It is part of the cinema ritual to eat and drink during the interval,' Anirudh said through a mouthful of crunchy popcorns.

'Well, I guess it is.'

When the movie was over at 6 PM they went to Jyotsna's house at Jai Ganesh Wadi. This was their first visit to this place since they got married and Jyotsna's mother was delighted to see them.

'You have changed a lot in few days,' gushed Jyotsna's mother.

'In what sense?' Jyotsna asked.

'You don't look like a girl anymore. You look like a wife.'

'Isn't that what I now am?'

'Does my daughter take good care of you?' Jyotsna's mother asked Anirudh.

'I have gained 5 kilos since I started eating food cooked by her,' Anirudh said patting his tummy.

Jyotsna laughed. After sometime Anirudh went out to meet his friends leaving the mother and daughter alone to indulge in their private chitchat. He met Wahab Mia at the tea stall on the roadside.

'How is life after marriage?' Wahab Mia asked.

'Had I known that life after marriage would be so good, I

would have married much earlier,' Anirudh said jovially.

'Marriage can be very pleasant, if one finds the correct life partner.'

'I am glad to have found Jyotsna.'

‡

Five

The narrow-gauge train rumbled inexorably forward, drawing him closer and closer to the land of his forbearers. He sat silently on the berth, his head bent low, eyes focused somewhere on his lap, brooding about the relatives and friends he would soon meet, the places he would soon see, the experiences he would rekindle. There was ecstasy in his mind at the prospect of being back in Sarita, but with ecstasy there was also the nagging fear, borne primarily from the suspense about what he was going to find in Sarita. Whether he would be welcome as an adult in the home where he was once a much-pampered toddler! He was barely seven when he left, now he was returning as a 27 years old. Would his relatives and friends recognize him as the same Anirudh? Would they still love him as they once did? Would the village be very different from how it had been when he lived there? The sprawling brick house standing in a sea of rice fields – had his house changed? Who all would be living there? Were grandfather and grandmother still alive? They had been quite old when he lived with them, now they would be older still. He hoped that they would be there to meet him, but what if they had passed away?

What about his father? What would his reaction be when he learned that his son had returned home after almost two decades? Would he be pleased or… Maybe he has become used to life without me and my going back would only serve to complicate his life, Anirudh told himself. What would stepmother's attitude towards him be? He hoped that her attitude would not be hateful. Would Hari and Jhankana recognize their cousin and childhood friend? Would they still love him or would they hate him for having left them so abruptly twenty years ago? He buried the thoughts quickly, telling himself that everyone would welcome him with open arms. His greatest fear was that he might fail to find any of his family members in the village? After all, twenty years was a lot of time… A lot could have changed during that period… What if he found some other family living in his house? His relatives could have sold the house and moved elsewhere… Or the house itself gone, demolished, to pave way for new construction … Suspense was turning him into a bundle of nerves. He wanted but one thing at this moment to reach his village quickly and learn the truth.

Jyotsna was sitting beside him, gazing wistfully at the endless vista of cultivated fields out of the window. Peasants working among the crops with bent backs seemed like giant beetles hovering on a sea of greenery. Electricity and telephone lines strung parallel to the tracks raced along the train, crossing and parting and then crossing again. Clusters of nondescript huts or brick houses came into view from time to time before the green fields took over again. Anirudh understood quite well that the emotions crisscrossing Jyotsna's mind were analogous to his own. Few hours ago when the train started from Bombay station she had betrayed her sentiments by saying, 'I hope your relatives like me.' Though she tried to pretend that she had spoken those words in jest, he knew that she was pondering relentlessly about what awaited them at the village. 'They will all be proud of you,' he had said, 'They will congratulate me on my choice.' 'They would better be proud of me,' she had laughed, 'I yearn to be a pampered daughter-in-law for as long as we stay in Sarita.'

Jyotsna withdrew her gaze from the window to look at him. Their eyes met and they gave each other sympathetic smiles. 'Cheer up,' she said, 'You will soon be among your people.'

'I hope they still consider me as one of their own,' Anirudh mused, 'So many years have passed…'

'They will,' Jyotsna interrupted, 'You are of their flesh and blood. How can they forget you.' As if she was not sure of her own words, she looked at him and asked, 'Well, won't they.'

'Of course they will,' he hastily replied and smiled softly. In so many ways she was like a child she wanted to be pampered and liked by everyone. For her sake he hoped that they would receive all the love and care in Sarita. Since their marriage how wonderfully patient she had been with him. She did her best to identify with the issues of consequence to him. She was curious about his relatives. It was she who had prodded him into undertaking this journey. One day when they were at home and he was being nostalgic, she asked him to plan a journey to Sarita. Her quick decision took him completely by surprise. She insisted that she wished to become acquainted with her husband's side of the family. It was her feeling that he would not have peace till he came to terms with his village past. Now barely two months had passed since his marriage and he was taking his bride to his ancestral village. They hoped to spend ten halcyon days in Sarita, basking in the company of his old relatives.

The compartment was chock-a-block with passengers and their

luggage. Those unable to find space on the few berths were sitting on various pieces of luggage. Some were squatting directly on the begrimed floor. There was also no dearth of standees. Much of the conversation in the compartment was flowing in Bhojpuri. 'It's a sweet language that the people of this state have,' Jyotsna said and then added with a chuckle, 'I say that even though I cannot make head or tail of Bhojpuri.'

'Bhojpuri is a simple language. You can pick it up in no time.'

'When we are in Sarita, your relatives will teach me Bhojpuri,' Jyotsna declared playfully.

'You can teach them Marathi when they teach you Bhojpuri.'

'I might as well do that.'

‡

Two hours later the train was lumbering through Sarita. Anirudh and Jyotsna looked out of the window anxiously. Parallel to the tracks ran a road, on which small handcarts, scooters and trucks were plying. Beyond the road, cultivated fields were interspersed at regular intervals with huts, houses and shops. The train passed a large pond with brackish water in which buffaloes were bathing. 'Has the village changed much?' Jyotsna asked expectantly. His eyes focused on the unfolding vista outside the window, Anirudh said, 'I am not sure.'

The station was now only minutes away and he picked up the two suitcases that was their entire luggage and they moved to the door, already choked with passengers bound for Sarita. The train thudded into the station and screeched to a stop. There was a bit of scramble as many passengers in the train were trying to get off, while others at the platform attempted to board. Anirudh and Jyotsna shoved and pushed their way out of the compartment. At last they stood on the platform with their suitcases lying on the ground. They looked around perplexed. Were they at home or in some unfamiliar land? Anirudh hoped that he might recognize someone from his childhood, but no familiar face came to his view. The sun, high in the sky, was reducing all colors to half tones. The station seemed to have been dried up and discolored by the sun's rays. The walls looked faded and weathered. There was a stall selling tea and snacks, a magazine stall and a two-storey yellowish gray building that served as the office. Anirudh reminisced that during his childhood days the station was just an open area, utterly devoid of stalls, and the station office was in a hut made from bamboo and clay. Around the station there was evidence of further change. Buildings had cropped up. The buildings huddled close to each other and left no room to view the green fields. Three or four shoeshine boys were sitting at one end of the platform. When Anirudh was a child it was rare to find a villager wearing shoes.

The train gave a sharp whistle and rambled out of the station. Anirudh picked up the suitcases and they started walking. Sarita's market was still located along the road behind the railway station. The nature of wares sold seemed more contemporary, though many shops were mere shacks, jerry-built from wood, bamboo and mud. Colorful airbags, cheap cosmetics and jewelry, fashionable clothes were on display. There was at least one shop selling electronic appliances, TV, fridge, etc. The crowd in the market consisted of as many women as men; a definite sign that the village society had turned liberal. The traditional dress of dhoti-kurta seemed passé, as most men were in shirt-pant. Women were in sari or salwar-kurta with a duppatta flung over the shoulders, only few hid their faces behind veils. There was a sweet shop selling hot jalebis. 'I think this is the shop where I used to come with my grandfather to eat jalebis.' Anirudh said. 'Let's have some jalebis before we go to your house,' Jyotsna said. They went inside the shop and ordered two plates of jalebis. The portly man, who was sitting behind the counter, seemed too young to be Rewa. Maybe he is Rewa's son, Anirudh thought. When he finished eating, he went to the counter and asked the portly man, 'Are you related to Rewa?'

'Rewa? Who is Rewa,' the man at the counter asked disinterestedly.

'Rewa ran this shop, twenty years ago when I used to come here.'

'I purchased this shop only ten years ago. I have no idea who ran this shop twenty years ago.'

Anirudh was disappointed at the answer. He wanted to enquire from the shopkeeper about his family members but desisted from dread of hearing something unpleasant. He preferred to confront the reality with his own eyes rather than hear about it second hand. He came out of the shop with Jyotsna and they started for his home. He remembered the general direction of the house and did not bother to inquire for directions. The huts made out of straw, mud and bamboo poles were there but somehow they looked more like city slums rather than village dwellings. Few buildings had come up where earlier there used to be cultivated land. These buildings, built in the style of cities, seemed incongruous in the village landscape. The school building was no longer a one-room affair. It was a long brick-colored building with many rooms. Few children wearing indigo and white dress were playing in the playground outside the school.

‡

They reached the point from where the agricultural land began and were soon walking on a narrow mud path meandering through fields with crops swaying in the breeze. In the maze of the fields Anirudh started getting confused about the direction. It seemed the fields had multiplied or the path led not to a house but to some wooded area. He wanted to inquire the way from someone but could find no one in the fields. They kept walking, hoping to find someone who could direct them or, better still, chancing upon the house itself... A little ahead the mud path turned sharply to the right and as they turned they came upon it, all of a sudden, and Anirudh stood with heart thumping in his breast and tears welling in his eyes. There it was! His home! No longer lost in the mists of time, it stood in front of his eyes. It seemed so familiar that he felt as if he had left but yesterday. The walls, the roof, the rectangular windows, the small verandah in the front were just as he remembered. Any moment he expected his family members to emerge from the house and call his name.

Memories flashed through his mind as he shuffled forward in a sort of dreamy haze. Soon his eyes started discerning changes that time had wrought. Grass and weeds were growing rampantly in the front ground. The outer walls were discolored and cement had peeled in many places exposing bricks, which seemed to be on the verge of crumbling. A portion of roof over the verandah had caved in and the floor was chipped and cracked in many places. No sound came from the house and the open windows gaped forlorn. It seemed as if the house was uninhabited.

'Why was my house allowed to deteriorate to such an extent,' Anirudh uttered, his voice thick with emotion. 'Maybe your relatives moved elsewhere and now there isn't anyone to take care of this old house,' Jyotsna said. There was no padlock outside the door, which opened when Anirudh pushed it. They entered. The interior was only little better than the exterior, the walls were discolored here as well. However the floor looked swept. There were signs of life in the courtyard, some freshly washed clothes drying on a string, a bed whose mattress bore the imprint of a human body, in one corner a bucket half full of water, beside it a utensil with chopped vegetables. But if someone did live in this house, where was he or she?

There were rooms around the courtyard. Anirudh remembered clearly the layout of the rooms. The room on the left used to belong to his father and mother. He rushed to it only to find it padlocked. His grandfather's room was not locked. He walked into the room. The high four-poster bed seemed quaintly familiar. Was it the same bed on which he used to sleep next to his grandfather? On a shelf beside the bed, among other bric-a-brac was grandfather's hookah. The hookah appeared dusty and old, as if it had not been used for a long time. Close to the bed was a rickety side table with a clay pitcher and an aluminum glass. He poured water into the glass and drank. The water tasted fresh, more proof that someone was living in the house. But where was that someone?

Jyotsna said something, her voice quivering with apprehension. He looked in the direction she pointed. On the opposite wall were two photographs, yellowed with age, hanging on wooden frames. Garlands of flowers adorned both the photographs. Anirudh's face turned ashen. 'Who are they,' Jyotsna whispered. 'My grandfather and grandmother,' Anirudh said. Suddenly the house felt like a sepulcher; it was not his past but the ruins of his past that lay in it.

‡

There was a rustling behind them and they turned to find an old woman, small and thin, wearing a rumpled white sari, her white hair arranged in pleats at the back of her head standing at the doorstep. There was fear in her eyes as she peered at them. Her frail body shivered a little. Maybe she took them to be a couple of robbers. 'Wh...who are you people' she stammered.

Could she be Gautami, the mother of Hari and Jhankana? Anirudh asked himself.

'What do you want?' the old woman asked suspiciously.

'I am a child of this house,' Anirudh said.

The old woman drew one or two steps backward, now definitely frightened of the intruders. 'You are not a child of this house,' she uttered, 'You have come to a wrong house. Go away.'

'They are my grandfather and grandmother,' Anirudh said, pointing to the two garlanded photographs on the wall.

The words affected the old woman in a queer way. Her eyes opened wide in amazement and she gasped, 'My God, are you Anirudh?'

'Yes, I am Anirudh.'

Fear vanished from the old woman's face, its place taken by brightness. She exclaimed, 'You are back, you have returned after all those years.'

Anirudh stepped forward and touched the old woman's feet. 'I always believed you will be back one day. Let me see how you look,' she pulled him closer and focused her eyes on his face. 'Yes, in your face I can recognize the small Anirudh I once knew. You are definitely my Anirudh. Do you remember who I am?'

'You must be Gautami chachi,' Anirudh said.

'You have forgotten me,' the woman said, 'I don't blame you, after all you knew me only for few weeks. I am Malti, your second mother.'

The relative to welcome him in his ancestral house turned out to be the one he had fled from twenty years ago. The bizarreness of the situation was not long in dawning on him, and he was overwhelmed by the caprice of fate. But Malti didn't look cruel, as he had imagined her to be. As she stood in front of him, she seemed full of compassion. This frail old woman could not harm anyone. He had believed in the stereotypical image of a stepmother and had developed absurd notions about her. A baseless fear had forced him to flee his house and had kept him away for all those years. 'It was such a tragedy that I went away,' he mumbled sadly and then pointing towards Jyotsna, said, 'She is my wife, Jyotsna.'

'I had guessed as much,' said Malti.

Jyotsna stepped forward and touched Malti's feet and said, 'I am happy to see you.'

'I used to live all alone in this sprawling house,' Malti said,

'Now suddenly I find that I have a son and a lovely daughter-in-law. God has mercifully brought my family together.'

'But why do you live all alone?' Anirudh asked with some uneasiness, 'Where is everyone else? Where is my father?'

Malti swallowed and said, 'The long journey must have tired you. Both of you must take some rest and after that I will tell you about your father and rest of the family.'

'No please, I would like to hear everything now.'

'Your father died two years ago. He believed that you would return someday. Before his death he made me promise that I would never sell the house and wait for you here.'

'These photographs of grandfather and grandmother on the wall mean that they too are…' He could not make himself pronounce the word dead.

'They passed into the next world more than a decade ago,' Malti replied, 'They died yearning for a glimpse of their grandson. But fate had decreed otherwise, their yearning went unfulfilled…' Malti wiped tears from the corner of her eyes, 'Both of you come with me. I will show you your father's room.' Like many village women she kept the house keys tied in a thread around her waist. One of the keys opened the lock on the door and they entered the room. Thin cotton curtains hanging on the widows were blowing softly in the breeze. The bed, the cabinet for clothes, a large tin trunk, a kerosene lamp lying on the side table, everything was as Anirudh remembered. But there was one change – On one wall hung the garlanded photographs of his father and his mother. 'I didn't come here to find everyone deceased,' Anirudh uttered. They sat down on the bed. 'My uncle Sambhu, aunt Gautami, and cousins Hari and Jhankana, where are they?' Anirudh asked.

'After your grandfather and grandmother died, your uncle sold his share of the property and shifted with his family to Madras. They used to write regularly and visit the village at least once every year. The last time they came here was when your father died. But after that I have not heard from them. I wrote few letters but there hasn't been any reply,' Malti said and then added with a hurt air, 'Maybe they don't consider me as close a relative as your father, that is why they stopped writing and visiting.'

Anirudh sat hushed and still. Nostalgic memories of how he, Hari and Jhankana used to run about the various rooms, came flooding to his mind. Now he lived in Bombay and they lived in Madras and their ancestral house was left unkempt and forlorn.

‡

A while later they got up to see other parts of the house. Since her husband's death Malti had started sleeping on a small cot arranged in the kitchen, and the other rooms were mostly kept locked. The house that once bustled with the activities of a large family was now an empty shell. All its vitality was gone. There were no cows or goats in the shed but troughs from which the animals used to feed were still fixed on the floor. The shed itself was not a patch of its former self. Its gravel surface was gone, spiders had woven huge cobwebs on all its walls, and a thick film of dust coated the pile of trunks that lay heaped in one corner.

Nature had come to its own in the back garden and in a steady insidious way encroached upon every inch of available space. The guava, mango, coconut trees were still there but they stood in a sea of weeds growing crowded, dark and uncontrolled. The neatly planted beds of flowers and vegetables that he remembered had yielded their place to wild shrubs and plants, existing cheek by jowl, branches intermingling in a strange embrace. The boundary wall around the garden was in a dilapidated state and had completely crumbled at one or two places. Malti explained that she was too old to take care of the house and there was no one to help her.

At night when Anirudh slept he dreamed that he was back in his house, not in the present one, but in the house as it was in the past. It was Holi and all the family members were dousing each other with colored water. Holi revelers were singing and dancing outside the house and the mouth-watering aroma of food being prepared in the kitchen filled the air. Suddenly he woke up and realized that he was lying on the bed in his father's room. Jyotsna was sleeping beside him. He got up and walked to the window. The window opened into the garden and as he stood in a dreamy haze, the moonlight played tricks on his fancy. He felt that the souls of his dead parents and grandparents were trapped in the branches and the roots of the monstrous shrubs and weeds. They were pleading with him to set them free. He was horrified by the imagery crafted by his mind's eye and retreated from the window hastily.

When the day dawned Anirudh and Jyotsna involved themselves in the chore of setting the house in order. Jyotsna worked in the rooms dusting and tidying up the furniture, trunks and other household bric-a-brac, whereas Anirudh started his work in the garden. He pulled out all the weeds and shrubs and then with some gardening tools that he found in the shed, started digging. Malti cooked flavorsome local dishes for her son and daughter-in-law. By the time dusk set in, the garden had acquired some semblance of order and Jyotsna, too, had managed to clear the clutter from two of the rooms. Next day they started working from where they had left. When Anirudh finished his work in the garden he set himself on patching the crumbled portions of the boundary wall.

And it was not just toiling around the house that kept them busy. Things like meeting old acquaintances and visiting different parts of the village provided a welcome break from the tedium of taxing labor. Chandu, Anirudh's childhood friend ran a grocery store in the village market. He heard from someone that Anirudh had returned and came to see him. Anirudh found it difficult to believe that the corpulent man in front of him was the same slim and small Chandu that he once knew. One day Anirudh took Jyotsna and his mother to the Hanuman Tekdi. The landscape of Hanuman Tekdi had hardly undergone any change. The same hillock with a temple on top was there, surrounded by a large open area with leafy shrubs, tall banyan, pipal, neem, mango and casuarina trees.

An important change in the temple was that the old priest was no longer there. He died few years ago and the task of taking care of the temple was passed on to his son. Anirudh, Jyotsna and Malti prayed at the temple for few minutes before returning home. On another day they went to their rice field. The crops had been cut few days ago and now the field was only an open area, much smaller than it was before, as Anirudh's uncle, Shambhu, had sold a part of the land before he shifted with his family to Madras. Malti herself was in no position to manage the land. Her younger brother who lived nearby looked after the cultivation and gave her part of the produce with which she subsisted.

‡

Aspirations rarely fructify into reality. Jyotsna had dreamed of being a pampered daughter-in-law when she came to the village, Anirudh had imagined of being cheered by numerous relatives. They had hoped to spend halcyon ten days with their relatives in their ancestral home. The reality of their experience in the village was so contrary to their expectations that time and again feelings of bewilderment came to haunt them. Often they were haunted by thoughts of what could have been if this house hadn't lost so many lives... if only circumstances had not been so meager.

Anirudh, working in some part of the house, would suddenly pause his work and start wondering if this was really his house, or was he somewhere else. He would try to think when was the last time his grandfather or father sat under this tree in the orchard or slept on the bed in any of the rooms. On hearing a sound behind him he would turn back expecting to find someone from his past walking up to him. Jyotsna cleaning up some room or checking the contents of some trunk would stop and start wondering how it would feel if the house had been packed with a cheerful crowd of old and young people... At times she would smile and laugh by herself, imagining amusing exchanges with doting relatives. But such moments of languor lasted only fleetingly and then they went on with whatever they were engaged in.

Soon it was their ninth day in the village. The house was in a far better state now. The weeds and shrubs cleared from the garden, the boundary walls repaired, the walls whitewashed, the various rooms dusted and cleaned. They had done all the work themselves. No way they could afford the luxury of spending money for hiring labor. Next day they had to leave. Their tickets were purchased and their bags were packed. It broke their heart to leave the old woman behind, and they offered to take her with them to Bombay, but Malti maintained that she had lived in the village for so long that she could not be comfortable anywhere else. Jyotsna promised her that they would write letters regularly and also visit the village at least once every year. Now as dusk was falling on their last day in the village, Anirudh and Jyotsna sat in the verandah, talking wistfully about their experience in the village.

Suddenly Jyotsna said, 'You haven't told me about how you left the village and reached Bombay.'

'I think it was about six months after my mother died, that my father decided to remarry,' Anirudh said looking wistfully at the cultivated fields that stretched ahead. 'My mind was filled with some absurd notions about my stepmother. I thought that if I remained at home she would beat me and even poison me... If only I knew what a heart of gold she had, I would never have left...'

‡

Six

Six months had passed since his mother's death. It was evening and Anirudh was playing ludo in the verandah with Jhankana and Hari. He heard his father calling him from the courtyard and went inside the house. Father made Anirudh sit beside him on the cot and asked, 'Do you remember your mother?'

'Yeah, I do,' Anirudh uttered.

'You want her back. Don't you?'

'It would be nice, if she were back,' Anirudh said. 'But grandmother told me that no one ever returns from heaven.'

'I am going to bring a new mother for you.'

'Really?' Anirudh exclaimed.

'She will not look like your old mother, but she will love you.'

'Will she play with me and tell me bedtime stories?'

'Sure, she will.'

'I will tell this good news to Hari and Jhankana,' Anirudh laughed and ran out.

'I learnt a secret,' he said to the two children.

'What secret?' Jhankana asked.

'Please tell it to us Anirudh?' Hari pleaded.

'It is good news,' Anirudh said to tantalize them further.

'Tell us,' Jhankana said. 'We always tell our secrets to you.'

'My father is getting a new mother for me,' Anirudh chuckled.

'That is no secret,' Jhankana said with some meanness. 'I have known that for days. Mother told me.'

Anirudh was piqued that Jhankana already knew. In order to make up for the lost ground, he said pompously, 'My new mother will give me sweets. She will play with me and tell me stories.'

'Says who?' asked Jhankana spitefully.

'Says I,' Anirudh thundered.

'You know nothing. Your father is getting a stepmother for you and stepmothers are always nasty. She will beat you mercilessly for slightest fault. Who knows, she may even try to poison you out of hatred. I won't be surprised if she did something of that sort. Stepmothers are known to do that. My mother has told me all about stepmothers,' Jhankana said.

'You are a liar,' Anirudh cried.

'She is not a liar,' Hari said, 'Your stepmother is going to beat you and one day she will poison you.'

Anirudh burst into tears and ran inside the house. Grandmother was sitting in her room. He fell into her lap sobbing.

'What happened, child?' she asked anxiously.

'I don't want a stepmother. I am frightened of her.'

Grandmother tried to assuage his fears by telling him how nice the stepmother would be to him.

One day Anirudh's stepmother arrived. When Anirudh went to see her, he was shocked to find that there was not the slightest resemblance between her and his mother. He took the lack of resemblance as proof of what Jhankana had told him about stepmothers. He felt sure that his stepmother was wicked. He hated her desperately.

Next day and in the days that followed, Anirudh did his best to keep away from his stepmother. He cowered behind his grandfather or grandmother whenever she called and if she attempted to hold him, he shouted and thrashed his hands and legs till she was forced to let him go.

‡

It was noon. The men had gone to work in the field. Gautami and Malti were working in the kitchen and Anirudh was sitting in the courtyard with grandmother. Suddenly, Jhankana and Hari came running from the verandah, screaming.

'What is the matter with both of you?' asked grandmother anxiously.

'Someone is at the door,' Jhankana gasped.

'He is a ghost. A demon,' Hari cried.

'These children have gone out of their mind,' grandmother muttered, getting up to find out for herself, who or what had frightened them. Anirudh was scared stiff, but the desire to discover what a ghost or a demon looked like, impelled him to follow his grandmother at close distance.

The open door framed a tall and muscularly built man. He was naked; his skin gray with ash and his matted hair fell in thick knots to his waist. In one hand, he held a trident from which fluttered a small piece of saffron cloth and in the other, a bizarre bowl made of human skull. 'Om Namah Shivay,' the man thundered, 'Is there any devotee of Shiva in this house, who will feed the Jungali Baba.'

The sight of this ferocious ascetic at her doorstep alarmed grandmother. 'All the men are working in the field at this time,' she gulped. 'There is no one here to feed you.'

'Om Namah Shivay, why can't you feed the Jungali Baba?'

'I have many things to do. Please forgive me. Go elsewhere.'

'I have undergone severe penances for Shiva. No one dares to send me away empty handed.' The ascetic's large red eyes glared at grandmother.

She shrank back with the fear of losing her soul and changed her attitude hastily, 'Please come and sit down in the courtyard. I will get something for you.'

'Om Namah Shivay,' Jungali Baba said and entered the house. He sat down in the courtyard on a mat that grandmother spread for him on the floor. Hari and Jhankana ran into their room and hid themselves under the bed. Anirudh remained beside grandmother.

'Is he a demon?' Anirudh whispered to his grandmother.

'No, he is a devotee of God,' grandmother said.

'Does God listen to what he says?'

'I think so,' grandmother mumbled.

They went into the kitchen. Gautami and Malti helped grandmother arrange a hasty lunch for Jungali Baba. When the plate was ready, Anirudh said, 'I will take the plate to Jungali Baba.'

'Aren't you afraid of him?' grandmother asked.

'No, I am not,' said Anirudh. 'Why should I be afraid of a devotee of God?'

'He is a brave boy,' Malti said.

'Hold the plate carefully or you will drop it,' grandmother said.

'Don't worry. I am careful,' Anirudh said, picking up the plate with both hands. Grandmother followed him to the courtyard with a pitcher of water.

'Jungali Baba does not eat from a plate. Put the food inside the holy bowl,' the ascetic said, holding the bowl made out of a human skull in front of Anirudh.

'I will do that,' grandmother said. She placed the pitcher of water on the ground and emptied the rice, pulse, vegetables and curd from the plate into the bowl. 'If you need any thing else, let me know.'

'That will be enough, old woman.'

Anirudh sat down on the ground a few feet away from Jungali Baba. 'Come with me Anirudh,' grandmother said.

'I will sit here and watch Jungali Baba eat,' Anirudh said.

Grandmother shrugged and walked off to the other end of the courtyard.

'What is your name boy?' Jungali Baba asked.

'Anirudh.'

Jungali Baba nodded and continued to eat from the bowl. When he finished eating, he drank half of the water in the pitcher and used the rest of it to rinse his mouth and hands.

Grandmother came forward with folded hands and said, 'This house belongs to poor farmers, Jungali Baba. I hope you are satisfied with our rustic fare.'

Jungali Baba raised his trident and said, 'Om Namah Shivay. For this hospitality the blessings of Shiva will be on you and your family.' With these words, he marched out of the house.

Grandmother and Anirudh stood at the doorstep and saw the ascetic wander off into the narrow mud path passing through the rice fields. When he disappeared from view, grandmother went inside the house, while Anirudh sat down on the verandah.

‡

The ascetic remained in his mind. 'Can he make mother return from heaven?' he asked himself. 'Grandmother had said that God listened to Jungali Baba. If Jungali Baba asked God to let mother return from heaven, won't God agree? If mother were with me again, I won't have to worry about stepmother. Mother would know how to handle her.' He looked longingly in the direction in which he had seen Jungali Baba go. Suddenly he got up and ran on the path going through the fields of rice.

Frantic with worry that he may miss Jungali Baba, he ran as fast as his small legs could carry him. He ran for many minutes before he espied the ascetic down the path, walking with the trident in his hand. 'Jungali Baba,' he shouted. He was relieved, when he saw the ascetic stop and look towards him.

'What is the matter boy?' the ascetic asked. 'Why have you come after me?'

Panting for breath said Anirudh, 'I need your help.'

'What do you want?'

'My mother has gone to heaven. Will you bring her back.'

There was a faint softening of the ascetic's fierce visage and he sympathetically asked, 'When did your mother go to heaven?'

'The day on which we celebrated Holi,' Anirudh answered.

'No one ever returns from heaven. You will have to learn to live without her.'

'But you can bring her back. You must...'

'Time will teach you to accept her loss and get on with your life. Now, be a good boy and return home.'

This was not the kind of response that Anirudh had been hoping for. 'If mother does not come back from heaven, my stepmother will beat me,' he cried.

'Has your father married again?'

'He has brought a stepmother,' Anirudh moaned.

'Does she mistreat you?'

'She is wicked. I know that she is planning to poison me. Save me from her. Take me with you.'

'It is not easy being an ascetic. I walk for miles each day, eat whatever I get as alms, remain naked in hot or cold weather and sleep in the open. You will not be able survive such hardships.'

'I can bear every hardship. Take me with you. I want to become a devotee of God.'

Jungali Baba's eyes peered into Anirudh's. 'Do you desire to devote the rest of your life to God, boy?'

'Yes.'

'Then it is my duty to help you. I will take you with me. Take off your clothes and throw them into the rice field. You won't need them any longer.'

Without a second's wait, Anirudh discarded his clothes into the rice field.

'Chant after me, Om Namah Shivay,' Jungali Baba said.

'Om Namah Shivay,' Anirudh uttered and felt strangely peaceful as he did so.

'Om Namah Shivay.'

'Om Namah Shivay,' Anirudh repeated.

'We will have to leave this village quickly,' Jungali Baba said, 'Your family members will soon start searching for you.'

‡

Jungali Baba took Anirudh's hand and they walked away with hasty steps. They came out of the rice fields and went down the mud path that led to the market. People they encountered on their way moved aside to avoid bumping into the two ascetics; nobody wished to cause affront to devotees of Shiva, the destroyer. In his naked state Anirudh appeared to be a child sadhu and no one could have guessed that he was a child of this village. They came out of the market and crossed the small railway station and the railway tracks to enter another stretch of cultivated fields. They passed the last field and reached the edge of the village. A dense forest lay beyond. Jungali Baba's pace did not falter as he guided Anirudh through a maze of thorny shrubs, tall grass and trees overgrown with wild jasmine and lantana creepers. Anirudh felt afraid of snakes and wild animals, and clutched Jungali Baba's hand.

In order to calm the child's fears, Jungali Baba started intoning in a deep voice, 'Om Namah Shivay, Om Namah Shivay…'

Anirudh focused on the chant and miraculously his fears dissipated. It was late in the evening when they reached the banks of a small stream. A dense pipal tree with gnarled branches flowing in all directions was growing on the bank of the stream.

'We will spend the night under this tree,' Jungali Baba said. Exhausted by the long march, Anirudh was only too pleased to hear that.

Jungali Baba filled his bowl with water from the stream and gave it to Anirudh to drink. The boy drank hungrily. When the ascetic, too, had his fill of water, they began scouring the nearby forest to find edible roots and berries. Frightened of getting lost in the dark jungle, Anirudh followed the ascetic closely. Few minutes later they were sitting under the pipul tree eating the roots and berries they had gathered. Soon after Anirudh lay down on the ground, his head on a mattress made out of dried grass. Till he fell asleep, the ascetic's reassuring voice kept humming, 'Om Namah Shivay, Om Namah Shivay…'

‡

The orange glow of the sun had barely started painting the sky when they woke up and having washed themselves in the stream, started on their journey again. Noon found them in another village, where they met some peasants working in a field, who cheered them lustily with, 'Jai Shiv Shankar, Bhole Nath ki Jai.'

'Jai Shiv Shankar,' Jungali Baba shouted back, 'Can anybody direct me to the cremation ground?'

'I will take you to the cremation ground,' one of the peasants said.

'Jai Shiv Shankar! May the blessings of Shiva be on you.'

A pyre was blazing at the cremation ground. A small crowd of relatives and friends sobbed and moaned around the blazing pyre.

The air was heavy with smoke that carried the acrid smell of burning flesh.

'Why are these people crying?' Anirudh asked.

'Someone has died and they are consigning his body to flames,' Jungali Baba said.

'But why are they burning the body?' Anirudh asked incredulously.

'A dead body has to be burned on a pyre. Your mother's body, too, was fed to flames after she died.'

The boy was anguished. He stared at the blazing pyre through a film of tears and said, 'That cannot be true. Grandmother said that mother was in heaven.'

'Only the soul goes to heaven. The body gets destroyed on earth.'

'What is the soul?'

'It is the essence of life. It is the divine spark, which imparts life to body. When the soul and body are separated the person dies.'

Anirudh was too bewildered to say anything.

'I have brought you to the cremation ground to initiate you as a devotee of Shiva,' Jungali Baba continued, 'Shiva is the lord of death and unless you overcome your fear of death you cannot be his devotee. We will stay at the cremation ground, till you are able to stare at the face of death without fear or pain.'

'Bhole Nath ki Jai,' the dom whose job it was to attend to the pyres walked towards them. A dom is considered unclean and untouchable by most Indians, as he handles dead bodies and lives in the cremation ground. But for Jungali Baba, who was a worshipper of death, the dom was a kindred soul. He touched the

dom's forehead with his right hand in benediction and said, 'The blessings of Shiva be with you.'

‡

There was a pond at the edge of the cremation ground. Jungali Baba and Anirudh bathed in the pond. When they came out of water the crowd of mourners had departed, leaving a smoldering pyre behind them. The ascetic picked up a fistful of ash from the pyre and after divesting it of glowing embers, pieces of bones and flesh, smeared it on Anirudh's hair and body. Then he smeared ash on his own hair and body. The air tasted of burnt flesh and Anirudh felt nauseous. Somehow he controlled his urge to vomit.

'You are a brave boy,' Jungali Baba said. 'Someday you will be a great devotee of Shiva. Bathing with ash from a recently burnt pyre cleanses the soul and brings the devotee closer to the God of death.'

Thus smeared in ash they sat down in a secluded corner of the cremation ground. Jungali Baba taught Anirudh how to sit with his legs crossed in a lotus position. 'Close your eyes, remove all thoughts from your mind and chant after me, Shiva-o-ham, Shiva-o-ham…'

Anirudh closed his eyes and mumbled, 'Shiva-o-ham, Shiva-o-ham…' He did not know the significance of what he was chanting but as he chanted he felt as if his mother was close to him. He opened his eyes expecting to see her. But she wasn't there. Instead he found Jungali Baba peering at him.

'Why did you open your eyes?' he asked.

'I thought she was here,' Anirudh uttered.

'Do you know the meaning of the mantra that you are chanting?'

'I don't.'

'Shiva-o-ham means, I am Shiva. By chanting this mantra you were attempting to dissolve the barriers between you and Shiva, the eternal destroyer. If you had chanted the mantra while concentrating on Shiva, you would have experienced the delight of nearness to the eternal destroyer himself. But as your mind was full of thoughts of your mother, you got a feeling of closeness to her instead. Death is a necessary reason for life to exist. In due course of time you will understand that and then you will accept your mother's death as part of the cycle, which creates life on earth. Close your eyes and while concentrating your mind on Shiva chant after me: Shiva-o-ham, Shiva-o-ham…'

They prayed for many hours. After that they went to the dom's hut, which was located at one corner of the cremation ground.

'Is there anyone in this house who will feed two devotees of Shiva?' Jungali Baba said.

The dom and his wife came out of the hut immediately and prostrated themselves at the feet of Jungali Baba. 'I am an untouchable. How can I offer food to a saint like you?' the dom pleaded.

'For a devotee of Shiva no one is untouchable,' Jungali Baba declared.

The dom hastily brought food from the house and placed it in Jungali Baba's bowl. Anirudh and Jungali Baba ate out of the bowl.

‡

For nine days they stayed at the cremation ground. Every day, after a bath at the pond, they rubbed fresh ash on their hair and body and prayed for hours. At nights they slept in the open, with the ash that covered their bodies, as the only shield against mosquitoes.

The dom was a poor man and Jungali Baba refrained from accepting food from him again. Instead, for few hours everyday he and Anirudh went to the village to beg for alms. Often people moved aside and children ran in fear when the two naked sadhus marched through the village. Anirudh was surprised at the fear that he and Jungali Baba invoked. Once he asked, 'Why are they afraid of us? We are not going to harm anyone?'

'Our ash covered bodies are terrifying reminders of death to people. No one wants to contemplate death.'

One or two cremations took place at the cremation ground daily. A routine of witnessing blazing pyres and relatives and friends mourning for the dead, gave Anirudh a fresh perspective on death. For few hours everyday Jungali Baba would speak to him about the Hindu philosophy of life and after-life. Slowly Anirudh realized that what had happened with his mother was nothing unique and he accepted her death as the end of one cycle and the commencement of another.

‡

On the ninth day, when they finished their morning ablutions, Jungali Baba said, 'Today you will pick up the ash and apply it on your body with your own hands.'

They went to a pyre where a corpse had recently been burnt.

Smoke was still rising from the smoldering pyre, filling the morning air with a pungent smell. Anirudh grabbed a fistful of ash and divested it of half-burnt pieces of flesh and bone, and glowing embers of wood, as he had seen Jungali Baba doing for the past many days. There was no fear or disgust on his face as he bathed his hair and body with the ash.

The ascetic smiled and picking up a fistful of ash to apply to his own body, said, 'Now, you are able to handle the remains of a pyre without any fear or disgust. Death does not awe you any longer. The first part of your training as a devotee of Shiva is complete. Tomorrow at the first light of dawn, we will leave the cremation ground.'

'Where do we go from here?' Anirudh asked.

'To Rishikesh.'

'Where is that?'

'It is far from here. We have to walk for many weeks to reach there.'

'Why can't we take a train?'

'A devotee of Shiva refrains from using modern means of transport, unless he is in a hurry to reach somewhere.'

At dawn they left the cremation ground on a journey that would take them more than two months to complete. They traveled for few miles daily and when dusk fell they took shelter wherever they could and fell asleep. They passed through all kinds of landscapes – jungles, fields, villages, towns and cities. Among humans everywhere, they were regarded with curiosity. Some people avoided them out of fear, while others sought their blessings. Jungali Baba placed a tilak on the forehead of those who sought blessings.

In the vicinity of towns or villages they begged for alms and ate whatever they received, and when they were passing through jungles, where there weren't any humans to provide alms, they foraged the woods for food. Jungali Baba had fine familiarity with edible wild fruits and leaves, and also with bulbs and tubers, all of which were abundant in the forests. The wild fruits and leaves they ate raw, but the bulbs and tubers had to be cooked before they could be consumed. The boy would watch patiently as the ascetic roasted the bulbs and tubers over a small fire of twigs, and often was surprised by how good they tasted. Jungali Baba taught him how to drink milk directly from the teats of wandering cattle. They collected cow dung and left it to dry in the sun. Jungali Baba burnt the dried dung and then crumbled it into powder between the palms of his hand. They smeared their body with the powder from burnt dung to keep mosquitoes and insects away.

The forests kept Anirudh busy with its elephants, monkeys, monitor lizards, leopards, snakes and birds. He learnt to identify different animals by looking at their footprints or by hearing their cries. The animals often came close to Jungali Baba, but as he was not afraid of them they, too, did not feel threatened by him. The steady drone of Jungali Baba's chanting was sufficient to calm any wild animal. On some nights Anirudh would hear hyenas and leopards snarling, but he knew that the animals would not harm him as long as he was with Jungali Baba.

‡

They reached the banks of river Ganga after a fortnight's journey. The rivers that Anirudh had seen in his lifetime were hopelessly small compared to the mighty Ganga. The churning, tossing and swirling mass of water filled him with awe.

'We shall go to the other side of the river,' the ascetic said, 'From there we shall walk along the river's bank and reach Rishikesh.'

'How far is Rishikesh from here?'

'We still have to walk for many weeks. But the journey along the banks of the river Ganga will not be tiring.'

A boat with many passengers was going to the other side of the river. The boatman readily agreed to take the ascetic and his young companion along. When they reached the other side, the boatman asked for blessings instead of money.

The ascetics bathed in the cool waters of the Ganga. 'Ganga is the holiest river,' Jungali Baba said. 'A dip in its waters cleanses a man of all his past sins.' After they finished their bath Jungali Baba meditated on the riverbank, while Anirudh sat beside him, gazing at the undulating waves of the river. Some pilgrims brought food for them, which they ate.

When the night fell the verandah of a decrepit temple overlooking the Ganga provided them the place to sleep. At daybreak they resumed their onward journey.

‡

Rishikesh, located at the height of about 1360 feet above sea level, in the Tehri-Garhwal region of Uttar Pradesh, is one of the holiest places for Hindus in India. The holy Ganga, emerging from the mountains, not far from here, runs deep and silent, through thickly wooded hills that straddle this area. According to legend, sage

Raibhya undertook staunch penance in this area to propitiate God. In reward for his meditation, God appeared before him manifested as Rishikesh and it was from this manifestation that the area got its name. Rishikesh also represents the site where Vishnu vanquished the demon Madhu.

Modern day Rishikesh is home to many temples, ashrams and dharamshalas. Pilgrims come here throughout the year, to bathe in the Ganga and to pray in the temples. The rope bridge, Lakshman Jhula is a major landmark. According to ancient scriptures Rama's brother Lakshman had crossed the river using the rope bridge. Tapovan, which is located on the other side of the river, houses a magnificent temple. It is believed that Lakshman carried out penances here. Situated at the height of 1700 feet, the Neelkanth Mahadev temple commands a stunning view of the region. According to mythological accounts, during Sagar Manthan, Lord Shiva drank all the effluent venom which turned his throat blue.

Jungali Baba didn't stop in the bustling town of Rishikesh. They continued to trek till they reached a quiet forest grove nestled by hills on three sides and the flowing Ganga on the fourth. It was a perfect place to live in harmony with nature and contemplate God.

'We have reached our destination,' Jungali Baba said. 'We will live here.'

'Is this the most holy place?' Anirudh asked.

In answer to the boy's question, the ascetic mused, 'Certain areas are more sacred than others, some on account of their situation, others because of their sparkling waters and others because of the habitation of saintly people.'

'Does that mean this place is the holiest?'

'It does. We will built our hut under this tree,' Jungali Baba said pointing towards a banyan tree so ancient that many of its branches had formed new roots on the ground.

Anirudh joined Jungali Baba in collecting banana leaves. The ascetic used his trident to cut few bamboos and then plunged the poles into the grassy ground under the banyan tree. They thatched the poles with banana leaves and bamboo sticks. Anirudh laughed with delight when a single room hut was completed.

'There is one last thing to do,' Jungali Baba said. 'Get some cow dung.'

Cattle, belonging to local villagers, were grazing in the vicinity. Anirudh loaded many pats of cow dung on a large banana leaf and brought it back to the hut. The ascetic smeared the floor and the walls of the hut with cow dung. 'That will keep mosquitoes and insects away,' he said. 'We can move in when the dung dries up.'

‡

After having their bath they sat down on a rocky outcrop overlooking the river and for the first time Jungali Baba talked with the boy about the rigorous austerities that he had undergone to become a naga sadhu.

'I was attracted to the divine force when I was a young man and left my home and my job in order to contemplate Shiva. I went to the Himalayas and after traveling through many snow-bound mountain passes, I reached a deserted temple dedicated to the God. As far as eye could see, there was nothing except snow and giant fir trees, the nearest human habitation being miles away.

For years I prayed to Shiva at this temple. The freezing cold, the snowstorms and the frost, would plunge me into delirium, but I never gave up on contemplating the God of death. I slapped and rubbed, rubbed and slapped, while continuing to chant the name of Shiva, as waves of mist and wind-driven snow buffeted me. I ate frozen chunks of food, as there was never enough wood to cook. Time and again I was only a whisker away from freezing to death but the Lord of death in his magnanimity always spared my life. Years later when I emerged from the mountains my body was immune to the extremes of clime.'

'Can I learn to survive in such cold?' Anirudh asked.

'Yes, you can. There are yogic exercises, which slow down the metabolic process in the body, so that one is not affected by the extremes of weather. I will eventually teach you all I know,' Jungali Baba said. 'After emerging from the mountains, I joined an academy for naga sadhus, where I was taught how to use a trident. I practiced mind control, which gave me the power to throw down an opponent without even touching him. I learnt to communicate with wild animals. I learnt to overcome my horror of snakes and to control and charm them. I learnt how to go without food and water for many days.'

'I wish to learn all that, too.'

'When you have developed an unwavering devotion for Shiva, I will take you to the Naga Academy.'

‡

In the days that followed a routine that was idyllic and somewhat monotonous established itself. They woke up at dawn and after bathing in the Ganga sat down for prayers. They got their food through foraging in the forests or by begging in the town of Rishikesh, a few kilometers away. Daily, for three or four hours Jungali Baba taught Anirudh different yogic exercises and to read and write. At nights, he narrated stories from Hindu scriptures and only when Anirudh fell asleep did the ascetic began his meditations. On many a night, when Anirudh woke, hearing the cry of a wild animal, he found Jungali Baba sitting in a lotus position and chanting in deep voice, 'Shiva-o-ham, Shiva-o-ham...'

As the hut was far from any human habitation, most of the time they were left to themselves. Shepherds who grazed their cattle in nearby forests were occasional visitors. They brought pitchers of milk to the two ascetics and sought blessings. Infrequently groups of pilgrims from Rishikesh reached the hut. They gawked with eyes full of curiosity and veneration and spoke with each other in hushed whispers. Some pilgrims would come forward and touch the feet of the two ascetics in a gesture of supplication. Anirudh felt embarrassed when grownups touched his feet, but he soon got used to the situation and learned to apply tilak on the forehead of the supplicants.

The balmy days of summer passed and the rainy season arrived. The sky was camouflaged with dark monsoon clouds. When it started raining the air was filled with the pleasing scent of wet soil. The thatched roof of the hut was not an effective shield against the rains and water dripped from every corner. During heavy downpours, the surging waters of Ganga regularly flooded the banks and waves hurrying on waves churned through the trees and rocks to invade the hut. On such days, Jungali Baba and Anirudh found shelter in a nearby rock cave, located on higher ground. One day when the flooding was particularly bad and the hut submerged by nearly a feet, the boy thought that his home was now done for and asked, 'Will our hut get washed away?'

'The hut will survive. The water will now recede,' Jungali Baba said. That is how it happened. After one or two hours the water started receding.

Winters in Rishikesh are bone chilly. Icy winds blow from the snow-covered Himalayan Mountains and the temperature drops to near freezing lèvel. The regimen of yogic exercises, to which Jungali Baba and Anirudh adapted, enabled them to bear the cold. During nights, they basked themselves in the heat of smoldering cow dung and twigs.

In the first year of their stay at the hut, Anirudh followed Jungali Baba wherever he went, but after that as he grew familiar with the area, he became bolder and started venturing out on his own. While the ascetic meditated, Anirudh explored the forests looking for interesting birds and animals or foraging for wild fruits and berries and tubers. Some boys of nearby hamlets, who came to the forests to gather firewood or to graze cattle, became his friends and he began meeting them regularly. With the passage of time the range of his excursions kept widening, until he started traveling up to Rishikesh without Jungali Baba. He treated such excursions as pleasure trips and did not engage in soliciting alms; instead he roamed through the streets looking at different people and places. Jungali Baba never asked him how he spent his time, but often reminded him that one should not forget Shiva wherever one went.

‡

Things that are interesting to a child often start seeming mundane and trivial by the time the child grows up into a young man. Anirudh was only seven years old when the trauma of his mother's death thrust him into the arms of a naga sadhu. At that age he was too young to decide for himself and followed the sadhu blindly, just as a dog follows its master. He accepted an ascetic's way of life not out of conviction, but because he wished to imitate Jungali Baba, whom he regarded as his savior. But his feelings for Jungali Baba, in the end, could not keep him bound to asceticism forever and the time dawned when Anirudh found himself longing for a life as normal as the one he had run away from when he left the village.

When he walked through the streets of Rishikesh, he used to be dazzled by the goods displayed in shop-windows and by the well-dressed and well-fed people he met going about the place. Desires, as fierce as physical hunger would seize him and make him stop dead in his tracks. He craved to be like the people who filled the streets of the town. He longed to have a normal life, have a normal home. Sometimes he did try to fight back his desires. But his efforts to convince himself that an ascetic way of life was superior – something that Jungali Baba kept harping about – failed. The religious ceremonies and austerities that Jungali Baba underwent and made him undergo could not, in the mind of the young boy, stand up to the sights and sounds of normal living. In the battle in his mind Jungali Baba was squarely beaten by every man on the street that was properly attired, lived in a proper house, ate proper food. Anirudh was fed up of subsisting on alms, living in a hut that dripped every time it rained, fed up in particular about being different from all the people he saw in Rishikesh.

One day, when he went to Rishikesh, a few boys of his age made fun of his nakedness. This incident woke him up to the fact that it was barbaric to walk about naked in a town filled with fully clothed people. For the first time, a sense of shame at his nakedness dawned on him. He did not tell Jungali Baba about this incident. But a day later he found a pair of clothes in the hut. Somehow the ascetic had learned of his craving for clothes.

'I thought you felt uncomfortable without your clothes. That is why I got these,' the ascetic said.

After that Anirudh never ventured out without his clothes on. But mere clothes could not stem the tide of disenchantment that brewed inside him against the kind of life that he was leading. Whenever he noticed someone of his age enjoying the fruits of normal human society, he yearned to be like him. He desperately desired material comforts; small things, like living in a brick house, wearing proper clothes, going to movies, eating in restaurants, were what his wildest dreams were made off. The idea began catching hold of him that he could not have normal life while being an ascetic. With this realization came a trenchant hatred for all that asceticism represented. He lost faith in God and stopped praying.

‡

With a gloom writ large on his face, Anirudh sat brooding at the riverbank. He had just returned from a hike through the streets of Rishikesh. The wide gap between what he wanted and what he had was making life unbearable for him. He knew he had to find a solution to his dilemma quickly. His desperation to divest himself of every trace of asceticism and return to the real world, where normal beings had regular lives, was driving him crazy. Jungali Baba had ceased to count for anything. These days Anirudh was seized with a feeling of disgust every time he saw the ascetic.

Youth, hot on a different scent, cannot understand the craving for God and Anirudh didn't. Damn it! He didn't want to be a saint. He was going to make a bolt for it someday and go someplace where he could fulfill his dream of being a normal human being. He heard footsteps behind him and turned to see Jungle Baba approaching.

'I thought you were meditating,' Anirudh said.

'I got up when you came,' the ascetic said sitting beside Anirudh.

Anirudh remained quiet and continued to gaze pensively at the river.

'You are thirteen years old now,' Jungali Baba said. 'During the six years that you have been with me, I have seen you change not just physically but also mentally. I can see that you are no longer satisfied with the life you are leading.'

'That's true.'

'Have you decided anything about your future?'

'I haven't.'

'Life as naga sadhu is hard. It is not for everyone. Do you desire to return to a materialistic life?' In the ascetic's heart there was a hope that the boy would somehow insist on remaining with him.

'I wish to lead a normal life, but I don't know how I can.'

Now that Anirudh's intentions were in the open, Jungali Baba had to be supportive. 'I can take you back to your village...to your relatives.'

The fear of stepmother was still alive inside Anirudh. There was also much anger in his heart against his village relatives, who allowed her to become part of the family. There was no way he would go back to them. He said, 'It has been so many years since I left home. By now my father would be having children from stepmother. The other relatives must have got used to life without me. I don't think they will welcome me. No, I don't want to return home.'

'It is a fundamental rule of asceticism that an ascetic should not become affectionate towards anyone except the divine lord. I have broken this rule in your case. Since I found you, I ceased to be an ascetic, for I developed affection for you. I am telling you all this because I want you to understand that if I could betray asceticism for you, then there is nothing that I won't do to help you.'

Anirudh brooded for a few moments and then spoke about the secret desire that he had been harboring in his mind for a long time – the desire to go to Bombay. 'Can I go to Bombay?' he asked.

'Bombay?' Jungali Baba had no idea till now that Anirudh wished to travel as far as Bombay, to achieve his heart's desire. 'What is there in Bombay? Do you know someone there?'

'I don't know anyone there. I only heard about the city from some boys I met in Rishikesh. It is a big city. Jobs are available. I could go there and find something to do,' Anirudh explained.

'It is not a bad idea to go to Bombay. There you might find the happiness that has eluded you till now. But I don't want you to go without any preparation. You must give me sometime, so that I can find someone to take you there and support you during your initial days in the city.'

Anirudh's face brightened up and he asked, 'Will you help me to go to Bombay?'

'I will. Don't worry, you will be in Bombay in a few days,' said Jungali Baba, looking pensively at Ganga, flowing a little distance away from them.

‡

A fortnight later a middle-aged man came to see Jungali Baba. Anirudh was sitting outside the hut at that time. The man touched Jungali Baba's feet and said, 'Bless me, Swamiji.'

'Om Namah Shivay,' Jungali Baba said and applied ash on the man's forehead.

'I heard from some people in Rishikesh that a devotee of Shiva resides in these forests. Somehow I managed to find your abode.'

'Your long walk from Rishikesh must have tired you. Sit down on the mat,' Jungali Baba said, pointing towards a hand-woven straw mat lying on the ground. The man sat down.

'What is your name?'

'People call me Ashok Pandit. I came to Rishikesh on pilgrimage.

'Where are you from?'

'Bombay.'

'What do you do there?'

'I am a transporter. I own two trucks. I need your blessings so that I can expand my business, buy more trucks.'

'You will be able to expand your business. I can see the glow of Shiva's blessings on your face. Shiva wants you to succeed.'

Ashok Pandit's face lit up with happiness at these words, 'Your words have boosted my morale.'

'I want you to do something for me.'

'Tell me.'

'When you leave for Bombay take my disciple Anirudh with you,' Jungali Baba said, pointing towards Anirudh, who was sitting nearby, listening to the conversation with anticipation. 'Give him a job in your transport company and a place to stay.'

'But he is a mere boy. I think he is too young to work in a transport company.'

'He may be young in age, but he is capable of doing a man's work. I am giving you this boy as a lucky charm. He is going to bring you luck. When he begins working in your organization, your business will grow beyond your wildest dreams.'

Lured by the prospect of expansion of business Ashok Pandit folded his hands and said, 'Swamiji, I am prepared to do your bidding. I will take him with me when I leave for Bombay tomorrow.'

A smile appeared on Anirudh's face.

'Om Namah Shivay,' Jungali Baba said.

‡

The train by which Ashok Pandit planned to leave for Bombay departed from Rishikesh's railway station at 12 PM. Anirudh, jittery at the prospect of missing the train, got ready by 8 AM itself. He would go to Ashok Pandit's hotel and from there accompany him to the railway station. He didn't have much to pack. All he was taking with him were some clothes and a stone image of Shiva. He packed these things inside a cloth bag.

Jungali Baba sat outside the hut lost in meditation. When

Anirudh was prepared to depart, he went to the ascetic and said, 'I am ready to leave.'

The ascetic opened his eyes instantly and said, 'Have you packed all your things?'

'My clothes and the idol of Shiva are in my bag,' Anirudh said patting the bag that was hanging by his side.

'There is something else that I want you to take with you,' Jungali Baba said and slowly rose to his feet. He went inside the hut and returned with a copper container, which he opened in front of Anirudh's eyes and let him see that it was full of coins and currency notes of small denominations. 'This container has little more than 2000 rupees. I saved this money from the alms that I got over a period of many years. Use it in time of need.'

'Keep the money with you. You may need it more than I.'

'Don't refuse me. I want you to have this money.'

Silently Anirudh received the container and placed it in his bag.

'Work hard and be honest in your dealings. The blessings of Shiva will always be with you,' Jungali Baba said.

'I will come here every two or three months to meet you.'

The ascetic smiled and said, 'You won't find me here again. I had built this hut for you. Now that you are going away, I don't need to remain here any longer. Tomorrow morning, I will depart for the Himalayas.'

'But how will we meet again?'

'If Lord Shiva wills then we will come together again. But you must never attempt to find me. From today our ways are separate.' Jungali Baba applied tilak on Anirudh's forehead and said, 'Now leave, or you will be late.'

This was the moment of parting. Anirudh thought that he should feel sad. But strangely he felt nothing. He bent forward and touched the ascetic's feet.

'Om Namah Shivay,' the ascetic intoned.

Anirudh turned and walked down the narrow mud path that led to Rishikesh. Few hours later he was train bound for Bombay. A new destiny awaited him there.

‡

Ashok Pandit kept the word that he had given to the ascetic and gave Anirudh a job when they reached Bombay. He made Anirudh a cleaner of one of his trucks.

It was Anirudh's duty to clean the truck every morning and then travel with it to different parts of the city for picking up and delivering cargo. He learnt how to load and unload the truck and to guide the driver through busy traffic intersections. The duty hours were long and exhausting. But Anirudh was used to hard life and did not complain. The truck became not just his place of work but also his home. When the day ended, he slept inside the driver's cabin.

The numerous cars that he encountered on Bombay's roads everyday gave him the idea that he should drive something like that. He was seventeen years old when he got his driving license and began his career as a taxi driver.

Seven

Anirudh and Jyotsna were back in their home in Bombay. For years Anirudh's past had been frozen at the point of time when, as a child he left, his village. Now the past had thawed, allowing him to understand what all had transpired in his ancestral home during those years when he had been at Rishikesh and Bombay. No longer would he spend hours trying to imagine how his relatives in the village were. The journey had also brought him closer to Jyotsna, for he shared with her not just his present and future but also his past. Most important of all, the journey had forged a new relationship for him, with his stepmother, who no longer horrified him. He loved her as much as he had loved his own mother. Jyotsna, too, cherished Malti. A day after she was in Bombay, she wrote a long letter to Malti, inquiring about her welfare and letting her know that her son and daughter-in-law had reached Bombay in comfort.

They had labored hard to repair the village house. Their tired bodies yearned for rest. But having spent quite some money on the journey, not to speak of the income they had lost while they were in village, they could not afford the luxury of relaxing at home even for a few days. The next day itself Anirudh's taxi hit the roads and Jyotsna resumed her nursing duties at the hospital. Bombay felt strange to them, used, as they had become, to the balmy atmosphere of the village. When Jyotsna returned from her first day at the hospital she joked, 'Those ten days in village have turned me into a real villager. It felt strange working in the hospital.' 'It felt weird driving on roads thick with traffic,' Anirudh laughed, 'I kept wondering where all the open spaces have gone.' In another day and two they regained their bearings and were once again the quintessential city dwellers they had been before going to the village.

Ten days passed. Anirudh came home after driving his taxi and found a toddler playing on the bed.

'Where did this brat come from?' he asked.

'Don't you remember? You saw him while we were taking a morning walk that day.'

'Uh oh then he is your nurse friend's son?' Anirudh said with a flash of recognition.

'Yes. He is Vimla's son.'

'Good morning,' the boy said.

'Good morning,' Anirudh said and added, 'Don't you think, it should be good evening or good night after sunset?'

The boy stared vaguely.

'Good morning is the only greeting he knows,' Jyotsna said. 'He is only four.'

'What is your name, boy?' Anirudh asked.

'Atul,' the toddler lisped.

'Where is your mother?'

'She isn't well,' Atul declared.

'Vimla is down with malaria. She requested me to take care

of her son till she recovers,' Jyotsna said.

'Is there no one else at home to look after her son?'

'Oh, hers is such a tragic story. I learnt about her case only yesterday. It is very bad, actually.'

'What is so bad?'

'Let's go to the balcony. I don't want the child to hear,' Jyotsna said secretly.

When they were in the balcony, Jyotsna said, 'Two years ago Vimla's husband left her for another woman. The scum does not bother about his son either.'

'Are they divorced?'

'They are in the process of getting it. Imagine, walking out on a wife and a four-year-old child for the sake of some despicable woman. What scapegrace men are?'

'Are you branding all men as scapegrace,' Anirudh asked suspiciously, 'for the crime of one individual?'

'Men always betray their women,' Jyotsna said peevishly.

'I won't.'

'Would you still be in love with me when I am an old hag?'

'You won't be an old hag if you listen to me and start bathing in lux,' Anirudh said, with a sly smile.

'You and your lux,' said Jyotsna spitefully. 'I hate it when someone acts over smart.'

'Who will take care of Atul when you are at the hospital? Don't expect me to stay home and baby sit.'

'Don't overestimate yourself. I won't trust you with a child. Vimla has enrolled him in a crèche, where he stays during the day. I will drop him there in the morning and pick him up in the evening,' Jyotsna said and marched inside the room. Anirudh followed her.

'Where did the child go?' Jyotsna exclaimed.

'He was on the bed few minutes ago,' Anirudh uttered.

They checked the bathroom and the kitchen. Atul was not there. The door was locked so he could not have gone out.

Anirudh dropped to his hands and knees, and peered under the bed. 'There he is, hiding under the bed,' he said. 'Come out, you prankster.'

'He is playing hide-and-seek,' Jyotsna grinned. 'You know, it was my favorite game when I was a child.'

Atul crawled out. 'Atul ride horsie,' he said.

'You should not have dropped to your hands and knees. Now he thinks that you are a horse,' Jyotsna said.

Anirudh snorted like a horse and said, 'Come on I will show you what a racehorse I am.'

Atul climbed on Anirudh's back. Anirudh scampered about the room making the child laugh.

'You take to children very well,' Jyotsna laughed.

'All the more reason for us to have children,' Anirudh said.

Jyotsna left Anirudh and Atul to their games and went inside the kitchen to cook. At dinner time Atul refused to let the adults feed him. 'If you drop anything, I will spank you,' Jyotsna said.

The child took the warning as a compliment and laughed with glee. He refused to eat at the table and sat on the floor. In spite of Jyotsna's warning, he dropped on the floor almost as much as he ate.

'I guess, kids will always be messy with food,' Jyotsna said.

'He needs to be taught table manners,' Anirudh replied.

'Floor manners, you mean.'

When the dinner was over, Anirudh asked, 'What is going to be the sleeping arrangement today?'

'Three of us won't fit into the small bed,' Jyotsna said thoughtfully.

'I will sleep on the floor, you sleep on the bed with the child,' Anirudh offered.

'What if he rolls over in sleep and falls from the bed,' Jyotsna fretted. 'It will be better if I slept on the floor with him and you occupy the bed.'

'Help yourself,' Anirudh shrugged and then added fretfully, 'Damn! This buster is separating me from my wife.'

'Don't worry. This arrangement will last for two or three days only,' Jyotsna said, smiling at his discomfiture.

‡

Next day Anirudh brought Atul and Jyotsna to the crèche in the taxi.

'Don't leave me here,' Atul whimpered.

'We will pick you up in the evening. Don't worry,' Jyotsna said.

'Don't be late.'

'I won't.'

'It breaks my heart to see that little boy so sad,' said Jyotsna, when she and Anirudh came out of the crèche.

'When we have a child, he too will have to live during the day in a crèche,' Anirudh said pensively.

'No, he won't. My mother will take care of him while we are working.'

'Yes, that sounds like a better arrangement.'

Jyotsna caught a bus for the hospital from the bus stop outside the crèche. Anirudh went to his taxi.

‡

It was a sunny noon when Anirudh was parked at Lamington Road. He heard the familiar cry of, 'taxi, taxi', and saw a young woman hailing him from the other side of the road. He took a u-turn and reached her. 'Where to, miss?' he asked, opening the backdoor of the cab.

The woman slipped inside. 'Take me...' she started but interrupting herself abruptly, she ejaculated with amusement, 'hey! I know you.'

Anirudh realized that his new passenger was the same woman, who according to Janki and Shalini was a harlot. 'We live in the same building,' he said, 'Don't we?'

'Sure.'

'Where do you want to go?'

'Take me to our building. I have to pick up a dress from my house and go to Natraj Studio.'

Anirudh started the taxi and said, 'You are a film actress?'

'No, a dress designer.'

'A dress designer! Someone told me that you were a dancer.'

'You must have got that rubbish from Janki and Shalini,' she said fretfully. 'I saw you were chatting with them, in the morning, that day. What else did they say about me?'

Anirudh didn't want to hurt her feelings by talking about the unpleasant rumors he had heard about her. 'Nothing except that you were a dancer.'

'Janki and Shalini are a real thorn on my side. They are always spreading rumors. I am even contemplating leaving the building and going elsewhere.'

'But why do they bother you?'

'Janki and Shalini came to me one day and said that they wanted to borrow my costumes for wearing at a marriage party they were invited to. My costumes don't come cheap since I use the best materials. Only film stars and other rich people can afford to wear my dresses. How could I run the risk of lending something so costly to them? They might damage the dresses by accidentally spilling food, and if that happened they would have found it difficult to compensate me. So, naturally, I refused. Since then Janki and Shalini have borne a grudge against me.'

'You did the right thing by refusing them the dresses,' Anirudh said.

'They have made my life hell for doing the right thing.'

'Why don't you confront them and tell them to stop harassing you?'

'Ha! As if those two frustrated housewives would listen to me.'

'Don't worry, next time if I catch them spreading canards about you, I will give them a piece of my mind.'

'Thank you for your support,' she said gratefully.

'No problem at all, miss.'

'My name is Urvee.'

'I am Anirudh Shukla and my wife's name is Jyotsna.'

'Your wife works somewhere, doesn't she? I see her leaving the building every morning.'

'Yeah. She is a nurse.'

‡

When the taxi reached their building, Urvee said, 'Will you take me to Natraj studio, or do you have some other work?'

'I can go to Natraj.'

'Give me ten minutes to fetch the costumes from my flat.'

'I will wait here,' Anirudh said.

'Fine,' she said and went inside the building. She returned in a few minutes, carrying a neat bundle of clothes. She placed the clothes on the backseat and sat down on the front seat, beside Anirudh.

'You came back very fast,' Anirudh said. 'It is not even ten minutes since you went inside.'

'Yeah, I came as quickly as I could,' she said, panting for breath. 'The shooting is held up at Natraj for these costumes. I have to reach there quickly.'

Anirudh started the taxi and then asked, 'Who will wear these dresses?'

'Some TV stars! They are making a TV serial at Natraj. I met Janki on the stairs. What a nasty look she gave me? I hate that woman.'

'You should stop being bothered by her. She is, as you rightly said, a frustrated housewife. She hates you not just because you refused her the dresses, but also because you are an independent working woman.'

'That may as well be the case.'

'Janki and Shalini are jealous of your commercial success.'

The words were music to Urvee's ears. She smiled and said, 'You and your wife should come to my flat someday.'

'We can have a get together whenever you wish.'

They reached Natraj Studio. 'How much do I have to pay?' Urvee asked.

'It does not feel nice to take money from a neighbor,' Anirudh said.

'Driving taxi is your profession. If you took a dress from me I will definitely want to be paid.'

'85 rupees.'

She handed a hundred-rupee note. He returned the change.

‡

When Anirudh returned home at 8 PM, Atul jumped up and down on the bed and shouted happily, 'Horsie, horsie.'

'Let me have a minute of rest. After that I will be your horsie.' Anirudh sat down on a chair and said, 'Fetch a glass of water for me Jyotsna.'

'Get it yourself,' thundered Jyotsna, and giving him a nasty look, walked off into the balcony.

'What is the matter with her?' Anirudh asked looking at Atul.

'Did you do anything to annoy her?'

The boy shook his head from side to side.

Anirudh went to the balcony and asked, 'What happened, Jyotsna?'

'Don't you talk to me,' she hissed.

His umbrage was raised at the uncalled-for harshness in her attitude. He said with some resentment, 'Is this the way to treat your husband, when he returns home after a tiring day?'

'You deserve worse treatment,' she shot back.

'Tell me, why.'

'What were you doing during the day?'

'That is a stupid question.'

'I asked a question and I deserve an answer,' Jyotsna shouted.

'There is no need to shout,' Anirudh said heatedly. 'You know I was driving taxi.'

'With whom?'

'For God's sake! With many different passengers.'

'Don't try to mislead me. I know all about your peccadilloes.'

'What peccadilloes?'

'Were you not with that woman?'

'Which woman?'

'The harlot who lives on the third floor.'

All of a sudden Anirudh realized what this was all about, and he shouted, 'What the hell!'

'Janki told me that you brought Urvee to this building at around noon and after that both of you went somewhere,' Jyotsna shouted back.

'That pest! I will teach her a lesson that she won't ever forget.' Anirudh moved menacingly to the door.

'Come back,' she cried. 'Do you want to create a scene?'

Confused by the heated exchanges, Atul started crying on the bed. Jyotsna turned towards him and snapped, 'No one is shouting at you. So keep quiet.'

'You are coming with me to Janki's place,' Anirudh said.

'What for?' she asked obstinately.

'A man has to assert himself once in a while,' Anirudh said and taking hold of Jyotsna's hand, he pulled her after him to Janki's.

‡

Janki's husband, a tall, dried up, stick of a man, middle aged, with graying hair, who worked as a junior level clerk at the rationing department, opened the door.

'We would like to come in for a moment,' Anirudh said.

Taking this to be a social visit, Janki's husband said pleasantly, 'Of course, do come in.'

Janki's ten-year-old son was studying at the table. He picked up his books and went into the balcony when the guests arrived. Anirudh and Jyotsna sat down on the sofa-cum folding-bed. Janki emerged from the kitchen with a frozen smile on her face, her hands coated with flour. Without any preliminaries, Anirudh said, 'I want you to tell everyone in this room about what you saw at noon.'

The smile on Janki's face turned into a frown. 'I don't understand,' she uttered.

'Is there something wrong?' Janki's husband said, looking first at Anirudh and then at his wife.

'A misunderstanding has been created between me and Jyotsna because of something that Janki claims to have seen at noon today,' Anirudh said to Janki's husband. 'I came here to get that misunderstanding cleared.'

'What is this about, Janki?' her husband asked.

'Yes...but...' Janki fumbled for words.

Jyotsna took Janki's fumbling as an admission of her guilt and said harshly, 'Tell the truth, about how you saw my husband with Urvee.'

'His taxi brought Urvee here at noon. She went inside the building while the taxi waited at the gate. She returned a few minutes later with some dresses and then left in the taxi,' Janki said meekly.

'I was waiting for a passenger at Lamington Road,' Anirudh said, presenting his side of the story. 'Urvee needed a taxi. It was a coincidence that the taxi which she hailed, turned out to be mine. She had to deliver some costumes at Natraj Studio. She asked me to drive her to our building, from where she picked up some costumes and after that I dropped her at Natraj Studio. I received the correct fare from her. If I have ferried a woman to her destination, does it mean I am having an affair with her? It is my job to take people wherever they have to go. I can't refuse someone, just because busybodies in my building don't like her.'

'It wasn't my intention to create misunderstanding between you and Jyotsna,' Janki said, impulsively clasping and unclasping her flour coated fingers.

'But you succeeded in doing just that by the sly way in which you narrated the episode to me,' Jyotsna said furiously.

'Why are you always poking your nose in other peoples, affairs Janki?' Janki's husband asked.

Janki was out of countenance. 'I am sorry,' she mumbled sheepishly.

'You should say sorry to Urvee as well for spreading canards about her. Urvee is as decent, as any of us in this room,' Anirudh said. He rose and said to Jyotsna, 'Let's go.'

'Never speak to me again about my husband,' Jyotsna glared at Janki and followed her husband out of the house.

‡

When they were inside their flat, Anirudh asked, 'Is my reputation restored now?'

'Yes, it is,' Jyotsna smiled. 'When you went to Janki's house, I was anxious that in a fit of anger, you might curse her. But you did well. You made your point without being impolite. I feel proud of you.'

'At last you are beginning to notice my better qualities,' Anirudh grinned.

'I should not have fought with you because of what I heard from Janki. I should have waited for your explanation. I am sorry.'

'I hope you will refrain from making such a mistake in future.'

'Do forgive me.'

'I am surprised that you could suspect me.'

'Just say you forgive me. Do you want me to fall on my knees?'

'I will grant my forgiveness when I feel that you have repented sufficiently for your misdemeanor,' the husband said haughtily.

'In that case, I can do without your forgiveness,' Jyotsna retorted.

'Are you two still fighting?' Atul asked.

Anirudh and Jyotsna laughed. 'We are not fighting,' Jyotsna said. 'We are playing a game called pointless arguing.'

'I want to play horsie.'

'Come on,' Anirudh said, getting down on his hands and knees. He shook an imaginary mane and neighed like a horse. Atul yelled with delight and climbed on his back. Jyotsna watched them scampering about the room for sometime and then went into the kitchen to prepare dinner.

‡

Next day, when Anirudh returned home, he found Vimla in the house.

'Namaste, bhai sahib,' Vimla said.

'How is your malaria now?' Anirudh asked.

'I am much better. I came to relieve you of Atul.'

'Relieve me of Atul? But that is so unfair. I was looking forward to spending few more days with Atul.'

'He is a charming boy,' Jyotsna said. 'Don't you want to stay with me, Atul?' she said patting the boy.

Atul smiled, 'I will go with mother.'

'You traitor!' Jyotsna said in mocked anger.

'I am so thankful to both of you for taking care of my son,' Vimla said.

'It was a pleasure having him,' Anirudh said.

After Vimla left with Atul, Anirudh said, 'Vimla is a decent sort. It is too bad that her husband has left her.'

'I feel sorry for her. She will find it difficult to bring up her son on her own.'

'That is the case,' Anirudh said and went to the bathroom to wash.

When he came out, Jyotsna said, 'Before you came, Vimla was with me for more than an hour and we talked about a lot of things.'

'It is good to have company.'

'She told me that she purchases her provisions from Deepa Store, located round the corner from here. She was full of praise for that store. The prices are lowest, goods of best quality and measure is always correct.'

Anirudh knew what response she expected from him and he obliged. 'In that case we should start buying our provisions from Deepa store.'

'I knew you would see my point. We could save a few rupees every month by shopping from Deepa.'

'Since you are more adept at saving money I am going to make you my finance manager from today. I will hand over my earnings to you and you can do whatever you like with it.'

'I don't mind taking over that responsibility if you want me to.' She tried to show as if she were making a great sacrifice by taking on herself the cumbersome responsibility of managing the finances but her eyes, glittering with happiness, betrayed her pleasure.

Anirudh took out a bundle of currency notes from his pocket and started counting. Jyotsna gazed hungrily at the notes. Anirudh knew that she was impatient to lay her paws on the cash and he took his time in counting. The bundle contained fourteen hundred rupees. 'This is what I have earned during the past few days,' he said. 'I will deposit thirteen hundred with you and keep the rest.'

Jyotsna took the thirteen hundred rupees and said, 'Of course, you should keep at least 100 rupees with you. You will need it for tea and lunch during the day.'

'That is true.'

'I saved a thousand rupees from my last salary. That added to this money from you makes two thousand three hundred rupees with me,' Jyotsna said, with satisfaction.

'You are a rich woman now.'

'Why don't we deposit our money in a bank?' Jyotsna asked eagerly.

'What for! We will have to withdraw it when we need it for expenses.'

'Withdrawal doesn't take more than few minutes. Many people keep their money in bank and withdraw it whenever they need it.'

'But why go through that hassle? Isn't it better to keep cash at home?'

'In the bank, our money will earn interest which it won't at home.'

'Interest is usually a pittance.'

'Howsoever small the interest may be, it is going to amount to something. Even if the bank gives us rupees 2 as interest, it will be an additional income. Why should we forgo that?'

Anirudh realized that she was now determined to have a bank account, so he decided to let her have her way. 'If you insist, I don't mind having a bank account.'

'Just imagine we will be earning money without having to do anything.' Jyotsna chirped. 'But that isn't the only reason why we should have a bank account.'

'What is the second reason?'

'It feels good to own a bank account. All important people have one.'

Two days later, they went to a nearby branch and opened a joint saving account.

Eight

Jyotsna was gripped with the idea that she was overdue and with this came a numbing excitement that was part fear and part delight. But being overdue by two days didn't necessarily mean that she was pregnant. It had happened before when she was unmarried and after that things had adjusted themselves next month. Something similar might happen this time, she thought. She decided to wait till she was sure about her pregnancy before telling Anirudh. It didn't make sense to get him all keyed up over nothing.

When she was a week late, she knew that she was pregnant. But still she decided to take medical advice before speaking to Anirudh. Dr. Sinha was the resident obstetrician at the hospital. When he had seen his last patient of the day and was alone in his office, Jyotsna went to see him.

Dr. Sinha looked up from the medical report of some patient that he was reading and said, 'What brings you here?'

'If you can spare a few minutes doctor, I would like to discuss something with you.'

'Are you expecting?'

'How did you guess?' Jyotsna asked with surprise.

Dr. Sinha smiled and said, 'Experience. Only time women want to discuss something with me is when they are expecting.'

'I have a feeling that I am pregnant, but I would rather have that confirmed by you.'

'We shall soon find out. That is what I am here for.'

With some consternation, Jyotsna asked, 'Will I have to pay the normal fees?'

'Don't be a fool. I won't take money from this hospital's nurse.'

The verdict was out within minutes. Jyotsna was pregnant. Now that her suspicions were confirmed, she felt a desperate longing to talk to Anirudh. Momentarily, she was angry with him for not being beside her when Dr. Sinha announced the verdict. But in no time it dawned on her that she herself was to blame for his absence. Had she informed him of her suspicions he would surely have insisted on being with her.

She toyed with the idea of trying to locate him by going around the city in a bus or a taxi but quickly gave up the idea as ridiculous. After all there was hardly any chance of her finding him. He could be driving the taxi in any part of this vast and almost endless city. Locating him in the city would be like trying to locate a needle in a haystack. Only thing she could do was to wait till he was home and then break the news to him.

‡

On her way home, she stopped at the fish market and purchased a kilo of rahu. She would cook Anirudh's favorite fish today and they would have a fine celebration.

When Anirudh returned home at his usual time of 8 PM she was in the kitchen frying fish. 'I smell something fishy,' he said, theatrically sniffing the air.

'Do you?' asked Jyotsna buoyantly. 'I purchased rahu on my way home.'

'You acted sensibly,' said Anirudh, sitting down on the chair.

'Guess what? We have reason to celebrate today.'

'Don't keep me waiting.'

'We are going to have a baby.'

It took few moments for the import of her words to sink into his mind. He rose slowly, almost laboriously, from the chair and asked what most men in similar situation would have. 'Are you sure?'

'I got it confirmed by Dr. Sinha today. He told me that the baby was a month old. Just imagine, a life has been growing inside me for all this time.'

Anirudh sank back into the chair. Jyotsna waited for him to say something, but he didn't. His laid-back attitude was so different from the way she had expected him to behave. 'Aren't you happy?' she asked.

'You have a fine way of putting that to a man who is sated with happiness.'

'I would expect little more enthusiasm from any happy person,' she said sullenly.

'Sit here, on my lap.'

'What for?'

'I want to find out if our child has made you heavier.'

Jyotsna sat on his lap and he patted her stomach.

'Do you notice any difference in my weight?'

'I do. You feel heavier.'

'You must have a goldsmith's scale installed in your knees, if you can detect the weight of a weeks old baby.'

'When did you learn about your pregnancy?'

Jyotsna didn't want to get him angry by letting him know that she had been hiding the news from him for days, so she said, 'I learnt today.'

'You must have had some suspicion before you went to see Dr. Sinha.'

'This morning I had an intuition that I might be pregnant and I decided to see Dr. Sinha during the day. My intuition was more of a sixth sense stuff rather than anything else,' she said searching his eye, to see if he believed what she had said and was relieved to see that he did.

'You have a great sixth sense, I must say.'

'What is your guess? Will we have a boy or a girl?'

'You tell me. You are the one with sixth sense.'

'My hunch is our first child will be a girl. When she grows up she will be a doctor, a very important specialist, probably even a surgeon.'

'Why do you want her to be a doctor?'

'A doctor's is the best profession that one can aspire for,' Jyotsna said wistfully. 'When I was a child, I wanted to be a doctor. But my parents could not afford to send me to a medical college, so I ended up being a nurse. When I see doctors going about their work in the hospital, I often feel a pang that I could not be like them. My daughter will fulfill my ambition. Through her I will achieve my desire of being a doctor.'

'I am happy that you did not become a doctor.'

She got up from his lap quickly and said sharply, 'Why did you say that?'

'You would not have married an ordinary cabby if you had been one.'

'If I could be a doctor, then why couldn't you be someone equally important, someone like a powerful government official who deals in important matters?'

'Don't you ever feel ashamed of your or my profession,' Anirudh said vehemently. 'We are honest and hardworking. That is what matters.'

'Yes, I guess, that is so,' she said despondently.

For sometime they kept quiet, then Jyotsna asked, 'Do you think our daughter will be a doctor?'

'We will try our best.'

'I will ready the fish,' she said and went into the kitchen.

He went after her. 'I will help you. Now onwards you should stop exerting yourself.'

She was pleased by his concern but said, 'There is no exertion in cooking.'

'Yeah, I know that. Now give me the fish, I will marinate it.' He took the plate of raw fish and started marinating it. Jyotsna turned her attention to the rice that was boiling on the stove.

'What about your job? How will you manage that?' Anirudh asked.

'Nurses at my hospital are entitled three months of paid maternity leave. So there won't be any problem.'

'Will three months of leave be sufficient?'

'It has been sufficient for most of the nurses who have been pregnant before me,' she quipped.

'If I told you to leave your job and stay at home, will you listen to me?'

'I like working as a nurse. The work isn't tiring at all.'

'Alright.'

‡

Jyotsna woke up at dawn. Anirudh was snoring by her side. She shook him, saying, 'Wake up, its morning.'

'What happened?' he mumbled.

'We are going for a walk. I have heard from someone that walking is good for pregnant women.'

'Let me sleep. I am not the pregnant woman.'

'Stop being lazybones,' she said, shaking him again, a little roughly this time.

'Stop shaking me! You will shatter my ribs,' Anirudh said and sat up on the bed. 'What time is it?'

'It is the right time to get up, 5.30.'

'I could do with another half hour of sleep.'

'Do you want me to pull you out of bed?'

'I would rather leave the bed on my own.'

'Then, do so.'

They brushed teeth in the bathroom and came out of their flat. The dawn had scarcely broken and a dirty smear reflected on a pool of water caused by an overflowing gutter. The air felt mild. Many were walking briskly or jogging along the sidewalks.

'See, all these people are taking morning walk. Most of them do this daily,' Jyotsna said, making a point. 'They are not like us who manage a morning walk only once in a while and that, too, after lots of cajoling and shaking. From today we should make it a habit, come what may, we will walk for at least a kilometer every morning...'

'Will you please stop haranguing me,' he interrupted, 'I hate it, when anyone lectures me the first thing in the morning.'

'If I am haranguing you, it is only for the sake of our daughter. If I get daily morning walks, I will be healthy and if I am healthy, the child inside me will also be healthy. A healthy mother gives birth to a healthy child. Don't you know that? It is your duty, as the father of our daughter, to see to it that I walk for some distance every morning. You ought to encourage me to take morning walks, but...'

Anirudh caught hold of her long hair and tugged at it once. 'I swear by your hair that every morning I shall drag you out of the house.'

'Let go of my hair,' Jyotsna cried. 'People are watching.'

'Not before you promise that you won't lecture me any further.'

'Lecture? I won't even speak to you,' Jyotsna said with pique.

Anirudh released her hair and they started walking again.

'I am surprised at the way you behaved on a public road,' Jyotsna said grumpily.

Anirudh kept quiet.

'Don't speak to me again,' Jyotsna said.

'I hate to remind you that you have already spoken twice since you declared you won't speak to me.'

Jyotsna glared at him and lapsed into a sullen silence. After walking for some distance they noticed a woman who was coming from the opposite direction, pushing a pram with her hands.

'Isn't that a beautiful pram?' Anirudh said.

Jyotsna's anger had dissipated by now and she simpered, 'I was thinking the same thing. We will buy a similar pram when our daughter is born. Every morning we will wheel her with us, like that woman. Won't that be nice?'

'It will be great.'

'I wonder how much a pram costs.'

'We can ask her.'

When the woman with the pram drew near, Jyotsna smiled looking into the pram and said, 'What a pretty baby.'

The woman stopped and said good-naturedly, 'Aren't all babies pretty?'

'Is she your daughter?'

'He is my son,' the woman answered simply.

'Oh! I am sorry. He looks so cute. Just like a girl.'

'He is only a year old.'

'I am going to have a baby myself,' Jyotsna said.

'Really? When is your baby due?'

'In six months.'

'Where did you get your pram from?' Anirudh asked. 'We would like to buy a similar pram for our child.'

'From Bombay Central market.'

'That isn't far from here,' Anirudh said.

'How much did you pay?' Jyotsna asked, admiring the pram's fine upholstery.

'850 rupees.'

'850 rupees,' Jyotsna gulped. 'That's costly.'

'Cheaper prams are available but they are not as durable or good looking as this one.'

Jyotsna looked at Anirudh with a question mark on her face.

'Don't worry about money,' Anirudh said bravely. 'We will get the best pram available for our daughter.'

'Yeah, we are not going to cut corners, where the interest of our child is concerned,' Jyotsna said.

'Do you stay close by?' the woman asked.

'In that building over there,' Jyotsna said pointing towards her house, which was visible from where she stood. 'Where do you stay?'

'My flat is on the first floor of the pale yellow building opposite your building.'

'It is nice to know we are neighbors. My name is Jyotsna and he is my husband, Anirudh Shukla.'

'I am Aditi and I call my son Nitin.'

'Come to my house whenever you have the time. I will feel delighted to receive you.'

'It is good to make your acquaintance,' Jyotsna said.

After sometime Aditi went ahead wheeling her pram and Anirudh and Jyotsna resumed their walk.

'Aditi is another friend that I now have in this area. One gets to meet such nice people in the morning,' Jyotsna said.

'That is one more reason why we should potter around every morning.'

She looked at him suspiciously. 'Are you being sarcastic?'

'I only said what you were eventually going to say.'

She thought that he was trying to be sarcastic and it angered her, but she let it pass and didn't say anything. They reached the point where the road divided into two branches and took the right turn.

'Looks like Vimla and Atul are not out this morning,' Anirudh said.

'Vimla is an occasional morning walker, just like us.'

'How is Vimla keeping these days? Does she come to the hospital regularly?'

'She does.'

'It has been quite a while since I saw Atul. I wonder if he remembers me?'

'Have no doubt that he remembers you. A boy seldom forgets his horse.'

'I miss that boy.'

'Why don't we invite Vimla and her son for lunch on Sunday.'

'That would be a good idea.'

When they returned to their building, they saw Janki and Shalini chatting at the gate.

'These two gossiping vixens are at the gate again,' Jyotsna said with pique.

'I can't understand what they talk about.'

'About everything that does not concern them.'

Janki had not been on talking terms with Anirudh and Jyotsna since the dressing down she had that day. She avoided making eye contact with them. But Shalini greeted them warmly. Jyotsna and Anirudh returned the greetings in a perfunctory manner and without pausing to exchange any words, entered the building.

'Did you see how confused Janki was when she saw us?' Jyotsna said. 'She didn't even greet us.'

'We should invite her and her family for lunch on Sunday along with Vimla and Atul.'

'How can we invite Janki?' Jyotsna asked contemptuously. 'That woman tried to create misunderstanding between us.'

'We should be generous and let bygones be bygones. She is a neighbor, one ought to have good relations with neighbors.'

'I am not generous and I will not invite her for lunch.'

'But....'

'Drop the subject. Janki is not worth having good relations with. When I love or hate someone, I do so for life.'

'You will make a bad enemy.'

'But a good friend,' she answered confidently.

‡

They were getting ready to leave for work when there was a knock on the door. Anirudh opened the door and was surprised to see Urvee.

'Hello there! How are you,' Urvee said brightly.

'Fine, thank you,' Anirudh said. 'Please come in.'

Urvee stepped into the room but did not sit down. 'I have to reach Filmistan Studio urgently,' She said. 'Can you drop me there in your taxi?'

'Yeah, I can. But you will have to give me five minutes to get ready.'

'Okay.'

Jyotsna's voice came from the bathroom. She asked, 'Whom are you talking to?'

'It's Urvee,' Anirudh answered.

Within moments Jyotsna emerged from the bathroom and, looking guardedly at Urvee, asked, 'What do you want?'

Urvee was bewildered at the antagonism in Jyotsna's voice. 'I came to hire your husband's taxi,' she uttered.

'She has to reach Filmistan Studio urgently. I will drive her there,' Anirudh explained.

'Our home is not a taxi stand. Why can't she get a taxi from the road?' Jyotsna demanded.

'There is nothing wrong if I take her to Filmistan,' Anirudh retorted, confused by the harshness in Jyotsna's tone.

'You can't do that,' Jyotsna said obstinately. 'I don't feel like catching a bus. You will have to drop me at the hospital.'

'Excuse me,' Urvee injected. 'I will take another taxi. Sorry to bother you.' She marched out in a huff.

Anirudh closed the door after her and then turned towards Jyotsna to let her have it from him. 'For Gods sake!' he hollered. 'The sky wouldn't have fallen down, if she traveled in my taxi. Why did you behave in such a ridiculous manner?'

'There was nothing ridiculous in the way I behaved,' answered Jyotsna.

'You acted as if Urvee came to entice me.'

'I don't suspect either you or Urvee.'

'Then why didn't you allow me to take her in my taxi?'

'Because I want you to take me to the hospital.'

'Speak the truth,' Anirudh said in a strong voice, 'I will respect you if you do that.'

'You want the truth?' Jyotsna said. 'Well, the truth is, I know you will never be unfaithful to me, but at the same time I don't want to take any chances.'

'Women! I will never understand women.'

'I think it is my job as a wife to keep my husband away from temptations,' she said smugly and then marched into the kitchen. When she returned with two cups of tea, she found Anirudh sitting on the edge of the bed and smiling to himself. 'We are getting along quite well now, Anirudh, you and me,' she said.

He said softly, 'Yes, we are.'

‡

On Sunday, Vimla arrived with Atul to lunch with the Shukla couple.

'Hi,' Atul said buoyantly, when Anirudh opened the door.

'Oh! My young horse rider friend is here,' Anirudh chuckled. 'Do you remember me?' Atul shook his head up and down in the affirmative. Anirudh laughed and picked him up.

'He often talks about you,' Vimla said.

'And what about me! Have you forgotten me Atul?' Jyotsna asked.

Atul smiled, but didn't say anything.

'Say 'hello' to aunty,' Vimla said.

'Hi,' Atul said.

'Let me hold him for a moment,' Jyotsna said. 'I want to see how it feels.'

'You are not supposed to lift anything heavy. He weighs as much as a baby elephant.' Anirudh said. 'Don't you, Atul?'

'Yeah, I am a baby elephant,' Atul declared.

'He has great fascination for all kinds of animals,' Vimla chuckled.

'All kids are like that,' Anirudh said.

'Give him to me,' Jyotsna said. 'I am sure that he will not weigh as much as a baby elephant. A monkey, maybe.'

Jyotsna was too thin and didn't have enough hip. Still Atul tried his best to get into the saddle. He twined his legs around her waist and grabbed her neck with both hands.

'Hey! You are choking me,' Jyotsna spluttered.

Atul let go of her neck and clutched her hair.

'Give him back to me before he pulls out all your hair and turns you bald,' Anirudh said.

'No, I am comfortable now,' said Jyotsna. She carried the child around the room few times and then dropped him on the bed. 'Who says, I won't be able to carry my daughter,' she said triumphantly.

They had chicken briyani for lunch.

‡

On another Sunday, Jyotsna went to visit Aditi. When Aditi opened the door there was some confusion on her face, as she tried to remember if she knew the woman standing at her door smiling pleasantly.

'Do I have to introduce myself Aditi?' Jyotsna said. 'We met in morning that day, don't you remember…'

'Oh! It's only you,' said Aditi with a flash of recognition. 'Welcome to my house.'

A dour looking man, wearing a cotton gown, was sitting on a chair with a magazine in his hand. Aditi introduced him as her husband Vijay Goel. Jyotsna greeted him warmly, but all that her greetings elicited from him, was a disinterested glance. She felt rebuffed by the cold response and wondered if she had arrived at a wrong moment. 'I hope I am not intruding,' she said.

'Of course not,' Aditi said cheerfully. 'I am pleased to see you.'

'I work as a nurse at a hospital. So it is difficult for me to go anywhere except on Sundays.'

'I thought you were a housewife like me.'

'How is Nitin?'

'He is fine. He is playing with his toys in the next room. Come, I will take you to him.'

Aditi's house was a two room flat. The second room was the bedroom. Nitin was sitting on the bed, mumbling to a 6-inch tall plastic clown that he held in his hands. Around him lay a toy train, a plastic ball and a teddy bear.

Aditi picked him up from the bed and placed a slobbering

kiss on his cheek. 'What were you saying to your clown?' she asked lovingly.

'Hi, Nitin,' Jyotsna said taking his hand. 'Has he started talking?'

'Not yet, but he has started calling me mama.'

As if to prove what his mother had said, Nitin uttered mama.

'See, what did I tell you?' Aditi said with pride, 'He knows I am his mama.'

'Let me take him,' Jyotsna said.

Aditi gave her son another kiss before turning him over. Jyotsna rocked the child in her lap and he giggled. His hands examined her face and he pushed one small finger into her nostril. 'How am I going to breathe if you do that?' Jyotsna said cheerfully. She placed him back on the bed. Nitin resumed playing with his toys, while Jyotsna and Aditi sat down on the bed to chat.

'Your husband seems a very quiet person,' Jyotsna said.

'He was not always like that but since he lost his legs he has changed a lot.'

'Lost his legs?' Jyotsna gasped. 'My God! I didn't know that.'

'Didn't you notice, when you met him in the living room. His legs end at his knees.'

'I didn't notice. But how did he lose his legs? Was he involved in an accident?'

'He was a subedar in the army. During counter insurgency operations in Kashmir, militants lobbed a grenade. Both his legs were blown off.'

'Is he still in the army?'

'A man without legs can be of little use to the army,' Aditi said sadly. 'He was discharged. Now he is unemployed. We live on his pension and insurance policies. But I am not complaining. I am thankful to God for sparing his life. Had he died, it would have been a disaster for my son and me.'

Jyotsna had a sudden insight into Vijay Goel's feelings. She thought that he didn't want anybody to know that he had lost his legs and his job, and feel pity for him. That is why he acted in a grouchy manner. 'Your husband is a brave man, Aditi,' Jyotsna said.

They chatted about different things for some more time and then Jyotsna got up to leave. Vijay Goel was still reading a magazine in the living room. This time Jyotsna noticed that the chair on which he was sitting, was actually a wheelchair and that his legs ended at his knees.

'Mr. Vijay Goel,' she said, 'Aditi told me about how you lost your legs while combating the militants. I want to tell you that your sacrifice was not in vain. Due to your bravery this country has become safer. I am proud to know you.'

There was a faint softening in Vijay Goel's grim demeanor. He nodded at Jyotsna and then resumed reading his magazine.

‡

That night when they lay down on the bed, she told Anirudh about Vijay Goel.

'That is too bad. I hope his pension and insurance money is sufficient for his needs,' Anirudh said.

'It is not about money,' Jyotsna said thoughtfully. 'That man has lost an important part of his body. Just think, how his lifestyle must have changed since his amputation. Simple chores like getting up from the bed, going to bathroom, getting up or down the stairs, taking the baby out for a walk or getting vegetables from the neighborhood grocer, are difficult feats for him. How cumbersome his life must have turned?'

'He has sacrificed his legs for the country.'

'Yeah, I know that. But that is something most of us would prefer not to do.'

'Most of us are not in the army. When Vijay Goel decided to join the army he must have taken into account the risks involved.'

'Don't be cynical.'

'I am not being cynical. I respect Vijay Goel for what he has done for the country. But it is also a fact that it was his job to fight for the country.'

'It is never anyone's job to get his legs blown off.'

'I don't like it when my wife thinks of another man at 11 PM in the night.'

She pulled herself up on the bed and looking into his eyes, said, 'I don't believe this. Are you jealous of Vijay Goel?'

'Only as jealous as you are of Urvee.'

'Damn it! How dare you think of Urvee at this time of the night?' Jyotsna demanded furiously.

'When you stop thinking of Vijay Goel, I will stop thinking of Urvee,' Anirudh said peevishly.

'Vijay Goel and Urvee are not the same. Vijay Goel is a patriotic soldier, whereas Urvee is a…' She let the sentence linger in the air and lay down on the bed.

'Is a what?' Anirudh asked menacingly.

After a moment's thought, Jyotsna whispered, 'We can't be absolutely sure that she isn't what Janki said she was.'

'What the hell!' Anirudh shouted.

'Don't holler at me.' she shouted back. 'Otherwise I will say something mean to you and hurt you real bad.'

'Try it. I am as eager to get the quarrel underway as you are.'

There was a dangerous silence. Jyotsna spoke first. 'We should not fight at bedtime.'

'Yes, not at bedtime,' he said with relief. 'Moreover expectant mother's should not get angry. It is bad for their baby. We must stop fighting till you have your baby.'

'This is not the first time we made this resolution,' Jyotsna said.

'This time we will keep it.'

‡

When Jyotsna went to see Dr. Sinha for the second time, Anirudh was with her. He waited impatiently in the corridor while Jyotsna lay on a stretcher in the examining room, where Dr. Sinha gave her a complete physical examination – heart, lungs, metabolism, blood pressure, liver and so on.

After almost an hour Jyotsna emerged from the examining room. She said, 'Dr. Sinha will see us in his office.' They went to Dr. Sinha's office.

'Jyotsna is four months pregnant,' Dr. Sinha said. 'The child in her womb is healthy and there is nothing to worry about.'

He gave a list of what to eat and what to avoid, and some other important instructions as well. '…Don't lift heavy furniture or buckets filled with water. Take short walks daily, but avoid exerting yourself. Drink a lot of water…'

'You didn't take any fees when Jyotsna visited you last time. But from now onwards, we would like to pay,' Anirudh said.

'You want to know my fees?' Dr. Sinha said.

'Yes.'

'It is 500 for every examination. But you don't have to pay that much. From nurses of this hospital, I charge 100 rupees per visit.'

'Thank you, doctor.'

'I presume that Jyotsna will be having her child at the hospital.'

'We have not made that decision,' Anirudh said looking at Jyotsna.

'My advice is she should have the child at the hospital. She is quite small in the middle and as a result could have a difficult childbirth.'

Jyotsna felt a quiver of fear.

'Do you think it will be a difficult childbirth,' Anirudh asked with apprehension.

'On the contrary! I didn't mean to frighten both of you. I am quite certain that Jyotsna will have an easy childbirth, but as a matter of policy, I always advise having the child at a hospital, where the best medical facilities are available. Being a nurse Jyotsna already knows about all that.'

'We will have our child at the hospital,' Anirudh said quickly.

'Normally the hospital bills amount to around 1000 rupees a day. She will have to stay here for at least four or five days.'

'That means four or five thousand rupees.'

'Yes, and that will be money well spent.'

'We will manage the money, doctor.'

‡

When they came out of the doctor's office, Jyotsna said, 'Do you seriously want me to have my daughter at the hospital?'

'Didn't you hear the doctor?' Anirudh said looking at her. 'It is safe having a child at the hospital.'

'The midwife at Jai Ganesh Wadi charges only 250 rupees for delivering a baby.'

Anirudh gave a contemptuous snort, 'I won't risk your life for any amount of money.'

'5000 is a big amount. Why pay so much when the midwife can accomplish the task at a fraction of the cost?'

'In that case our daughter will end up as a nurse like you.'

'Why did you say that?' Jyotsna asked with shock.

'If our daughter is to become a doctor, we have to give her the best things in life from the very beginning. Our daughter will not be born like a slum child in the hands of an illiterate midwife. She will be born at a first-rate hospital, where kids from good families are born.'

The words spoken by her husband acted as a catalyst, which all of a sudden brought together and fused separate thoughts and desires and revealed an entirely new line of reasoning. 'Your way of thinking is somewhat convoluted,' she said. 'But despite all that you have me convinced we should have our child at the hospital.'

‡

Anirudh came home at the usual time. In his hand was a small packet.

'What is in the packet?' Jyotsna asked.

'Guess?' he challenged.

'Is it something for me?' she asked eagerly.

'For both of us.'

She snatched the packet from his hand and opened it hastily. Out came a twelve-month calendar with beautiful photographs of toddlers.

'I thought you would like to have a calendar with such photographs in the house,' Anirudh said.

'The babies are so beautiful,' she gushed, leafing through the pages of the calendar. 'I can keep seeing them all day.'

'I have heard from someone that if expectant mothers look at photos of beautiful babies everyday their children turn out to be beautiful.'

'I will hang this calendar opposite the bed so that I can look at it even when I am lying down.'

'Let me do that.' He brought a nail and hammer from the toolbox in the balcony and after fixing the nail on the wall, hung the calendar.

'Perfect,' she said.

'Another thing has come to my mind?'

'What?'

'We should find a good name for our daughter?'

'I have already done that,' Jyotsna declared complacently.

'Without even asking me?' he said with a hurt air.

'I am sure you will like the name that I have chosen.'

'What name?'

'Reema.'

'What is so special about this name?'

'I just happen to like it.'

'You have dictatorial streak inside you,' Anirudh frowned. 'You always try to impose your views on me. You should have taken my suggestion before deciding a name for our daughter. After all, I am the father. It is my right, too, to choose a name for my daughter.'

'Let us not fight over our daughter's name. I like the name, Reema. Let me call her by that name,' Jyotsna pleaded.

Anirudh brought his face close to Jyotsna's stomach and dramatically said, 'Hey you in there! Do you wish to be called Reema?' He looked up at Jyotsna's amused face and said, 'She says the name is alright.'

‡

Rainy season in Bombay comes all of a sudden, as if it had been waiting round the corner all the time. From the sea, dark monsoon clouds float into the city casting a thick veil over the sky. When downpour begins it does so with the ferocity of a deluge. Waterlogged streets, overflowing gutters, disrupted local train schedules, frequent traffic jams and cancelled flights, are a norm for the season.

But the denizens of the city always welcome the rains with open arms, in spite of all the inconvenience in its wake. The rain replenishes the lakes that supply water to the city. It also provides a welcome break from the sweltering summer heat and cleans up the city by washing away the garbage that its citizens have created through the year. Some locals assert that the rains cleanse the city of not just the muck, but also of the sins of its inhabitants.

Around the middle of June, when it was six in the morning, and Anirudh and Jyotsna were still in the bed, the first downpour began. They left their bed quickly and came into the balcony to greet the rains. Bolts of lightning streaked across the overcast sky and raindrops pitter-pattered on the earth in a steady drizzle. A cool breeze, saturated with minute droplets of water blew. The faint glow of the rising sun, peeping softly through the thick cloud cover, could be made out.

'When I was young, I used to play in the rain,' Jyotsna said jauntily, extending her hand out of the balcony to catch the raindrops descending from the sky.

'You are still young enough to play,' Anirudh said mischievously.

'Not with my advanced pregnancy,' Jyotsna said caressing her protruding stomach with her wet palm.

'You are lucky. If the rain had come two hours later, it would have caught you in the street.'

'Looks like I will get caught in the rain quite often, since the rainy season is here.'

'Not if you do as I say. I don't want you to clamber up and

down the slippery steps of a bus while it is raining. That will be too risky for you and for our baby. I will drop you to your hospital every morning right through the rainy season.'

'O yeah! And what do you expect me to do, when I have to return home in the evening. You can't come to pick me up every day.'

'If it is raining in the evening, you can catch any taxi that is available outside your hospital.'

'All that fuss only amounts to much ado over nothing,' she said shrugging her shoulders. 'Many pregnant women travel in buses while it is raining. Why can't I do the same?'

Her obstinate attitude got on his nerves. 'Why can't you see my point of view even once?' he grumbled. 'I don't want you to travel by bus and that's it. You will have to obey me. I won't take 'no' for an answer.'

'Okay, I will do what you say. Cool down now.'

They lapsed into silence and looked into the street. People sheltered by umbrellas were walking hastily along the sidewalks. Some, who had been caught unawares by the first rains of the season and did not have an umbrella with them, were scurrying about for cover. School children draped in colorful raincoats were waiting for their school bus at one corner of the street.

'Reema will be with us by the time this rainy season is over,' Anirudh said.

'I can't bear to wait for the day when she will be in my arms,' Jyotsna said wistfully.

‡

Two days later, it was raining cats and dogs when Jyotsna came out of the hospital in the evening. For a few minutes, she waited under the hospital's awning, hoping that the rain would stop. But the rains showed no sign of relenting. She realized that it could carry on for quite some time and walked into the street, clutching her open umbrella. Around her, people under umbrellas some resplendent in colorful raincoats, marched to and fro.

A long line of taxis was parked on the road outside the hospital compound. She thought of taking a taxi, then quickly decided against it. The taxi fare to her house would be at least 20 rupees, whereas a bus would charge just 2 rupees. 'Anirudh does not need to know that I took a bus,' she told herself and went to the bus stop. The bus soon arrived. Though it was a bit crowded, she somehow managed to squeeze inside the compartment.

A middle-aged man, who probably noticed her pregnant state, offered her his seat. She thanked him and sat down. The rain intensified by the time the bus reached her stop. Her house was about 100 meters away from the bus stop and the downpour being too thick for her umbrella to handle, she decided to wait somewhere till the rain thinned or stopped. She found shelter in a grocery store adjacent to the bus stop.

Like her a few others had also sought shelter inside the grocery shop. The grocer sat behind a long counter laid out with different kinds of vegetables. Jyotsna thought of buying some vegetables for her kitchen while she was here.

'What is the price of tomatoes?' she asked the grocer.

'8 rupees a kilo.'

'That's costly.'

The grocer shrugged, but didn't say anything.

'What about the peas?' Jyotsna asked.

'10 rupees a kilo.'

'Is this shop newly opened? I haven't seen it before.'

The grocer nodded disinterestedly. He obviously was not interested in pursuing a conversation.

What makes him so grouchy, Jyotsna wondered? He probably hates to have customers. In that case why has he opened this shop? She noticed that the shopkeeper was staring at her. Why is he staring at me? She thought. The impudent fool, I will never come to his shop again.

'Have I seen you before?' the shopkeeper opened his mouth to ask.

'I don't think so,' said Jyotsna gruffly.

'Are you Aditi's friend?'

Suddenly Jyotsna realized who the grocer was. He was Aditi's soldier husband, Vijay Goel. Her attitude transformed right away, from one of spite to that of goodwill. 'Mr. Vijay Goel,' she exclaimed, 'Sorry I didn't recognize you. But you should not blame me for that. This is the last place where I could have expected to see you.'

'You wanted to know if this shop was newly opened. I opened this shop two days ago.'

'I am so glad that you have got busy in this enterprise.'

'One has to do something to make a living. I got a loan sanctioned from a bank and with that money I opened this shop.'

'It must be difficult for a man in your condition to manage,'

Jyotsna said sympathetically and immediately realized that by making an indirect reference to Vijay Goel's handicap, she may have hurt his feelings. She cursed herself for her faux pas. 'I admire your courage in trying to rebuild your life,' she added.

'I got false legs fitted to my stumps. Now I am able to walk.'

'Oh really!' Jyotsna exclaimed. 'That is great news.'

'Let me show you how I walk.'

Jyotsna was gripped with the apprehension that he may lose balance and hurt himself and then she would be held responsible. 'Please don't exert yourself for my sake,' she said hastily.

He read her mind and said, 'Don't worry, I won't fall down.' He got up and took a few steps around the shop.

'You walk like a soldier,' Jyotsna cheered.

She knew and he knew that that was not the case. His steps were unsteady. But it was a nice thing to say – that he walked like a soldier.

'Do you want to buy tomatoes and peas?' Vijay Goel asked.

'Yeah. I will take a kilo of each.'

Vijay Goel weighed the merchandise she wanted. 'The total comes to 18 rupees, but from you I will take only 15.'

'Why such magnanimity?' Jyotsna asked.

'I always charge less from special customers.'

Jyotsna was pleased to hear she was a special customer and she said smilingly, 'In future I will purchase all my vegetables from here. Your shop is special to me.'

'You are welcome.'

Jyotsna inquired about Aditi and Nitin. Vijay Goel assured

her that they were fine. By then the rain had become a trickle. Jyotsna left for home.

‡

'Vijay Goel has opened a grocery shop in our neighborhood,' Jyotsna exclaimed.

'Is he someone I know?' Anirudh asked.

'Didn't I tell you about him? The solider who lost his legs while fighting militants in Kashmir.'

'You are talking about Aditi's husband.'

'Who else? Imagine him managing a grocery store.'

'How does he do that without his legs.'

'He has got false legs fitted to his stumps and he can walk with them. What a strong character he has, to be able to bounce back after the calamity of losing his legs.'

'Yeah. I guess he must be all that.'

'He is a man of true grit.'

'You are not planning to sing paeans to Vijay Goel through the night. Are you?' He said teasingly. 'Because if you do that, I will retaliate by talking about Urvee.'

'You are thinking of Urvee,' Jyotsna said with disgust.

'If you can think of that solider friend of yours, why can't I think of Urvee?'

'I admire Vijay Goel for the sacrifice he has made for the country and for his courage, whereas your admiration for Urvee hinges on something else.'

'What do I admire Urvee for? Let me know.'

'For...you know what,' Jyotsna said with pique.

'To get your mind in order, I will have to spank you someday.'

'You won't dare.'

'Wait and see,' Anirudh said with intent.

'Don't get me angry. You know it isn't good for expectant mothers to be angry.'

'You are the one who started this conversation.'

'That's right I started a conversation, but you turned it into an argument.'

'Let's change the topic,' Anirudh said. 'How did you find Vijay Goel's shop?'

'When I got down from the bus, it was still raining. So I went to a shop behind the bus stop to take shelter from rain and the shop turned out to be Vijay Goel's. He told me he opened the shop two days ago.'

'But why did you return from the hospital in a bus when it was raining? Haven't I told you to take a cab?'

Jyotsna realized that she was trapped. 'The taxi costs 20 rupees, whereas the bus ticket is 2 rupees,' she said guiltily.

Anirudh was livid. 'You never listen to me,' he hollered. 'In a crowded bus, you could have been pushed on your stomach. I don't have to remind you how dangerous that can be.'

'I am sorry. I won't act like that again.'

But he was in no mood to forgive. 'I don't care about saving 18 rupees,' he thundered.

'I won't repeat the mistake.'

He kept quiet.

'Ouch,' Jyotsna cried.

'What happened?'

'Reema kicked me.'

Anirudh placed his hand on Jyotsna's stomach and felt the child's movements. 'Even our daughter realizes that you deserve to be kicked,' he said happily.

‡

Fifteen days later, they met Urvee while on their morning walk. Urvee, draped in a figure-hugging tracksuit was jogging towards them. Her large and firm breasts wobbled visibly as she jogged. Her shapely waist and longlegs were clearly outlined by her tight dress. Her bob cut hair appeared like a halo around her head.

'Why can't she dress in a respectable manner?' Jyotsna said making a face.

'Who?' Anirudh asked innocently.

'Don't pretend you have not noticed her,' Jyotsna glared.

Anirudh whistled lightly adding to her annoyance.

Urvee stopped beside them and said, 'Hello both of you.'

'Good morning,' Anirudh said.

'It's nice to see you,' Jyotsna said, managing a smile.

'Did I tell you that I am going to Madras next week?' Urvee asked.

'No, you didn't,' Anirudh said. 'Why are you going there?'

'Madras is my hometown. I am going to get married,' Urvee said with a coy smile.

'Congratulations,' Jyotsna said. 'You will be returning to Bombay with your husband, I presume.'

'No, I am shifting permanently to Madras. The person I am marrying owns a boutique there. I will help him in his business.'

'Oh, it's sad you are leaving Bombay. We will miss you,' Jyotsna said.

'I, too, will miss you and everybody else.'

'What are you going to do about your costume business in Bombay?' Anirudh asked.

'My costume business will go with me to Madras. I will design costumes for my husband's boutique.'

'I feel sad that you are leaving us,' Jyotsna said.

'I guess that is how life is. I have to go where my destiny takes me,' Urvee said philosophically.

'I wish you all the luck in the new life that you will be beginning in Madras.'

After exchanging few more words, Urvee jogged away and Anirudh and Jyotsna carried on with their walk.

'She is such a nice girl,' Jyotsna said.

'That was not your impression till a few minutes ago,' Anirudh remarked sarcastically.

'I accept that I made a mistake about Urvee.'

'Mistake? You made a blunder. You believed in all sorts of things about her.'

'I have accepted my mistake and that is a very courageous thing to do. Not many people accept their mistakes,' declared Jyotsna with her head held high.

'Instead of being contrite, you are using your mistake for self-glorification. I don't think you will ever repent for anything. You will make a fine politician.'

'I will let you have the last word on this, but only because I am not in mood for a debate.'

'You are letting me have the last word because you know that you can't win.'

'Have it your way.'

‡

Janki and Shalini were talking animatedly with Urvee at the gate.

'Looks like Janki and Shalini have buried their hatchet so far as Urvee is concerned,' Anirudh said.

'Life never ceases to amaze me,' Jyotsna mused.

When they reached the gate, Janki said, 'Do you know Urvee is leaving us?' There was not the slightest hint of animosity on her face. Her rivalry, it seemed, was over not just against Urvee, but also against Jyotsna and Anirudh.

'She told us about her marriage plans a few minutes ago,' Jyotsna said with similar friendliness.

'It felt so nice to have someone modern and sophisticated living in the building. Without her this building will lose its lustre,' Shalini said, conveniently forgetting that she used to call Urvee a hooker because of her modern lifestyle.

'I was telling Urvee that she should not forget us once she goes to Madras. We must keep in touch through letters,' Janki declared.

'How can I forget the love and respect I have received from all of you,' said Urvee emotionally. She, too, seemed to be suffering from amnesia and had forgotten or chosen to overlook the numerous insults that Janki and Shalini had regularly heaped on her. 'I will write letters every week.'

'You must consider the whole building as your home,' Shalini said. 'Whenever you come to Bombay, you can stay with any one of us.'

'Yes the door to my flat will always be open for you,' Janki said.

'When does your train leave for Madras?' Jyotsna asked.

'On the 18th at 6 PM,' Urvee said.

'My husband will take you to the railway station in his taxi,' Jyotsna said good-naturedly. 'He will see you safely into the train.'

'I am overwhelmed by the kindness everyone is showering on me,' Urvee said.

'We are concerned that you should reach Madras safely,' Janki spouted. 'You are like a sister to us.'

When they were inside their flat, Anirudh asked, 'Why did you talk to Janki today, when you had promised that you would never in all your life?'

'That was then,' Jyotsna said with surprise, 'Don't you see how the situation has changed now. Now that Urvee is departing for Madras, there is no reason for us to quarrel.'

'Women!' Anirudh uttered and, shaking his head, went into the bathroom to get ready.

‡

On another day when Anirudh returned from driving the taxi Jyotsna announced proudly, 'Today I went to the bank to have our passbook updated.'

'How much does your kitty amount to, now?' asked her husband.

'Little over 10,000 rupees,' Jyotsna said happily. 'I will show you the passbook.' She brought it out from the cupboard and opened it in front of him.

'Not bad,' Anirudh murmured. 'We managed to save a substantial sum.'

'Look at this entry,' Jyotsna said, pointing with her index finger to one entry in the passbook. 'It says interest 21 rupees. Isn't it nice of the bank people to give us so much interest.'

'This is the first time in my life that I have earned interest. It was such a good idea to open a bank account.'

'It was my idea,' Jyotsna said, barely trying to conceal the sense of victory that was after all hers.

'I am prepared to give you credit where it is due.'

'It is too bad that we will have to withdraw almost 5000 rupees to pay the hospital bills. I would have liked to maintain a balance of 10000 rupees in our account, as it is now.'

'Don't you go about grudging that 5000 rupees. What is money for, if we can't spend it when it is required?'

'Yeah, that is true,' she whispered.

‡

It was a Sunday on the day when Urvee had to catch the train for Madras. Anirudh helped her load the luggage on the taxi's carrier and the dickey. Many residents of the building had come out of their homes to bid fond farewell to the woman, who due to her different lifestyle fuelled so much gossip. Janki and Shalini dabbed tears from their eyes as they told Urvee how much they were going to miss her. Urvee sobbed and hugged them. Anirudh watched the cloying melodrama in silence.

Finally, after lots of hugging, crying and banal expressions of love, Urvee slipped into the backseat of the taxi. Jyotsna had not gone to the hospital. She insisted on seeing Urvee off and sat beside Anirudh in the front. Anirudh thought that Jyotsna was tagging along because she did not trust Urvee with him, even at this juncture. But he kept his thoughts to himself.

The taxi reached the station around 5.30 PM. Anirudh and Jyotsna accompanied Urvee to the platform. The train arrived within few minutes.

'Write to me when you reach Madras,' Jyotsna said.

'When your daughter is born send me her photograph,' Urvee said.

Anirudh and Jyotsna waited at the platform till the train departed.

‡

Nine

The rainy season ended prematurely in the middle of August. The cloud cover disappeared and it was bright and sunny once again. This was Jyotsna's last month of pregnancy. Her stomach was now bloated and moving around was difficult for her. She availed of maternity leave and started staying at home.

For someone who has been working as a nurse for many years, this sudden confinement in the house was difficult to bear. She missed the hustle and bustle of the hospital, especially the interaction she had, with the patients, doctors and other medical staff. The hours, during which Anirudh was out driving taxi and she remained alone in the house, were the most difficult ones for her. She felt lonesome without anyone to talk to. But when he was at home, she gave him hell by carping about being housebound. Anirudh often offered to take her to movies or to restaurants, but with her pregnancy so obvious, she flatly refused to accompany him anywhere. The only time she ventured out was when she went to see her neighbors, Janki, Aditi and others, or to shop at nearby stores.

She was more argumentative than ever before and picked up a quarrel at the drop of a hat. She begged Anirudh to tell her, what he would like to have for dinner and when he made a suggestion she contested it fiercely. If it was fish he wanted, then this was not the season for having fish. Rajma was too heavy for the stomach, potatoes had cholesterol and green vegetables were contaminated. Even the smallest issue would irk her. Once she nagged Anirudh for an hour, just because he left the kitchen tap running. Anirudh knew that her tantrums were the result of her pregnancy. He worried a lot about her health and at times had nightmarish thoughts of something going horribly wrong.

He tried his best to keep her happy. He kept himself restrained and let her have the last word in every argument they kept having from time to time. Often when he returned home, he brought her gifts; small things like, sweets, flowers, fruits, makeup materials or toys for their yet-to-be-born daughter. When she praised his efforts, his heart would swell with joy. However, on some days when the combined pressures of driving for 8 to 10 hours and returning home to an irritable wife became too much to bear, few strong words would slip out of his mouth. She would sulk in a corner when that happened until he begged for forgiveness.

Jyotsna's mother visited them for few hours, once or twice every week. She helped in the housework and advised her daughter on pregnancy related issues. That her daughter was having the child at a hospital and not through midwife at Jai Ganesh Wadi was a sore point with her. In her view giving birth was a natural function, which the body was quite capable of executing on its own. A midwife was required only for tying the cord and catching the baby as it popped out. Doctors, she claimed, exaggerated the gravity of the simple process of childbirth, as they hoped to pocket a big fee. Anirudh felt bored by his mother-in-law's views and took consolation from the fact that Jyotsna did not take her mother seriously.

‡

The long wait was finally over and the day came when Jyotsna packed her bags and moved to the hospital. The general ward, where she was admitted, was a long hall containing ten beds, all of them occupied by different patients. Anirudh and his mother-in-law sat on steel chairs beside Jyotsna's bed. The hall smelled of carbolic acid and was filled with moans and groans of different patients. Nurses and doctors, in crisp white uniforms, moved briskly among the beds, checking blood pressure of this patient, fever of another and giving saline drip to someone else. Anirudh was surprised they could handle so many patients without becoming patients themselves. How did Jyotsna enjoy working in this chaotic place, he wondered.

The nurses at the general ward showed remarkable concern for their colleague. They frequently stopped beside Jyotsna's bed to inquire how she was and if she needed anything. Anirudh felt satisfied that at least his wife was getting some sort of a special treatment at this place.

Vimla was working in some other ward and came to check Jyotsna's condition. 'For how long do you plan to keep your daughter hidden from us?' she asked cheerfully.

'Not for long.'

'I spoke to Dr. Sinha before coming here. He said childbirth was hours away.'

'Oh, even now it is hours away,' Anirudh exclaimed.

'Don't fret needlessly,' his mother-in-law grumpily said. 'Everything happens in its own time.'

'I am not fretting. But I am concerned.'

Mother-in-law was not finished yet. 'Why don't you go and take a walk in the corridor. You look as if you could do with some fresh air.'

Jyotsna broke into laughter. 'Mother is right,' she said. 'You should relax in the corridor. I will be fine, don't worry.'

Anirudh got up and said with a martyred air, 'I know when I am not wanted.'

'It is not about your being unwanted,' Jyotsna reposted. 'You look blue in the face. You need fresh air.'

'I guess it will be a good idea for me to take a walk,' he said. He came out in the corridor and lounged on an empty bench. Anxiety had sapped his strength and he started feeling drowsy. In few minutes he was asleep.

‡

'They are taking Jyotsna to the maternity room,' mother-in-law said.

Anirudh sat up immediately. He rubbed his eyes and glanced at his wristwatch. He had slept for almost three hours. 'Where is she now?' he asked.

'They are preparing her in the ward.'

Anirudh got up and briskly walked towards the general ward. Jyotsna's appearance was ashen. Anirudh felt a quiet chill creep up his spine. 'It will soon be over,' he uttered.

She took his hand and pressed it faintly. Her hand felt hot and clammy. A fat nurse asked him to move away and then wheeled Jyotsna's stretcher out of the general ward. Anirudh followed the stretcher down the corridor till it disappeared behind the closed doors of the maternity room. Minutes later Dr. Sinha arrived with two nurses. He saw Anirudh's tense face and said, 'There is nothing to worry about. Jyotsna is in fine shape.'

'I trust you doctor,' Anirudh said.

Dr. Sinha and the nurses went inside the maternity room and the door closed behind them. Anirudh looked at the closed door for few moments, wondering what was happening on the other side. He sat down on a nearby bench beside his mother-in-law.

'I still feel the midwife would have been better than the fussy atmosphere of this hospital,' she said.

'This is not the time to talk about all that,' Anirudh said with exasperation. 'Now we can't pull Jyotsna out of this hospital and take her to a midwife.'

'Young people,' mother-in-law angrily mumbled, 'never listen to adults.'

Listening to mother-in-law carrying on in favor of the midwife even at this point of time, Anirudh realized that she was as argumentative as her daughter. Maybe Jyotsna has inherited her argumentative nature from her mother, he thought. Like mother, like daughter. Will this trait of argumentativeness be carried on to the next generation as well? Will my daughter behave like her mother and grandmother? He thought of Reema arguing about everything and laughed.

'What are you laughing at?' mother-in-law asked peevishly, thinking rightly that his laughter had something to do with her.

'Nothing,' Anirudh said, amidst laughter.

‡

An hour later Dr. Sinha emerged from the maternity room. Anirudh walked up to him and asked, 'How did it go, doctor?'

'Didn't I tell you that there was nothing to worry about?' Dr. Sinha beamed. 'Your wife gave birth to a healthy boy.'

'A boy?' said Anirudh incredulously. 'Are you sure?'

'Naturally.'

'The news of a boy's birth has taken me by surprise. Jyotsna had convinced me that we will have a girl.'

'Are you disappointed at having a boy?'

'Disappointed?' A smile manifested itself on Anirudh's face. 'I am the happiest person in the world. It never really mattered to me or to Jyotsna whether we had a boy or a girl. It was just a feeling that somehow crept into our mind that our first-born was going to be a girl. Can I see my wife and my son?'

'You will have to wait for sometime before you see them. Jyotsna is still under sedation and the nurse is taking care of the baby.'

'Thank you for all that you have done for us doctor.'

'My pleasure,' Dr. Sinha said and walked off in one direction.

'I was convinced from the day I learned about Jyotsna's

pregnancy that her child would be a boy,' mother-in-law announced, scoring a point.

'You never said that till now,' Anirudh said skeptically.

'I didn't want to get into an argument with Jyotsna. You know how argumentative she is.'

'She is your daughter,' Anirudh opined. 'Maybe she has inherited the trait from you.'

The old woman said nothing but the grimace on her face made it obvious that she was fuming.

‡

After sometime, when Jyotsna's sedation wore off, the nurse brought her to the general ward. Anirudh was there, waiting for her.

'I was so overwhelmed, when the nurse told me I had a son,' she said with a tired smile.

'You prediction about having a daughter has gone off the mark,' Anirudh winked. 'Maybe in future you will be more careful in predicting events.'

'Oh, come on! Stop trying to score points even at a time like this,' Jyotsna exclaimed. 'I wonder where they are keeping our son. I am eager to see him.'

'Your mother has gone with the nurse to bring him.'

'Why are they taking so much time?'

'Are we going to call our son Reema?' Anirudh smirked.

'Don't be silly. We will have to think of another name for him.'

A nurse, holding a baby in her hands, walked into the general ward, followed by Jyotsna's mother.

'There they are,' Anirudh said.

She sat up on the bed and said, 'Give him to me Ritika.' Ritika handed the child to Jyotsna. He felt light as a feather and his black eyes looked around with avid curiosity. His small mouth was tightly shut.

'Isn't he beautiful?' Jyotsna exulted.

'Yes, he is beautiful like a Kamal flower,' Jyotsna's mother injected.

'Why don't we call him Kamal?' Anirudh asked. 'I like that name.'

'Hey! It is my job to find a name,' Jyotsna exclaimed, but after a second's thought she added, 'Never mind. From today he will be Kamal. I like that name, too.'

‡

Jyotsna had to stay in the hospital till she recovered fully. Dr. Sinha suggested two-day hospital stay for her. Anirudh would have preferred to remain at the hospital till his wife and child were discharged, but that would have meant a break of three days from driving and Jyotsna refused to let that happen. 'Let us be sensible,' she said. 'We are already reeling under hospital expenses and we can't afford to lose more income. You have stayed with me on the day that I needed you the most. Now you have to start plying the taxi. Mother will take care of me. There is nothing to be worried about.'

On the third day Dr. Sinha discharged Jyotsna from the hospital. She sat on the backseat of the taxi, with Kamal sleeping in her lap. Her mother sat beside her and Anirudh drove them towards Jai Ganesh Wadi. They went to the slum's Ganpati temple, where the priest performed a small puja for Kamal's long life and fortune. Kamal slept peacefully throughout the monotonous chanting of mantras propitiating various Hindu Gods and Goddesses, but woke up when the priest sprinkled few drops of holy water on him. He thrashed his small arms and made sounds of discomfort. Jyotsna rocked and patted Kamal back to sleep. Anirudh gave the priest 111 rupees after the puja was over.

When they came out of the temple, Jyotsna asked in dismay, 'Why did you give the priest 111 rupees? 51 rupees would have sufficed.'

'Allow me a touch of profligacy on the day my son is coming home,' Anirudh said.

They went to Jyotsna's room at Jai Ganesh Wadi. Women from the neighborhood came to gawk at the child. They congratulated Jyotsna and made usual comments about how beautiful the baby was. Some of them felt that the baby's features were similar to that of Anirudh, while others maintained that he resembled Jyotsna. It was 6 PM when Anirudh returned home with his family.

‡

A small crib, bedecked with a mattress and a colorful bed-sheet, lay in the center of the room.

'Where did this crib come from?' Jyotsna exclaimed, gazing at Anirudh with bright eyes.

'The good fairy must have brought it for our son.'

'Oh, stop making fun of me,' she laughed, 'Tell me who got this crib?'

'Who else?' Anirudh smiled smugly, pointing a finger to himself, 'I got it yesterday while you were at the hospital. This kind of a baby bed is the safest for a child to sleep in. The railing around the bed prevents the child from falling out and the mattress is very soft. Feel it.'

Jyotsna felt the mattress with her fingers. 'Yeah. It is soft,' she said. 'You think of everything.'

'I am smart.'

Jyotsna laid the child down on the mattress. Small copper bells were hanging from the crib's railing. Anirudh jingled the bells and Kamal laughed at the sound.

'He likes this bed.' Jyotsna said.

'He laughs beautifully,' Anirudh said

'How much did you pay for the crib?' Jyotsna asked.

'300 rupees.'

Jyotsna frowned at the amount.

'300 rupees is not too big a price to pay for our child's comfort,' Anirudh said. 'Right?'

'Right,' Jyotsna said, her frown transforming into a smile.

'There is another reason, why I bought this bed.'

'Tell me?'

'I didn't want this buster to share our bed,' Anirudh winked.

'Don't you call my son, buster?'

'What if I do?'

She glared at him. 'You can cook your own food from today.'

'Oh, in that case I won't,' he said hastily.

‡

They wrote a long letter to Malti informing her of Kamal's birth. Malti's reply came a week later. She was filled with joy at the news. She asked Jyotsna and Anirudh to bring Kamal to the village at the earliest possible but before that they could at least mail her the boy's photograph. Jyotsna sent few of the photographs along with a letter in which she wrote that they, too, were eager to come to the village with Kamal but it was difficult to plan a train journey with a newly born child. She promised that when Kamal was one year old they would come to the village. Malti wrote back that she had held prayer meeting at her home for Kamal's long life. She also sent a lucky charm for Kamal to wear that she had got made from the priest of Hanuman Tekdi. These missives from their village were a source of great delight to Anirudh and Jyotsna. They made Kamal wear the lucky charm around his neck.

Meanwhile, the customary round of visits by neighbors and friends that are associated with the birth of a child took place. People from the neighborhood came visiting. They brought gifts. Kamal ended up with plastic rattles, plastic balls and packets of disposable diapers. Janki and Shalini, both mothers of grownup children, sat with Jyotsna for many hours and advised her on how to care for her child.

Aditi came with her son Nitin at noon, next day. She brought a colorful dress for Kamal. Jyotsna was rocking Kamal in her lap when they came. Nitin was excited at seeing someone smaller than himself. Though his balance was not yet perfect, he could make himself stand and take a few steps. He wriggled down from his mother's lap and stationed himself beside Jyotsna. He touched Kamal's hands and legs, and laughed.

'He probably considers Kamal to be a large toy,' Aditi chuckled. 'Do you know who he is, Nitin?'

'Babee,' Nitin said.

'Hey! He knows,' Jyotsna laughed. 'When did you learn that?'

'He is picking up new words at the rate of five everyday,' Aditi said with pride.

Jyotsna laid down Kamal in the crib and showed Nitin how to play the bells that were hanging from the railing. Ringing the bells was a fine amusement for Nitin. He stood beside the crib and shook the bells merrily, to the delight of the child lying on the mattress. Kamal laughed thrashing his little hands and legs.

'The children have developed a good rapport,' Aditi said.

'Looks like it,' Jyotsna said.

'Has your husband gone to drive his taxi?'

'He left in the morning itself,' Jyotsna said. 'How is Mr. Vijay Goel's vegetable business doing?'

'Business is not as good as we expected, but it is not very bad either. We are making a little amount of money.'

'I am sure the business will improve with time.'

‡

Vimla had already seen the baby at the hospital, but she came with Atul on Sunday.

'He was clamoring to see the baby,' she said.

'Where is he?' Atul asked eagerly. In his hand he was holding a plastic rattle, which he jingled continuously.

Jyotsna was pleased to see him. 'The baby is waiting for you in the crib,' she said.

Atul stood on the side of the railing and jingled the rattle loudly. Attracted by the sound, Kamal looked around with interest.

'He brought the rattle for your child,' Vimla said to Jyotsna.

Atul displayed the rattle proudly to Jyotsna.

'This is such a nice toy that you have brought,' Jyotsna said and planted a kiss on his cheek.

Atul placed the rattle on the bed beside the child. Instead of shaking the rattle, Kamal started putting it in his mouth. 'He is too young to know what to do with the rattle,' Jyotsna said. 'You jingle it for him.' She took the rattle from Kamal and gave it to Atul. Atul shook the rattle and also the bells hanging from the crib, creating a small amount of din.

Vimla and Jyotsna left the two children to their amusement and sat down on two chairs to chat.

'Do you still leave Atul at the same crèche?' Jyotsna asked.

'Yes. But from next month when he is four years old, I will have to admit him to a proper school. It will be very difficult for me to manage his school expenses with my meager nurse's salary. I don't know how I will make both ends meet,' Vimla said morosely.

'Something will come up to see you through,' Jyotsna said to console her friend. 'Maybe your husband will come to his senses and return home to you and his son.'

A scowl appeared on Vimla's face and she hissed, 'That bastard! I don't want that bastard to return home. He betrayed my trust. I will never let his foul shadow fall on my son.'

Jyotsna was taken aback by Vimla's livid retort. She could not understand, how any woman could call her husband a bastard. 'I am sure you must have reasons for hating your husband,' she said mildly.

'Reasons! I have enough reasons not just to hate him but even to... to kill him,' Vimla blurted. There were tears in her eyes.

'Oh, please don't get so upset. If he has wronged you God will punish him.'

'I very much doubt if God exists at all,' said Vimla, wiping her eyes with the end of her sari.

'I will get you a glass of water,' Jyotsna said and went to the kitchen. When she returned, Vimla said, 'My mother will come to stay with me from next month. She will take care of Atul, while I am working at the hospital. I will do overtime and earn extra money while my mother is with me.'

'That is a fine idea,' Jyotsna said.

‡

In the evening Anirudh came with Wahab Mia. Wahab Mia had brought a box of sweets as gift, which he handed to Jyotsna with words of congratulations. They had tea and talked about the affairs of Jai Ganesh Wadi.

When Wahab Mia left, Jyotsna said, 'Vimla was with me today. She told me that Atul would be joining a school from next month. She was so worried about his school fees. Poor woman. I feel sorry for her.'

'Her husband is responsible for her plight,' Anirudh said.

'That is true. If only he had been a gentleman like you.'

'Well, at least you have recognized the fact that I am a gentleman,' said Anirudh puffing up with pride.

She changed tack quickly. 'It was probably a slip of my tongue.'

'I like it when your tongue slips; it is only then that you speak truth about me.'

Jyotsna ignored the wisecrack changing the topic and said, 'I was thinking of my maternity leave. It will be over in less than two months.'

'Do you plan to rejoin your job?'

'I don't know, how I will pull myself away from Kamal. It will break my heart to be separated from him for so many hours daily.'

'You don't have to rejoin your job. I want you to stay at home.'

'We can't afford to lose my nurse's salary,' Jyotsna said playing nervously with the tassel of her gown. 'We will need all the money that both of us can earn to make Kamal a doctor.'

'Stop being so fastidious. Kamal is only a few days old. It will be at least three or four years before his education begins. We will have enough money by then. Trust me, we will.'

'Do you know how much a good school costs these days? It is very costly,' said Jyotsna with emphasis. 'Unless both of us contribute to the family kitty, it will be difficult for us to make the ends meet. For Kamal's future, I will have to keep my job. My mother will care for him in my absence.'

'You nurse the child three or four times in a day. How will he get his nourishment in your absence?'

'My mother will give him baby formula. Many kids grow up on formula these days.'

'I have heard formula is not as nourishing,' Anirudh maintained.

Jyotsna thought for a moment and said, 'Let us postpone the decision. We can decide whether I should rejoin my job or not, on the day my maternity leave expires. There are still two months for that to happen.'

'Take your time to decide,' Anirudh said.

Jyotsna went into the kitchen to ready the dinner. The baby woke up and started to cry. Anirudh picked him up from the crib and rocked him gently. But instead of quieting down, the baby cried more lustily.

Jyotsna emerged from the kitchen and said, 'Give him to me. He is hungry.' She took Kamal from Anirudh and brought his face close to her naked breast. The child started sucking hungrily.

'This buster has turned you into his kitchen,' Anirudh said.

'How many times have I told you not to call him buster?' Jyotsna asked.

'Let me guess, about 15 times.'

'Don't get me angry. It will spoil my milk.'

‡

Jyotsna had purchased disposable diapers for Kamal for that was the fashionable thing to do. But he soiled his diapers at an alarming rate. Almost six or seven diapers had to be discarded everyday. Within a couple of days, Jyotsna realized what was fashionable was not prudent. She stitched cotton diapers, which could be washed and used again.

However corners could not be cut everywhere. The baby soap, baby powder, baby oil were costly, but could not be done without. The doctor had advised her to eat fish, meat and fruits regularly, so that her milk could be abundant and nourishing. Their kitchen bills soared. The baby had to be taken to a child specialist at regular intervals. That meant medical expenses.

'At this rate, we will consume everything you earn. There won't be any fresh savings going into our bank account,' said Jyotsna one day when she and Anirudh were mulling over their monthly budget.

'I am planning to begin driving taxi for 15 hours daily.'

'I told you even before we married that I won't allow you to work for more than eight hours,' Jyotsna said vehemently.

'We are not rich people. Working for eight hours is a luxury, which we can ill afford. I have got to find a way of increasing my monthly income and the only way that comes to my mind is for me to work for longer hours.'

'I am not at all prepared to allow you to work for more than 8 hours. We will manage somehow, with my income and your income.'

'But you don't have to work as a nurse. Our child needs you

at home. It is a man's job to bring money to the house. Many taxi driver's work for more than 8 hours, without facing any problem. I can do the same.'

'I will never agree to that. I don't want my child to grow up without knowing what his father looks like. Which is what is going to happen, if you work for 15 hours and then return home late in the night.'

'You are taking a very extreme view.'

'My father used to do few hours of overtime regularly to earn extra money. Hard work and little rest sapped his strength and he died prematurely. I don't want something like that to happen to us.'

'I can understand your pain but that sort of a tragedy does not have to repeat itself. Everyone who works for more than 8 hours does not die prematurely.'

Suddenly Jyotsna was angry. 'Do you want me to shed tears and beseech you to make you see reason?'

'Oh, why do you lose your temper so quickly! I am not forcing the issue on you. If I can't work for more than 8 hours then we have to find some other way to augment our income. Whatever we decide we shall decide together.'

'Yes, it has to be a joint decision,' she said, no longer sounding angry but only sad.

To cheer her up, Anirudh said, 'We have to get a pram, remember.'

'It will be costly.'

'It will be just what we can afford to pay and you will proudly wheel Kamal around.'

A smile appeared on Jyotsna's face as she imagined herself wheeling Kamal in a pram.

'We will get the pram on Sunday,' Anirudh said.

‡

Anirudh returned home early on Sunday, at around 4 PM. Jyotsna, looking radiant with her hair dressed and be-flowered, face elegantly powdered, sat beside him in the taxi, with Kamal in her lap. She carried an extra pair of diapers with her, just in case the ones Kamal was wearing needed to be changed. Kamal started crying when Anirudh revved up the engine. Jyotsna rocked him in her lap and sang a lullaby to quiet him down. Under his mother's ministrations, the child got used to the noise of the taxi and the traffic around them and fell asleep. In 30 minutes, they were at Bombay Central Market. Anirudh parked the taxi and they got down.

'I will take Kamal,' Anirudh said. 'You will get tired walking with him in your lap.'

Jyotsna was not prepared to let go of her asset. 'He will wake up, if I give him to you,' she said. 'No need for you to worry, I can manage to carry him around. You take my handbag.'

Anirudh took the handbag from her and they walked along the sidewalk looking for a shop where they could buy a pram. Hawkers, selling wares from temporary stalls, encroached more than half of the sidewalk. To attract customers, they proclaimed the superior quality and cheap price of their goods in lusty shouts. The narrow stretch of sidewalk spared by the hawkers was full of pedestrians going to and fro, some in a hurry and others ambling along leisurely, gawking at the goods displayed in the shop windows and in the hawker stalls. The sound of the vehicles plying on the road, the shouts of the hawkers and the chattering of the customers and the pedestrians, blended without any discordant note and created what could rightly be termed, the music of the market.

They arrived at a large department store that carried the hoarding: Kids Emporium. In its window, among other things, was displayed a beautiful pram.

Jyotsna gasped with delight. 'This is what I had in mind for my son,' she said.

'Let's go and buy it,' Anirudh said.

Perfumed air-conditioned air struck them in their face when they opened the glass door of the shop and entered. Light music was wafting through the air. Numerous racks and shelves displayed dresses, toys, cosmetics, educational items, prams, cribs and many other things besides all that. Jyotsna and Anirudh were overwhelmed by the wealth of items on display. They felt depressed at the thought that they could not afford to buy all these fantastic things for their child. Immaculately dressed salesmen were attending to few affluent looking customers.

'This place looks forbiddingly lavish,' Jyotsna whispered.

'Our money is as good as anybody else's,' Anirudh answered stubbornly.

All the salesmen were busy with other customers. A fat lady with pomaded hair and a pearl necklace around her neck was purchasing dresses and cosmetics for her three-year-old daughter. A father was telling his five-year-old son that he could have one toy only. The son insisted on at least three. A couple was selecting a crib for their baby.

A salesman finally came to attend Anirudh and Jyotsna.

'I am interested in the pram displayed in the window,' Anirudh said.

'I will get it for you,' the salesman said. He went to one of the shelves and pulled out a pram that was similar to the one displayed in the window. He opened it on the floor and launched his usual sales pitch. 'This pram is made out of finest quality material. The body is of steel, the interior of soft leather and the wheels are made from vulcanized rubber.'

'What is the price?' Anirudh asked the question that was uppermost in his mind.

'3000 rupees,' the salesman said.

The price was way beyond anything that Anirudh and Jyotsna could have expected. In fact Anirudh had brought only 1000 rupees with him. 'My God,' Anirudh sputtered.

'Th...th...three thousand rupees.' Jyotsna spoke so quickly that her tongue got twisted and she could not speak without fumbling.

'We were hoping to buy something much cheaper,' Anirudh said.

'The cheapest pram we have costs 2300 rupees,' the salesman said condescendingly.

Anirudh looked at Jyotsna.

She looked crestfallen as she said, 'I guess we will have to go elsewhere.'

'Thank you,' Anirudh said to the salesman and walked out of the shop with his wife.

When they were on the sidewalk, Jyotsna said, '3000 rupees for a pram? That is banditry.'

'It is their prerogative to fix the price of goods that they sell in their shop,' Anirudh said.

'Their prices are high because they are covering the cost of the shop's lavish interior, music system, air-conditioning by overcharging customers. I would rather buy economically from an ordinary shop.'

'Did Aditi tell us the name of the shop from where she purchased her pram?' Anirudh asked.

'She didn't. We should have asked her,' Jyotsna fretted. 'She bought her pram for 850 only.'

'Anyway it must be accepted that her pram was nothing compared to the pram we saw in the store.'

'A pram is a pram,' Jyotsna said complacently. 'I will be satisfied with the kind of pram that Aditi has and so will be my child.'

‡

They made inquiries and reached a shop located in a back street of the market. The shop's floor was littered with small cycles, tricycles, prams and cribs. The shelves were full of toys and sports equipment. A middle-aged sardarji sat behind a dusty wooden counter.

'I want a pram,' Anirudh said.

Fearing that the Sardarji would show something beyond their budget, Jyotsna added, 'A cheap pram.'

'My prams are the cheapest and the best,' the sardarji declared with a flourish. He emerged from behind the counter, removed the plastic covering from a pram and opened it on the floor. 'This is our cheapest pram. It costs just 700 rupees.'

Jyotsna handed Kamal to Anirudh and started checking the pram's interior. Made out of ordinary upholstery, it didn't look very durable. She pushed the pram, but the wheels dragged instead of rolling. 'This pram is no good. I don't like it. Show me something better,' she said.

'For discerning customers, I keep better prams,' Sardarji said. He stripped another pram of plastic cover and opened it on the floor. 'Now this is what I call a real pram. A real work of art.'

This pram's upholstery was better. From its sides were hanging brass bells, which jingled when the pram was pushed. Its wheels rolled freely. Jyotsna pushed and pulled the pram and felt satisfied with its performance.

'What is the price?' she asked.

'Price is very cheap, considering the quality of this pram. It is of 1400 rupees only.'

'Why such a big leap in price?' Jyotsna exclaimed. 'The last pram you showed us was for 700 rupees only.'

'This pram is of export quality,' Sardarji said superciliously, hoping to impress his customers. When he noted that Jyotsna did not seem awed, he added, 'It comes with many extra features. The upholstery is, as you can see of very fine quality, soft and durable. Your child will never be uncomfortable while sitting or lying down in this pram. The wheels will always function properly and the bells – don't they sound delightful?' Sardarji brushed his hands against few of the bells, making them jingle.

'I like this pram, but it is way beyond my budget.'

'Buy this one. It costs only 700 rupees,' Sardarji said quickly, 'Or I will show you another priced at 900 rupees.' He opened another pram.

This pram's interior was black and Jyotsna hated black color. 'There is no way I will buy black pram. Tell me the last price you will charge for this one,' she said pointing towards the pram for which Sardarji had demanded 1400 rupees.

'For the sake of your beautiful baby, I will charge hundred rupees less. You can pay me 1300 rupees.'

'Let us get out of here. This shop is too costly,' Jyotsna said to Anirudh.

Not wishing to lose a prospective customer, Sardarji said, 'How much will you pay?'

'700 rupees,' Jyotsna said without batting an eyelid.

'700 rupees for a 1400 rupees merchandise,' Sardarji seemed shocked. He looked at Anirudh for support. 'Please convince the lady that her price is too low for me to accept.'

Anirudh felt surprised at the low price that Jyotsna had quoted but he did not react to Sardarji's entreaty.

'Are you prepared to give me 1000 rupees?' Sardarji asked.

'You heard me say 700 rupees,' Jyotsna said obstinately.

Kamal woke up and started crying in Anirudh's lap. 'Give him to me,' Jyotsna said. She rocked the child to make him stop crying. 'Is 1000 rupees your last price?' she asked the shopkeeper.

'If I sell lower than that, I will lose money,' Sardarji said and started packing the prams inside plastic covering, to show that he was not interested in any further bargaining.

'Very well, we will look elsewhere. Thank you for your trouble,' Jyotsna said. She and Anirudh started making their way out of the shop. They were barely on the street when the sardarji called after them, 'Will you pay 800? That is as low as I can get.'

Jyotsna looked at Anirudh and laughed. 'What do you say?' she asked.

'It is a good bargain at 800 rupees. I don't think we can get it any cheaper elsewhere.'

They turned back and Jyotsna said, 'Let me see if my son likes this pram.' She laid Kamal, who was still crying, inside the pram and then jingled the bells. The sound silenced him and he looked around with curiosity. 'My child likes this pram,' Jyotsna gushed. 'We will take it.'

'Should we wheel Kamal to our taxi?' Jyotsna asked enthusiastically, looking at Anirudh.

'There is too much traffic in the market for us to do that,' Anirudh said.

Reluctantly Jyotsna picked up Kamal from the pram. Sardarji wrapped the pram in its plastic covering. Anirudh paid him 800 rupees.

'You won't believe me, but the fact is that I am losing 200 rupees on this transaction,' Sardarji said, pocketing the money that Anirudh had paid.

'I have heard such statements before,' Jyotsna said shrewdly.

'I sold at such low price because I didn't want to deny a pram to your child. Come again if you need anything else from my store.'

'Be sure that we will,' Jyotsna said.

Anirudh picked up the folded pram and they came out of the store.

'You are a very good bargainer,' he chuckled. 'I never imagined the sardarji would sell at 800 rupees.'

'That is what these things usually cost,' Jyotsna said. 'I can assure you that Sardarji made at least 100 rupees on the transaction. I don't grudge him the 100 rupees. He deserves to earn that much, but any more profit by him would have been extortion.'

'Don't you think, this pram is better than the one that Aditi had got?'

'Of course, it is. But we paid 50 rupees less than what she paid for her pram.'

'We did a very smart thing.'

'Both of us know who is responsible for this smartness,' Jyotsna said.

'You like to drive home an advantage, don't you?' Anirudh laughed.

'There is nothing wrong in claiming credit where it is due.'

'Do you want to purchase anything else while we are here?'

'After spending 800 rupees, I don't have the heart even to look inside any shop,' Jyotsna said. 'Can we go somewhere, where it is calm and peaceful? I feel so eager to wheel the pram with my child in it.'

'It is 5.30 and we can reach Mud Island by 6. The beach there is a very good place to wheel a pram. I have seen people wheeling their children on the beach many times.'

'Let's go there,' Jyotsna said enthusiastically.

‡

Ten

Mud Island boasts of a clean beach, flanked not by concrete structures as most Bombay's beaches are, but greenery. The area looks picturesque with silvery sand, tall palm trees and clear blue seawater. The secluded environment of the beach is the main contributing factor in turning it into a lover's paradise. Couples can be seen strolling on the beach, hand in hand, or just whispering to each other in a grove of palm trees. Enterprising ones have built cottages in the near vicinity. Any couple, desiring more privacy, can book a room on hourly basis. The only furniture the rooms contain is a strong bed with mattress and a clean bed sheet; most couples are satisfied with these facilities. A few resorts, hotels and cold drink stalls have sprouted around the beach, but overall the area has managed to retain its innocence.

Anirudh parked the taxi on the road and they got down. A soft breeze that carried the tangy smell of the sea fanned them with butterfly wings. Kamal was awake in Jyotsna's lap.

'You like this place, don't you?' Jyotsna said, giving Kamal a kiss on his cheek. The child gurgled with delight and tried to catch her face with his small hands.

Anirudh opened the pram on the white sand and said, cheerfully, 'Kamal's buggy is ready.'

Jyotsna laid Kamal down in the pram and started wheeling it gently. The sand soaked with seawater had settled down into a comparatively hard surface and the wheels of the pram could roll on it without any hitch. Anirudh walked beside her. The bells hanging from the pram's body jingled with its movement, making the child ecstatic by their melodious sound. Kamal laughed and thrashed his hands and legs.

'How nice this feels?' Jyotsna whispered.

'Kamal seems to be enjoying the ride,' Anirudh said.

'I don't grudge the 800 rupees that we paid to the shopkeeper for this pram. Anything that makes our child so happy is worth purchasing.'

'There is hardly any doubt about that.'

A couple strolling along the beach peered into the pram and smiled at the child, before passing them by.

'They were admiring my baby,' Jyotsna said with pride.

'He is someone to be admired.'

They had strolled for little over half an hour when the sun started setting.

Looking towards the horizon, Anirudh said, 'I have always enjoyed visiting Mud Island, especially in the evening.'

'Why?'

'Because of its sunset! See it is taking place now.'

Jyotsna stopped pushing the pram and gazed in the direction of the setting sun. Towards the horizon the sky was an immense expanse of bright orange, in which floated wisps of clouds painted in hues of silver and orange. The sea had acquired all the tones reflected in the sky and they seemed to blend seamlessly. No one could have guessed where the sky ended and the sea began, it seemed as if the sun no longer reigned in the sky but sat on the sea, its flaming globe sinking slowly under the shimmering golden waters. 'The scene looks magnificent,' she said.

'I don't know why, but whenever I watched sunset at Mud Island, I felt one with the universe.'

'This sunset gives me a feeling of being one with you,' Jyotsna whispered.

Anirudh placed his hand around her waist and they stood in this position till the sun disappeared in the ocean. Kamal lay quietly in the pram with his eyes wide open. It seemed as if he too was enjoying the scene. When the sea had consumed the globe of the sun, Anirudh broke from his reverie abruptly and said, 'I think we should leave now. It is going to be dark.'

Jyotsna took Kamal in her lap, Anirudh picked up the pram and they made their way to the taxi.

‡

Night had set by the time they reached their taxi. A solitary yellow streetlight glowing on the roadside could only amount for limited visibility. Jyotsna slipped into the taxi with Kamal, while Anirudh loaded the pram in the dickey. A small kiosk selling cold drinks, cigarettes and fast food, stood across the road.

'Would you like to have some cold drink?' Anirudh asked, peering inside the taxi through one open window.

'Get a fanta for me,' Jyotsna said, from inside the taxi.

'Okay.'

A teenage boy and a girl were manning the kiosk. Both having similar features appeared to be siblings.

'How's business out here?' Anirudh asked good-naturedly.

The boy was a chatty sort and he replied eagerly, 'It is not as good as at Juhu Beach. But once in a while we do get paying customers like you.'

Anirudh laughed. 'Give me two bottles of chilled fanta.'

'Two chilled fanta coming,' the girl said cheerfully and opened the refrigerator to fetch the bottles.

'It is not even 7.30 and this place has a deserted look,' Anirudh said.

'People return to their homes soon after it turns dark. We will be closing the kiosk in a few minutes. You are probably our last customer for the day,' the boy said.

The girl placed the fanta bottles on the counter and opened them with the opener. 'Don't you want anything for your baby?' she asked looking towards the taxi. 'We have good quality chocolates in our store.'

'My baby is too small to eat chocolates,' Anirudh grinned. 'He is only few days old.'

'Buy chocolates from us when he grows up,' the boy said.

'Be sure that I will,' Anirudh said and picked up the bottles. He sat beside Jyotsna inside the taxi and both of them began to sip.

Kamal was looking around with his clear dark eyes and mumbling incoherent sounds in a monotonous drone. Anirudh clicked his fingers in front of Kamal's face and said softly, 'What are you saying boy?'

Kamal tried to catch hold of Anirudh's fingers.

'I could do anything for my child,' Anirudh said fervently.

'I am sure you would,' Jyotsna said

All of a sudden there was the sound of screeching tyres. They turned back and saw through the taxi's rear glass, the glowing headlights of a vehicle approaching at breakneck speed.

'Oh my God!' Jyotsna cried with horror, 'Is he going to hit us?'

The question was answered moments later, when the vehicle slammed into the kiosk, on the opposite side of the road. There was a shattering explosion and splinters of wood, iron sheets, cold drink bottles and cigarette packets flew in all directions. Instinctively Anirudh covered Jyotsna and the child with his body, to protect them from the flying debris.

When the explosion was over, he looked out of the taxi's window. The kiosk was utterly destroyed. Its four walls made out of wood and tin, had splintered into many pieces and lay scattered on the road, along with smashed cold drink bottles, broken crates, food items and an overturned refrigerator. A black Mercedes, with its engine still running, bonnet dented and windshield smashed, stood in the place, where the kiosk once stood. A young man, in his early twenties was sitting behind the steering wheel, gazing at the devastation around him with dazed unbelieving eyes.

The sight of this wanton mayhem made Anirudh's blood boil. 'Hey you,' he shouted at the Mercedes driver and jumped out of the taxi to confront him.

The Mercedes driver gave Anirudh a petrified glance and

straight away began reversing from the accident site. When the Mercedes was on the road again, it dashed forward at scorching speed. Anirudh had to jump aside quickly, to save himself from getting crushed under the vehicle's wheels.

'You bastard,' he shouted after the vehicle. He peered into his taxi and said, 'Take down the number of that car.'

Jyotsna, with shaking hands opened the glove compartment and took out a pen and paper.

'MLX 568, black Mercedes,' Anirudh said.

Jyotsna scribbled hastily. Kamal was screaming. 'Is he hurt?' Anirudh asked.

'I don't think so. He is frightened by the crash,' Jyotsna said. 'Where are the boy and the girl who were manning the kiosk?'

'Heavens,' Anirudh gulped. 'I had forgotten all about them.' He rushed to the other side of the road and kicked aside pieces of rubble. He saw a pair of legs sticking out from under the refrigerator. He pushed the refrigerator aside. The head was crushed flatter than a pancake. It was only the clothes that identified the body to be that of the boy. Somehow Anirudh controlled his revulsion and started looking for the girl. He found her lying in the grass at the roadside. Her neck was bent at an unnatural angle and her abdomen was ripped open. Her open eyes stared with vacuous indifference.

The gory scene was too much for Anirudh to bear. He took a few faltering steps away from the scene and vomited copiously. When he returned to the taxi, he saw that Jyotsna was sobbing. The child in her lap was crying, but she was doing nothing to comfort him.

'They are both dead,' Anirudh panted.

'The poor souls!' Jyotsna cried hysterically, shivering a little and holding her baby tightly in her arms. 'Why did all this have to happen in front of our eyes?' The same thought was haunting Anirudh's mind. What could be the explanation, except that quirkiness of fate had placed them at the wrong place at the wrong time.

'What are we going to do?' Jyotsna asked.

Anirudh sat down on the driver's seat and said, 'We are going to get away from here?'

Her tearful eyes stared at his face and she asked, 'Won't we call the police?'

'I don't want us to get mixed up in police business.'

'But we can't allow the Mercedes man to go scot-free after taking two innocent lives,' Jyotsna cried. 'It is our duty to tell the police what we know.'

'If I need your advice, I will ask for it,' Anirudh snapped. 'Attend to the baby. He has been crying for a long time.'

'There are two dead bodies few feet away from us. Think of them before reaching any decision,' Jyotsna said grimly and then began to rock Kamal.

Anirudh glared at her and started the taxi. He parked in front of the first PCO on the way and dialed 100, the number of police control room. After hearing his story, the policeman at the other end of the wire advised him to remain at the accident site, till police team arrived there. Anirudh put the phone down and drove back to the accident site.

‡

When they reached the place where the shattered remains of the kiosk lay, they found a small crowd of men and women gathered there. Exclamations of horror and angry vociferations came from the crowd. Jyotsna remained inside the taxi, while Anirudh got down. He found an avid audience in the crowd, when he narrated what he had seen.

'These filthy car owners! They drive as if they own the whole road,' one woman said.

'The driver must have been drunk,' said an old man, who himself appeared to be reeling under few glasses of toddy.

'If I had been here when the Mercedes crashed into the kiosk, I would have torn the driver into pieces,' a hefty young man thundered.

The crowd cheered at his violent words.

'The drunks who drive cars these days have no respect for human lives. They should all be murdered,' another young man said.

'We should ban the entry of all private cars into Mud Island. Let anyone who wants to be on the beach take a bus or walk on foot.'

'We will burn alive every guy who drives a black Mercedes in this city.'

The crowd was working itself into a towering rage. If any Mercedes black or of any other color, had arrived at the scene at that point of time, the driver would surely have been lynched.

'There come the parents of the deceased,' a woman said, pointing towards a middle-aged couple walking hastily towards them.

'How devastated they must be feeling?' someone said.

'Where are my children?' the father of the victims screeched.

The mother was beating her breasts hysterically and kept repeating in a monotonous drone, '...hai Ram, hai Ram...'

To Anirudh the lamentations of the bereaved parents felt like pincers, which opened painful wounds in his psyche. He avoided looking at them and his gaze remained fixed on the ground, as tears ran slowly down his cheeks. The crowd made way for the grieving parents. Bodies of the two children were still on the road. The parents flung themselves on the dead bodies and cried bitterly. Members of the crowd tried to console them ineffectually.

'The dead boy and girl were their only children,' someone said.

Anirudh could not stomach the heartrending scene anymore and turned back to the taxi. Jyotsna had closed her eyes and was resting her head on the back of the seat. Kamal had fallen asleep in her lap. When Anirudh opened the taxi's door she opened her eyes, 'We shouldn't have come to Mud Island.'

'We can't change what has already happened,' Anirudh said.

‡

A piercing siren was heard. 'That must be the police jeep,' Anirudh said.

'I hope they will take our statement quickly and let us go,' Jyotsna said.

A moment later the police jeep with flashing red light on its hood appeared down the road and parked itself beside the accident site. An inspector and two constables stepped out of the vehicle. They officiously went about the business of surveying the accident site.

Anirudh told the inspector what he had seen. The crowd raved and ranted against the man who was behind the accident and demanded that the police arrest him immediately. Few youths threatened to take matters into their own hands. The inspector did his best to pacify the crowd. He radioed to police headquarters the details that he had received from Anirudh.

Two other police jeeps and an ambulance arrived. Paramedics from the ambulance took charge of the dead bodies. The parents of the deceased wailed miserably when the dead bodies were loaded into the ambulance.

'My son, my daughter...' the woman groaned.

'I want justice,' the father cried. 'I want the man who did this to my children hanged.'

Kamal woke up due to all the commotion that was going on and made his displeasure known by crying loudly. No amount of rocking and cuddling that Jyotsna did seemed good enough to pacify him.

Anirudh went to the inspector and asked, 'Can I go home now? I have told you what I saw.'

'You will have to come to the police station to give a signed statement,' the inspector said. 'Your statement is important, as you are an eyewitness.'

'My baby is only a few days old. I can't keep him in the taxi for the whole night. My wife too, is having problems,' Anirudh said.

The inspector was a kind man. He said, 'You can do one

thing. Drop your wife and child at home and after that come to the police station to give your statement.'

Anirudh agreed to do that. He thanked the inspector and returned to his taxi.

'What did he say?' Jyotsna asked.

'I can drop you and Kamal at home. But after that I will have to present myself at the police station to give my statement.'

'Why does he need you at the police station when you have already given your statement?'

'He will take my signed statement at the police station.'

'He is only harassing you,' Jyotsna said resentfully.

'That is how the system works.' Anirudh started the taxi. Jyotsna fell into a glum silence.

‡

They were dead tired, by the time the taxi reached their building at 12 PM. Jyotsna went up the stairs with Kamal in her arms, and Anirudh came after her carrying the pram in his hand.

When they were inside their flat, Jyotsna said, 'I will fix dinner for you after I put Kamal to sleep.'

'I am not hungry,' Anirudh said.

'You must have something before you leave for the police station. Who knows how much time you will have to spend there.'

'I can't get the dead bodies out of my mind.'

'Why don't you have a bath? It may make you feel better.'

'I will do that.' He picked up the towel and went into the bathroom.

Jyotsna sat down on the bed to nurse Kamal. Within few minutes Kamal fell asleep and Jyotsna laid him down in the crib. When Anirudh emerged from the bathroom, she said, 'I will make chapatti and vegetable for you.'

'No, I can't eat all that. Give me a cup of tea and a few biscuits.'

'Will that be enough?' Jyotsna asked with concern.

'Yes.'

She went into the kitchen. In few minutes she returned with two cups of tea and a plate of biscuits.

'Why two cups of tea?' Anirudh asked. 'Have you, too, decided to skip dinner?'

'Like you I also have lost my appetite.'

They sat down at the table and started having their tea and biscuits. Anirudh left for the police station soon after.

‡

When Anirudh returned at 5 AM, Jyotsna was still awake. 'What took you so long?' she said. 'I felt so concerned. I could not sleep a wink.'

'Those policemen wasted lot of time in recording my statement,' Anirudh said, sitting down on the bed.

'I hope you won't have to go to the police station again.'

'I will have to go there to identify the Mercedes driver, if they manage to nab him. There will also be visits to the courts when the matter comes up for hearing.'

Jyotsna was aghast to hear this. 'Had I known that informing the police would get us into so much trouble, I would not have asked you to do so.'

'Don't blame yourself. We did the right thing by going to the police. Guilt is more difficult to endure than harassment. If we had not reported, guilt would have made us miserable for the rest of our lives.'

'Go to sleep. You must be very tired.'

'Yeah,' Anirudh mumbled. He changed his clothes and lay down on the bed. Jyotsna switched off the light and slept beside him.

Few minutes later he whispered, 'Jyotsna, are you still awake?'

'Yes.'

'I am concerned about the Mercedes driver.'

Jyotsna sat up on the bed. 'Why?' the urgency in her voice was obvious.

'Through the vehicle number that I provided, the Mercedes has been traced to Ved Rahi, one of Bombay's leading businessmen. Police officials suspect that his son was driving the Mercedes.'

'Has Ved Rahi's son been arrested?'

'Police officials are looking for him.'

Jyotsna voiced her gravest fear when she asked, 'Do you think Ved Rahi and his son will hurt us for providing information to the police about the accident?'

'It is not likely that they will try to hurt us, but they may do something to force me to change my statement. In our country people with money consider themselves to be a law onto themselves.'

'What are we going to do?' Jyotsna groaned with desperation.

'I didn't mean to frighten you. In my view this episode will blow away without affecting our lives in any significant way.'

'I will never ask you to get involved in police business again.'

'Have courage,' Anirudh whispered. 'Go back to sleep.'

‡

When Anirudh woke up it was 7. Jyotsna was attending to Kamal in the balcony. She saw him leaving the bed and said, 'Why did you wake up? I brought Kamal to the balcony, because I didn't want his crying to upset your sleep.'

'I have to get ready for work,' Anirudh uttered drowsily.

'But you hardly slept at all,' she said with concern.

'I will manage,' he said and shuffled towards the bathroom.

An hour later, they were sitting at the table, having breakfast of omelet and bread. They ate in silence, as they feared that if they started talking, the conversation might veer to last night's events, a topic which both of them wanted to avoid.

There was a knock at the door. Anirudh looked at Jyotsna. 'Must be Janki or someone else from the building,' said Jyotsna. 'I will check. You continue having your breakfast.'

A man in his middle thirties, fastidiously immaculate in gold-rimmed spectacles, pinstripe suit, tie and polished boots stood at the door, holding a costly leather handbag in his right hand.

Jyotsna caught a whiff of perfume – the scent of a man who has the means to be fashionable. She was surprised to see someone like him waiting at her door. 'Yes,' she said tentatively.

'Good morning,' the man said with a bright smile. 'My name is Vikram Singh. I am here to meet Mr. Anirudh Shukla.'

Anirudh came at the door and said, 'I am Anirudh Shukla.'

'Pleased to meet you Mr. Shukla, I am the personal secretary of Mr. Ved Rahi.'

Jyotsna felt emptiness in the pit of her stomach, when she heard the dreaded name of Ved Rahi. Her paranoia was such that she almost expected Vikram Singh to pull out a gun from his coat pocket or his handbag and start shooting at her and her husband.

'What do you want from me?' Anirudh asked.

'You have heard of Mr. Ved Rahi, I presume?'

After a pause of two or three seconds, which spoke amply of the confusion in his mind, Anirudh said, 'Yeah, I heard of him.'

'I have a message from Ved Rahi.'

'Tell me.'

'Won't you invite me inside your house,' Vikram Singh said with a smile, which somehow made him seem even more sinister to Jyotsna. 'I will not take more than few minutes of your time.'

Anirudh realized that he was being impolite by keeping Vikram Singh standing at the door. 'You can come in,' he said and stepped aside from the door to allow Vikram Singh to enter.

Jyotsna did not want any agent of Ved Rahi inside her house. But before she could come up with some appropriate excuse to keep Vikram Singh out, he had already stepped in. He saw the half-eaten breakfast and said, 'Looks like I am interrupting your breakfast.'

'Of course,' Jyotsna blurted spitefully.

'I can wait in the balcony till you finish your breakfast,' Vikram Singh said.

'Okay,' Anirudh said.

On way to the balcony, Vikram Singh peered into the crib for a moment or two. Jyotsna's heart skipped a few beats. Was this man planning to abduct her child to blackmail Anirudh from implicating Ved Rahi's son? Her mind was in a tizzy. She saw that Anirudh was gulping down the omelet and the bread without chewing. Was he, too, being racked by similar fear? She was filled with an overwhelming sense of physical repulsion for Vikram Singh; she wanted but one thing at this moment – to be relieved of his wearisome presence.

Anirudh finished the breakfast quickly and went into the balcony. Jyotsna stayed in the room with her ear perked to catch the conversation between her husband and Vikram Singh.

'Now you can tell me what this visit is all about?' Anirudh said.

'Mr. Ved Rahi would like to talk to you personally.'

'What for?'

Vikram Singh did not mince any words and came to the point directly. 'You are eyewitness to the accident that took place at Mud Island,' he said. 'Mr. Ved Rahi wants to discuss that accident with you.'

'There is nothing to discuss about that accident. I have already given my statement to the police and…'

Vikram Singh interrupted Anirudh by saying, 'You don't understand Mr. Shukla. Mr. Ved Rahi is a wealthy man. People like you and me will have to be very lucky, if we can make in our lifetime what he makes in a week. Fate has brought you in a position, where a man like Ved Rahi needs your cooperation. Don't squander this opportunity. This is your chance to improve your life and that of your family.'

'You rich people think that everybody in this world is up for sale,' Anirudh said with disgust. 'No amount of money can make me change the statement I have given to the police.'

'My request is that you should meet Mr. Ved Rahi and listen to what he has to say before reaching any decision. If you don't like his proposal, you can refuse. He will never force you to do anything against your will.'

'Okay, I will come with you. But I can't afford to waste more than 10 or 15 minutes with Mr. Ved Rahi.'

Vikram Singh smiled patronizingly, 'Believe me Mr. Ved Rahi's time is more valuable than yours. He won't hold you for a second more than absolutely necessary.'

Anirudh's decision to meet Ved Rahi horrified Jyotsna. A man like Ved Rahi could plumb to any depth for protecting his son. If bribery didn't work, he may resort to torture or even murder.

'You must give me few minutes to get ready,' Anirudh said.

'I will wait in my car. It is a white Honda parked outside the building's gate.'

'Okay.'

‡

When Vikram Singh went out of the house, Jyotsna said, 'You should not go with him.'

'It is important that I see Ved Rahi,' Anirudh said. 'I will tell him in clear terms that I am determined to get justice for the two teenagers, whose death I witnessed that night. So he may as well stop attempting to coerce me into changing my deposition.'

'You must be naive to think he will listen. His son mowed down two innocent people with his car and then drove away without a glance at the victims. What kind of a man would try to protect such a wayward son? If my son had been involved in this kind of crime, I would have handed him over to the police myself. Ved Rahi is the devil incarnate. He will do anything to save his son from a jail sentence. Instead of going to him, we should go to the police and demand police protection. I am afraid of what Ved Rahi and his son may do to us.'

'They won't dare to harm my family,' Anirudh said heatedly.

'I wish I could share your optimism.'

'I will know what he plans to do after I speak to him. If I feel that there is a danger, I will go to the police.'

'What if he gets angry and turns violent while talking to you?'

'I know how to handle violent people. Let me take care of this problem in my own way,' Anirudh said and stepped out of the house.

'Don't try to provoke him. Be diplomatic,' Jyotsna cried after him.

'Don't worry, have courage,' he said and climbed down the stairs.

When Anirudh disappeared down the stairs, Jyotsna mumbled to herself, 'Sometimes it seems, I have no more courage.'

‡

She went into the balcony and saw Anirudh get into a white Honda parked outside the building gate. Her eyes followed the Honda till it disappeared down the road. The morning sun was hot and there was no breeze on the balcony. But she could not make herself come back into the room and remained standing in the balcony, gazing pensively in the direction in which the white Honda had gone. She tried to think how much time it would take for Anirudh to return; 30 minutes for going to Ved Rahi's house, a maximum of 30 minutes to hear whatever Ved Rahi had to say and another 30 minutes to return. He should be back in about ninety minutes, she calculated. The time was 9 AM and she expected him back by 10.30 AM. She tried not to think, what she would do, if he didn't return by 10.30.

She told herself that there was no reason to be nervous. After all Ved Rahi was a responsible businessman. If anything, he was expected to be sensible about the whole thing. He was expected to believe in the rule of law. But what if he was not sensible and decided to take the law into his own hands? His son had mowed down two people in cold blood and then fled the scene. Like father, like son...She cursed herself for not doing enough to stop Anirudh from leaving with Vikram Singh.

A woman, fat and small, wearing an apron with gay polka dots, called from the middle of the road. It was Suchitra, whose husband ran a mutton shop few blocks away. 'Good morning Jyotsna,' she said. 'I have not seen you at the shop for sometime.'

Jyotsna leaned further out on the balcony and said, 'Morning Suchitra...I was at your shop only two days ago. I purchased a kilo of mutton from your husband, but you were not there at the shop.'

'Oh, was I not there,' said Suchitra thoughtfully, 'I must have gone somewhere for an errand.'

Talk began to flow backwards and forwards between the balcony and the road below. After Suchitra was on her way, Jyotsna came inside the room and her wide solemn eyes, clouded with worry, gazed into the crib, where Kamal was sleeping peacefully. How serenely he slept. He had no idea of the grave danger his father was in. She shook her head and sat down on the bed. She waited impatiently for the time to pass. On the wall clock seconds and minutes ticked away. By the time it was 10.15 her condition was absolutely unbearable. She told herself that there were still 15 minutes to 10.30, but her mind would not listen to her. She decided that she would feel better, if she waited outside the house. Kamal was sleeping in the crib. He opened his eyes and made some sounds of displeasure when she picked him up, but fell asleep again, when she patted him on his back. She locked the flat and came out of the building with Kamal in her lap.

‡

She looked on both sides of the road, but failed to notice any approaching white Honda. Janki, wearing a rumpled gown, which gave her a bedraggled appearance, came from somewhere carrying a bag full of groceries. 'What are you doing in the sun?' she asked.

'I am waiting for my husband,' Jyotsna said.

'Aha! The adoring wife,' Janki smirked, 'waits for her husband. I saw him leave in a white Honda in the morning. Where has he gone?'

Little happens in the building without Janki noticing it,

Jyotsna thought with pique. 'He has gone to meet someone.'

'Your husband has rich acquaintances. People who wear suits and drive around in a Honda.'

Jyotsna had too much on her mind to waste time on empty tittle-tattle. She kept quiet, hoping that her silence would shoo Janki away.

'At least you should do the waiting in the shade,' Janki said. 'Sun is bad for the baby.'

Jyotsna realized that she was standing under the hot sun. 'Thanks for reminding me of that,' she said and moved below the awning.

'I will go to my house. I have a lot of washing to do.'

'Okay.'

It was past 10.30 but the white Honda was still nowhere to be seen. The sound of any approaching vehicle filled her with anticipation that it may be the white Honda, which she awaited, but every time her hopes were belied. Was something wrong? Should she go to the police station and report that Ved Rahi's henchmen had kidnapped her husband? Oh, she was being paranoid. Anirudh may have got stuck in the traffic or his conversation with Ved Rahi could be taking longer than expected. She decided to wait for another half hour... and then another half hour...and then another half hour. Her legs were aching from standing through all this time, while holding Kamal in her lap. But despite the discomfort, she could not make herself go back to the room. She remained standing under the building' awning with her eyes fixed on the road.

‡

She was at the end of her tether, when suddenly a white Honda appeared and parked itself in front of the gate. She watched with breathless wonder as the car's door opened and Anirudh emerged. It was not her nature to be demonstrative and she tried to behave normally. But Anirudh knew that she was waiting for him. So he said, 'I have not taken too much time. I am back in only three hours.'

'I didn't come out to look for you, but to take a walk,' she said and then added immediately, 'Did he try to threaten you?'

'He was quite cordial actually.'

'What did he say?' she asked secretly.

'Let us go inside the house. I will tell you there.'

They climbed up the flight of stairs that led to their flat. Jyotsna laid Kamal down in the crib. Thankfully he was still sleeping and not hollering for her milk. She got water for Anirudh from the kitchen and both of them sat down on the bed.

'Vikram Singh took me to Ved Rahi's bungalow,' Anirudh said. 'Never before in my life have I been inside such a lavish bungalow. In the living room, where I sat with Ved Rahi, there was enough space to park 20 taxis. Can you beat that?'

'Really,' gasped Jyotsna.

'The bungalow had many rooms like that and a front garden with flowers and trees, and a lovely porch. The furniture, the carpets, the chandeliers, the decorative items were better than what we get to see in any movie. Ved Rahi lives in a palace fit for a king.'

'What did he say about the accident?'

'Ved Rahi allowed me to meet his son, Gautam, who had

been driving the Mercedes at the time of the accident. Gautam told me with tears in his eyes how devastated he was by the death of those two teenagers. He was driving at only little above the normal speed but somehow the car skidded out of control and rammed into the kiosk. Drivers sometimes do lose control of their vehicles. I should know that after driving a taxi for so many years. Ved Rahi, too, was sorry about the accident. In spite of being wealthy, they are decent human beings. They care for the lives of other people. They are traumatized by the death of the two teenagers.'

'Is that enough? Feeling traumatized,' snapped Jyotsna. 'A murderer cannot be allowed to go scot-free, if he feels traumatized after killing someone.'

'Gautam Rahi isn't a murderer. He didn't ram his Mercedes into the kiosk intentionally. What happened was an accident, a tragic accident. An accident can happen with any driver, including me.'

'Why are you pleading Gautam Rahi's case?' Jyotsna asked suspiciously.

'Gautam is only 20 years old. He has a bright future ahead of him. Should we spoil his life by sending him to prison.'

'Isn't that for the police to decide?'

'Ved Rahi offered money for changing my statement,' said Anirudh, looking away from her.

'You must have refused.'

'I didn't.'

'You didn't?'

'Ved Rahi offered 5 lakh rupees,' he turned towards her and

looked into her eyes, to gauge her feelings.

Jyotsna gasped at the sum.

'Five lakh is a huge sum of money.'

'But it would be unethical to...'

Anirudh interrupted her by saying, 'Let me tell you what we could achieve with 5 lakh rupees. Instead of living in a rented one room flat, we would buy a two room flat. Kamal would have more space to grow up in a two room flat. Our new home would be furnished with decent furniture and have modern appliances as freeze, TV, and washing machine. You would not have to cook food over a smoky, kerosene-burning primus stove. Our kitchen would have a gas stove. I would stop plying a rented taxi and buy a second hand taxi of my own. After purchasing all these things, we would still have some money left to deposit in the bank.' He paused and waited for her response. She remained silent. Her eyes carried a hazy look as if she were lost in some reverie.

'You won't have to work as a nurse again,' Anirudh continued. 'After we have purchased a flat and taxi, we will be saving 1000 rupees on the flat's rent and 5000 on the taxi's rental. Just imagine every month we will be saving 6000 rupees. We shall deposit that much money in the bank every month and use it later to pay for Kamal's education. We will not lack for resources to see Kamal through the school and medical college. Our son's future will be secure.'

'Your words sound like a dream,' Jyotsna whispered wistfully.

'It is upon us to make it a reality.'

'But what about the parents of the two teenagers who perished in the accident,' she mused sadly. 'We will be racked with guilt whenever we remember them.'

'Ved Rahi has assured me that he is going to pay a huge sum to the parents as well. He will also pay for the reconstruction of the kiosk.'

Money can't bring the dead back to life.'

'The dead are not going to come back to life even if Gautam Rahi goes to jail. What has happened cannot be undone.'

'When will Ved Rahi give us the money?'

'Tomorrow.'

‡

Ved Rahi was a man of his word. Anirudh received 5 lakh rupees next day. He went to the police station to keep his part of the bargain. He told the investigating officers that it was not a black Mercedes, but a tempo that mowed down the kiosk and that it was too dark at the time of accident for him to read the tempo's license plate. The police officials didn't create any fuss in recording the new statement. To protect his son, Ved Rahi had purchased not just the eyewitness, but also the complete legal machinery. Anirudh wondered how much money the police officials could have received.

When he returned home after finishing all the formalities at the police station, Jyotsna asked, 'Was there any problem in changing your deposition?'

'Everything went off without a hitch,' Anirudh exulted. 'Now we are free to begin our new life.'

'I am so happy,' Jyotsna murmured and in the wildness of her joy flung her arms around his neck and hugged him, laughing.

Eleven

Within another day, began the exciting chore of finding a flat that they could purchase. The chore entailed meeting many real estate agents, examining different flats and negotiating prices. After a fortnight's search they chanced upon one they liked. The flat was situated only seven blocks away from their present home, on the first floor of a four-storey building. It had a large living room, a bedroom, kitchen, bathroom and also a five feet wide cubicle, which Jyotsna thought, could be turned into a store. Broad windows and wide balcony gave the flat a general appearance of spaciousness and taste. The floor was tiled and the doors and windows looked fresh with paint. The owner demanded 3.25 lakh rupees. With some hard bargaining Anirudh and Jyotsna were able to get the price down to 3 lakh rupees. The deal was signed and they became proud owners of their new home.

There was very little furniture that they owned: a single bed, a wooden cupboard, a table, two chairs and a dresser with cracked mirror. The single bed was too narrow for them to sleep comfortably. They decided to sell it off at second hand price. Anirudh wanted to replace the other pieces of furniture as well, but Jyotsna viewed that to be an unnecessary wastage of money. It took them many days to buy everything. they needed to furnish their new home. It was mostly Jyotsna who had the final word in all their purchases, be it furniture or some other household item. Anirudh always supported her decisions.

She displayed her best bargaining skills. Before buying anything they would inquire at a number of shops and then buy from the shop where the best bargain was available. On some occasions their quest for best bargain made them spend the whole day roaming the market for just one item. It pleased Anirudh to watch her plan their new home. In the end their purchase comprised of a double bed, a chest of drawers with marble top, a TV with trolley, a steel almirah, freeze, gas stove, a sofa set, household linen, curtains for all the doors and windows and a set of new pots and pans. They felt as though at last they were making a serious start in life. From now onwards they would belong to the small elite group of those who are fortunate enough to own property. They now had an assured position in society.

They went to consult the priest from Jai Ganesh Wadi, the one who had solemnized their marriage. After poring over some tattered almanacs for few minutes the priest droned, 'Brishpati, Mangal and Surya are situated in the auspicious sign of the zodiac on the coming Monday. That makes this Monday most favorable for matters relating to property.'

Jyotsna looked at Anirudh and asked, 'Can we shift on Monday?'

'There are only two days left for Monday,' Anirudh said doubtfully.

'The next auspicious day is after one and a half month,' the priest droned.

'Oh, no,' Jyotsna said urgently, 'We can't wait that long.'

'We shall shift on this Monday,' Anirudh said.

'Can you come to our new house on Monday and conduct the puja for us?' Jyotsna asked the Pandit.

'I will come at noon, after closing my temple.'

'Thank you for your guidance,' Anirudh said.

The priest stared back. Anirudh placed 51 rupees in the priest's hand. The priest smiled.

‡

Coming Monday, they loaded all their worldly possessions on a handcart, locked up their old home, and handed the keys to the landlord. Jyotsna felt a bit embarrassed at the sight of her frugal belongings being displayed on the road. Thinking that the handcart man might think this was all she possessed, she said, 'We have much else at our new home.' The handcart man didn't oblige her by any signs of being impressed. He only nodded disinterestedly.

Jyotsna's mother was with them to assist their relocation. The family followed the handcart to their new home. By 11.30 AM, friends and neighbors started arriving for housewarming celebrations and to participate in the puja. Janki and Shalini were there. Aditi brought Nitin. Her husband could not make it, as he had to open the grocery shop. Vimla took the day off from the hospital and came with Atul. Wahab Mia took a break from driving his taxi and came with his wife.

Jyotsna essayed the role of a charming hostess to perfection.

Her face glowed with happiness as she received the guests. She seated everyone on the new sofa set and proudly made orange squash with cold water and ice from the new refrigerator. As all the guests were intimate friends, there was an air of jollity in the house, and the glasses of orange squash and plates full of sweets were being circulated around without ceremony. Janki admired the 21-inch color TV and the sleek TV trolley on which it stood. Aditi liked the velvet curtains. Vimla found the double bed and the refrigerator very interesting. Wahab Mia and his wife liked the smoke-free gas stove.

'If only I had been lucky enough to have lavish relatives like you people do,' mused Shalini, who appeared a trifle jealous of the sudden upward swing that Jyotsna's fortunes had taken, 'I too would have bought a flat and furnished it with all sorts of wonderful things.'

'My relatives are such misers that they would not part with a rupee, even if I were on my deathbed,' murmured Janki spitefully.

Jyotsna and Anirudh had not told anyone – not even Jyotsna's mother – the truth behind their sudden wealth. To assuage the inquisitiveness of their friends and relatives they had explained their riches as a bequest from one of Anirudh's relatives, who they claimed was a rich businessman based in Delhi. Jyotsna's mother suspected that her daughter and son-in-law were making a story. However, she was sensible enough not to voice her suspicions.

'It is strange that your rich relative is not here to attend the puja,' Aditi said, 'I would have liked to meet him.'

'Yes, it is too bad that he is not here,' Vimla said.

'Oh! He is a very busy man,' Jyotsna said quickly. 'He has a large business to look after, which hardly leaves him time to go anywhere.'

'The man who came to your house in a white Honda that day, was he the rich relative?' Janki asked cagily.

Jyotsna knew that Janki was prying for information and she hated her for that. 'No, that person was someone else,' she said.

'I have my suspicions Jyotsna that you are hiding your rich relative from us, as you fear we may borrow something from him,' Vimla said and then laughed at her own words.

'That seems likely to me, too,' said Shalini with a sly smile.

'Is that so Jyotsna? But why don't you want us to get rich as you did,' Janki ejaculated cunningly. 'Are we not your friends?'

Jyotsna managed a smile but said nothing.

Anirudh noted her discomfiture with the way the conversation was going, and to change the topic, he said, 'Kamal has been very lucky for us. Our time has changed after his birth.'

'Kamal must been born under a very auspicious planetary configurations,' Wahab Mia said.

'Maybe we are reaping the fruits of his marvelous destiny,' Jyotsna said with wonder.

Atul clamored for more orange juice. Jyotsna prepared another glass for him and for Nitin as well.

‡

The priest arrived. Jyotsna and Anirudh had planned to have the puja done on the floor of the living room. But the priest declared that since the bedroom was east facing, it would be more auspicious to conduct the puja there.

Jyotsna and her mother hastily scrubbed the bedroom floor with wet linen. The priest set himself on the mat spread on the floor and started arranging in front of him the bric-a-brac of a religious ceremony. Few minutes later he was chanting holy slokas in a steady drone. Jyotsna, her mother and Anirudh sat with their legs folded and listened to the hymns. Kamal slept in Jyotsna's lap. The guests waited in the living room for the puja to be over. Nitin and Atul stood at the bedroom door gawking at the priest.

When the chanting of hymns was over, the priest took out a large conch shell from his bag and after washing it with a fistful of water, blew into it several times, creating short bursts of sonorous sound. Nitin and Atul were ecstatic at the performance of the conch shell.

'Mother, I want to blow into the conch shell,' Atul said to Vimla.

'Hush! The priest will get angry,' Vimla said and pulled him away from the bedroom.

Kamal was not amused by the conch shell's performance. The sound woke him up and he started crying.

'Oh! The sound has disturbed him,' Jyotsna whispered and started rocking him.

'It is considered lucky if children wake up in the middle of a puja,' the priest droned.

Anirudh and Jyotsna were pleased to hear that. The priest got up and sprinkled holy water in all corners of the house and then declared that the puja was over. Everyone had lunch. Jyotsna had cooked pulav, two kinds of vegetables and dahi wada. Her culinary skills came in for much praise from all the guests.

After the lunch was over, the guests prepared to depart. The priest and Jyotsna's mother left for Jai Ganesh Wadi in Wahab Mia's taxi. Others lived close by and left on foot.

‡

When they had seen all the guests out of the house, Anirudh said, 'Finally we have our house to ourselves.'

'It seems unbelievable,' Jyotsna laughed, 'We have a house of our own, comfortable furniture, freeze, color TV, washing machine, gas stove and so many other things. Tell me that I am not dreaming. I need to be assured.'

He spread both his hands in a gesture to indicate everything around him and gaily said, 'This is the new reality, Jyotsna. This house and everything in it is ours. We have made a quantum jump in life.'

'Life is so beautiful,' Jyotsna gushed. 'Just imagine if we had not been at Mud Island when the accident occurred, we would not have had all these things.'

'Yeah, we were at the right place, at the right time,' Anirudh gloated.

The emotions expressed were not fully thought through, but even so they could not avoid owning the responsibility for what they had said. When the import of their words dawned on them, they gasped with horror. Jyotsna's feet were suddenly too weak to support her and she slipped down on the sofa. 'It is disgusting,' she groaned. 'We are feeling happy that the accident happened and the two teenagers died.'

'Please,' Anirudh pleaded, 'We didn't mean that.'

'Yes, we did,' Jyotsna cried. 'I will never again believe that poverty ennobles. We were celebrating the death of two people, because it alleviated our poverty.'

Anirudh sat down on the sofa, beside her, with his head in his hands. Jyotsna rose with Kamal in her lap and shuffled into the bedroom. Their mood remained somber for therest of the day.

‡

Next day Anirudh awakened at 5.30 in the morning. On the bed beside him Jyotsna was sleeping. Kamal slept in the crib. He thought of yesterday and how happy they had been, when suddenly a few inadvertently spoken words had soured their happiness. He could make out Jyotsna's features in the soft glow of the night lamp. Even now she appeared sad.

'Jyotsna,' he whispered and when she didn't respond he shook her softly.

She opened her eyes and mumbled drowsily, 'What?'

'This is our first morning in our new home.' He waited for her to say something but when she kept silent, he continued, 'Let's go out for a walk. We will take Kamal with us in the pram.'

'I don't feel like taking a morning walk,' she said dejectedly.

'We will feel better in the morning breeze. Get up.'

She lay still for a few moments, lost in sad thoughts and then slowly crept out of the bed. Both of them stood side by side and brushed their teeth in front of the washbasin. Few minutes later they were in the street with Kamal in the pram. Jyotsna wheeled the pram.

'What we said to each other yesterday was a tragic slip of tongue,' Anirudh said. 'Those words didn't represent our real feelings.'

'I am myself not sure, what our real feelings are,' Jyotsna snapped.

'It isn't just we who got money from Ved Rahi. The parents of the dead teenagers got money, too.'

'I am sure that the parents would not be gloating over their children's death, just because it earned them a few rupees.'

'We can't bring the dead back to life by making ourselves miserable.'

'That's true, but we shouldn't rejoice over people's death either.'

'I am ashamed for what I said yesterday.'

'I am also ashamed. We should not repeat our mistake.'

'Be sure, we won't. Now we should get this regretful episode out of our mind.'

'Yeah,' she sighed, 'That we should.'

Down the path they bumped into Aditi and her family. Aditi was wheeling Nitin in a pram. Vijay Goel walked beside her, somewhat stiffly, on his artificial legs.

'Mr. Vijay Goel,' Jyotsna said cheerfully, 'It is good to see you taking a morning walk.'

'My balance has improved,' Vijay Goel said. 'Congratulations on your new home.'

'Why didn't you come to my housewarming party?'

Jyotsna asked. 'I had been expecting you.'

'I have to open the grocery shop.'

'He hardly gets time to go anywhere since he opened the grocery shop,' Aditi said.

'How is business these days?' Jyotsna asked.

'Better than it was before,' Vijay Goel said.

'Nitin, aren't you old enough to walk on foot now,' Jyotsna said patting the boy on his cheeks. Nitin gave a sly smile and hid his face inside the pram.

'He calls the pram his horse buggy,' Aditi said.

'That makes you the horse,' Jyotsna chuckled.

'Jyotsna, let's not turn this morning walk into a morning chat,' Anirudh injected.

Vijay Goel and Aditi laughed at Anirudh's words. Jyotsna managed an awkward smile.

'See you then,' Jyotsna said. The two families parted company and went on their separate ways.

'Why did you embarrass me?' Jyotsna demanded.

'I didn't embarrass you,' Anirudh shrugged.

'You said something about not turning the morning walk into a morning chat.'

'I made a point. We woke up in the morning for a walk and not to stand in one place and chat.'

'Why don't you become a hermit if you don't like speaking to people?' asked Jyotsna spitefully.

'I don't like your being so familiar with Vijay Goel. After all he is another man.'

'So the truth has finally tumbled out of the closet. That is the real reason why you pulled me away from them. You felt jealous, because I exchanged a few kind words with Vijay Goel.'

Anirudh kept quiet.

'Answer me. Weren't you jealous?' Jyotsna thundered.

'I wonder if Urvee is happy with her husband in Madras,' Anirudh mused.

Jyotsna glared at him and said, 'You still remember Urvee?'

Anirudh broke into laughter.

‡

When they returned to their flat, Jyotsna switched on the TV and asked, 'What do you prefer to watch – news or film songs?'

'Definitely not a news channel! I don't want to know so many died of malnutrition here or so many were murdered by terrorists there, or hear some lousy politician making banal speeches. Film songs will be fine with me.'

Jyotsna browsed through few channels and settled on a channel broadcasting A R Rehman's songs. She pushed the volume to limit and the house echoed with A R Rehman's thunderous, fast paced music.

'Doesn't this sound wonderful,' she shouted loudly, to make her voice heard above the music.

'People, blocks away, must be hearing this song,' Anirudh laughed.

'Our TV in providing entertainment to the whole area,' she said with glee.

Anirudh picked up the towel and went into the bathroom to have his bath. When he emerged from the bathroom, the TV was still running but the volume was low. Jyotsna was lounging on the sofa. She said, 'Our neighbor, Rohini, was here.'

'What did she say?'

'Will you please lower the volume of your TV. My children are unable to study,' Jyotsna said, in a shrill peevish tone, mimicking Rohini's voice.

Anirudh laughed and said, 'I think she had the right to say that. The volume was too high.'

'Yes, in future we will have to remember to keep the volume low,' said Jyotsna.

‡

A week later, Anirudh came home from driving his taxi earlier than his usual time. 'What brings you so early today,' Jyotsna said.

'Don't tell me that you are not pleased to see me back early.'

'If you are back early it must be for a reason,' Jyotsna carried on in the same vein.

He announced dramatically, 'Guess what, I found a second hand taxi to buy.'

'That is jolly good news. At what price?'

'70,000 rupees! Its engine and body are in excellent condition. At 70,000, that taxi is a fantastic bargain.'

'We have spent 300,000 on the flat, 50,000 on the furniture and the appliances and now we have to pay 70,000 for the taxi.

That still leaves us around 80,000 in the bank account,' Jyotsna calculated quickly.

'Very good, Mrs. Accountant.'

'80,000 will be sufficient to see Kamal through the best medical college.'

'80,000 will earn interest and become a much larger figure by the time Kamal is of college going age. We are rich people now.'

'Being rich is such a good feeling. When do you plan to buy the taxi?'

'Tomorrow.'

'Then we can let go of the old taxi from tomorrow.'

'That's the idea. We shall save 5000 rupees every month that we pay as rent for the old taxi.'

'We will be able to deposit that much money in the bank every month,' Jyotsna simpered.

'Great, isn't it?' Anirudh said eagerly.

Suddenly Jyotsna's face became somber and she said, 'I wonder if the parents of the two deceased teenagers are as happy today as we are.'

Anirudh flared up quickly. 'For God's sake Jyotsna!' he said heatedly. 'Why can't you let the matter rest? Didn't we agree that we won't talk about all that again?'

'I am sorry,' Jyotsna uttered. 'I don't know why I said that. You change your clothes, I will fix tea for you.' So saying she left him and hastily went into the kitchen.

‡

In the excitement of moving to a new home, meeting new people and caring for her baby, Jyotsna had little time to think about her hospital job. Vimla came to meet her one evening and told her that the hospital superintendent was asking about her.

'Oh! I have kept so busy off late that the hospital went out of my mind completely,' Jyotsna said. 'My maternity leave will be over next week.'

'Will you rejoin your job?'

'I would rather spend my time caring for my son.'

'You should inform the hospital authorities about your decision.'

'I will do that in a day or two,' Jyotsna said. 'Why didn't you bring Atul with you?'

'He was playing Ludo with his grandmother when I came here.'

'How is his schooling going on?'

'He has learned to write alphabets from A to Z and numerals from 1 to 100.'

'He must be proud of his knowledge?'

'Very proud! He has scribbled all the walls of my house with alphabets and numbers,' Vimla laughed.

'When Kamal grows up, will he too write on the walls?' Jyotsna said, looking at the child in her lap.

'Be sure of that,' Vimla answered for the child.

'I am going to spank you if you scribble on my walls,' Jyotsna cooed lovingly to the child in her lap.

After sometime, Vimla left for her home.

‡

When Anirudh arrived at night after driving his taxi, Jyotsna said, 'My maternity leave will be over next week.'

Anirudh lounged on the sofa and said, 'We have already decided that your maternity leave is going to carry on forever.'

'I have changed my mind,' said Jyotsna without batting an eyelid. Anirudh raised his eyebrows. 'I plan to rejoin my job,' Jyotsna declared.

'O yeah, and who is going to take care of the baby while you flirt with the doctors at the hospital?'

'I don't flirt with the doctors,' Jyotsna said sharply.

'That is your story.'

She glared at him. He glared back. 'I am definitely going back to work,' she said. 'If you don't like it then lump it.'

'Are you serious?'

'Do I look otherwise?'

She did look serious and he was momentarily confused about what could be the reason behind her sudden decision to rejoin her job. 'What about the baby?' he asked.

'My mother will have to manage the baby.'

'There is no financial compulsion for you to take up your job.'

'The compulsion is not financial, it is something else.'

'Do tell me about it,' Anirudh said sarcastically.

'You will stop respecting me if I resign from the hospital and become an ordinary housewife.'

The realization dawned on him that all this talk was a pose. 'You want to keep your job to earn my respect,' he said with a sly smile.

Jyotsna nodded her head in affirmative. 'That's right. If you want me to resign, you will have to promise me that you will always hold me in esteem. You must never forget that I am capable of keeping a job and earning a living for myself.'

'Interesting set of demands,' Anirudh uttered and got up from the sofa.

'Where are you going?'

'To the bathroom for a wash.'

'Give me my promise first,' she said putting a hand on his sleeve.

'I never make a promise that I don't intend to keep.'

'Then I will be forced to take up my job.'

'Go ahead,' he winked.

Jyotsna tried to think of something nasty to say to him but nothing came to her mind, by then he was inside the bathroom.

‡

They were in the middle of dinner when Jyotsna said, 'Tomorrow, I will go to the hospital and resign from my job.'

'I have not promised yet,' Anirudh reminded mischievously.

'I don't care about your promise. If you ever be rude to me, I will deal with you.'

'We shall see about that,' Anirudh said menacingly.

'Finish your dinner quietly. I don't like people who talk while eating.'

'You are the one who started this conversation.'

'Now I am ending it.'

She was washing plates in the kitchen sink. Anirudh came from behind and said, 'I will take you to the hospital tomorrow in my taxi.'

'You can take me to my mother's place. I will drop Kamal with her and then go to the hospital on my own.'

'How long will it take you at the hospital?'

'Two hours at the maximum! Kamal can stay that long with my mother.'

'Yeah, he can.'

‡

At 8 AM next day, Jyotsna, with Kamal in her lap, sat in the taxi and Anirudh drove towards Jai Ganesh Wadi. When they arrived at their destination, Anirudh asked, 'When will you return home?'

'After finishing my hospital work, I will spend few hours with my mother. I should be back home at around 4.'

'Take a taxi while returning. I don't want you to travel in a bus with Kamal.'

'Of course, with Kamal I won't dare to travel in a bus.'

'We are rich now. You can afford to travel in a taxi, not just my taxi, any taxi.'

'As if I don't know that,' she said before stepping out of the taxi.

'I told you only because you have a tendency of trying to save money at all times. You always cut corners here and there even when it is not advisable to do so,' he said looking at her through the taxi's window as she stood on the roadside.

'I said that I will take a taxi,' she said with emphasis.

'Earlier also you had given me such promises only to hop into the first bus that caught your eye.'

'My God! What has come over you. You are very argumentative today.'

'I am not like you. I never argue without any reason.'

'As if I argue needlessly,' she said testily. 'Now be off to ferrying your passengers. You are losing money idling here.'

'There is one more thing that I have to tell you.'

'Oh, how many sermons have you got from me today.'

'Don't let the doctors or the nurses at the hospital pester you into continuing with your nursing job. Kamal needs you at home, never forget that.'

She made a face and started to walk away without saying anything.

He honked the horn and said, 'Hey did you hear what I said.'

She turned to look at him and said, 'I have a mind of my own. No one can pester me into doing anything. Now be on your way for God's sake.'

'Okay, I am on my way,' he said and drove off.

Twelve

It was evening and the Linking Road market was full of shoppers. Handsomely dressed men, women fashionably attired and charming kids in colorful dresses could be seen everywhere. Anirudh had brought two young women to the market and now he was parked on the roadside waiting for the familiar shout of, 'taxi, taxi…' It was normal for passengers to call him 'taxi'. In the eyes of most, he was an inseparable part of the taxi, like the steering wheel, engine, chassis, headlights and wheels. 'There is nothing wrong if they call me taxi,' he told himself. 'I am part of my taxi.'

The watch fixed on the taxi's dashboard said that it was 6 PM. By now Jyotsna must have reached home after resigning from her job at the hospital, he thought. Poor kid, she enjoyed being a nurse so much, but had to resign because someone has to stay at home to care for Kamal. He remembered the exchange that had taken place between them yesterday. Though the exchange had been nothing more than a harmless banter, he felt sorry for the lack of consideration he had shown for her feelings. Her demand for a promise that he would always respect her was not made out of any false sense of pride, but because she wanted to be reassured that he valued the sacrifice she was making by giving up her job. He should have empathized with her feelings instead of torturing her with jibes. What a boorish person he was? She would be within her rights, if she started hating him someday.

I have to make amends for my yesterday's boorish behavior, he told himself. He knew well that the best way to win a woman's heart is through gifts. It was his good luck that his taxi was parked just at the right place. On the other side of the road was the glass-fronted Hazel Boutique, very popular among Bombay's fashion-conscious, high society women. The store must be quite costly, he knew that, but he wanted to treat Jyotsna with something special, something that would show her, how much he cared for her. He locked the taxi and crossed the road to enter the shop.

'Show me something for a very beautiful woman,' he said to the saleswoman, surprising himself with his own flamboyance.

The saleswoman showed him many dresses. He selected an elegant maroon velvet gown, that had yellow flowers printed on it and had the dress gift-wrapped. He paid 1000 rupees for the dress – the costliest dress he had ever purchased. He could imagine how she would react to his gift. She would say a few words about his being too profligate, but in reality she would be pleased as a punch. He would make her wear the dress. How pretty she would look? He decided not to take any more passengers and drove towards home. He was eager to experience love and happiness with Jyotsna.

‡

He reached his building at around 7. A taxi was parked beside the building gate. He recognized Wahab Mia's taxi. Wahab Mia was standing beside the taxi, smoking a beedi. What is he doing here? Anirudh asked himself.

Wahab Mia saw him and walked towards him hastily. 'Park your taxi and come with me quickly,' he said frantically.

Anirudh could read the urgency in Wahab Mia's demeanor and was startled by it. 'What is the hurry?' he asked.

'Do as I say.'

Something in Wahab Mia's tone made Anirudh realize that this was not the time to argue. 'Okay,' he said. He parked his taxi inside the building compound and came out.

'Sit down in my taxi,' Wahab Mia said, 'We are going to the hospital.'

All strength drained out of Anirudh's body when the word 'hospital' fell on his ears. He shivered as he stepped into the passenger side of the front seat. Wahab Mia started the taxi. 'Are Jyotsna and Kamal alright?' he asked through a feeling of dread.

After a pause of few moments, Wahab Mia said, 'Jyotsna had an accident.'

Anirudh gulped. 'When? Where?'

'Around 2 PM she was standing on the road outside Jai Ganesh Wadi with her mother to catch a taxi, when a speeding car struck her.' Wahab Mia waited for Anirudh's reaction. There was none. 'I was not feeling well today,' Wahab Mia continued, 'So I was resting in the house. I came out when I heard the shouts. Jyotsna was lying on the road. I transported her to the hospital in my taxi.'

Instinctively, Anirudh turned and looked at the backseat. The backseat was drenched with blood. Jyotsna's blood! It is Jyotsna's blood splashed on the backseat, his mind screamed. He was horrified that Jyotsna had lost so much blood. 'Kamal,' he gasped. 'How is Kamal?'

'Jyotsna's mother was carrying Kamal. The car didn't strike them.'

'How is Jyotsna?'

'She was still alive, when I transported her to the hospital.'

Anirudh winced at the phrase 'still alive.' What a big difference there is between 'alive' and 'still alive'!

'The doctors are doing their best to save her.'

Anirudh nodded. 'What happened to the car that struck her?'

'Some bystanders told me that Jyotsna was hit by a silver colored Toyota. The driver didn't stop after the accident. He sped away. No one had the chance to read the vehicle's number plate. Had the bastard stopped, the crowd would have lynched him. I hope the police manage to apprehend the swine.'

‡

They arrived at the hospital. It was the same hospital where Jyotsna used to work as a nurse. Wahab Mia parked the taxi. Anirudh's face was a grim mask as he walked briskly into the hospital building. Wahab Mia followed him at close distance. The emergency ward for accident victims was on the second floor. The elevator was hovering between the fifth and the sixth floor. Instead of wasting time waiting for the elevator to descend, they took the stairs. The lobby of the emergency ward echoed with mournful wails of women. Anirudh saw his mother-in-law sitting on the floor, her hair disheveled, crying like a madwoman. Around her were huddled other women from Jai Ganesh Wadi. They were trying to console her, while they were themselves racked by sobs.

The sight curdled Anirudh's blood. 'Where is my wife?' he screeched. His voice sounded strange, not his voice at all.

His mother-in-law noticed him and her lamentations grew shriller. She punctuated her sobs with incomprehensible words.

'Can't any of you answer a simple question?' Anirudh uttered. 'I want to know where my wife is.'

He felt a hand on his shoulder and turned to see Vimla. Her eyes were red. 'Come with me,' she sobbed.

He followed her down the corridor, into a room, moderately lit by a tube light. The horrifying smell of death was in the air. In the center of the room was one bed, on which lay Jyotsna. Her body was covered with white cloth, only the face could be seen. Her eyes were closed. The upward crescent of her lips made it seem as if she were smiling in her sleep. An unearthly chill caught Anirudh as he gazed at his wife's inert body. His blood ran cold and his teeth chattered.

'...The doctors did their best to save her,' he heard Vimla say, 'But she had lost so much blood. Some of her internal organs were also damaged...'

'When did she...this happen?' He was unable to bring himself to pronounce the word 'die'. He could not make himself believe that his wife was dead, even though he comprehended clearly that it was her dead body lying on the bed.

'Somewhere between 6 and 6.15, she succumbed to her injuries,' Vimla moaned.

While his beloved wife lay dying at the hospital, he had been purchasing a dress for her at the shop. The absurdity of the situation struck him like a thunderbolt. He could not control his emotions any longer. A volcano erupted inside him. 'Why? Why? Why?' He wailed and fell sobbing on her body.

Since a violent accident was the cause of death, police were involved. An inspector and a constable arrived to prepare the FIR. With an indifference that was cruelly casual they interviewed the grieving relatives and friends of the victim. The body could not be released to the relatives till an autopsy confirmed the cause of death. Wahab Mia and few others pleaded with the police officials and the morgue officials to get the body released quickly. After some heated haggling on both sides, a deal was struck at 500 rupees. The officials received the money and an autopsy report was prepared within an hour. The world and its callous ways! An incident that brought pain to one group of people, was for others an opportunity to make profit. Thankfully Anirudh was left out of the sordid dealings. His friends handled everything.

‡

It was midnight by the time Jyotsna's body was brought to the flat. She was laid on the floor of the living room. It is a tradition that the body of the dead must always lie on the ground. Anirudh, Jyotsna's mother and few others squatted around the body. They wailed, they sobbed, they tried to console each other, and they talked about the dead. Kamal was in the bedroom. Vimla had cajoled him into sleep by feeding him baby formula. Never again would his mother nurse him, fondle him, rock him or speak to him. He would grow up without knowing what a loving person his mother was.

The priest was sent for in the morning. Neighbors and friends arrived to show their grief. The building echoed with lamentations from many throats. Aditi, Janki, Shalini and Rohini wept bitterly in the room where Jyotsna's body was kept. The eyes of the valiant soldier, Vijay Goel, were red with grief and he was heard muttering, 'I didn't feel as miserable even on the day when I lost my legs.' The cashier of the bank where Jyotsna had her account, the mutton shop owner, the provisions store man and many others came to pay their last respects. It was strange that someone dying so young had made a mark on so many people.

Anirudh was allowed a few minutes of privacy with his wife. He opened the new velvet dress that he had purchased for her yesterday and arranged it on her body. While selecting the dress in the boutique yesterday, he had wondered how she would look wearing it. Well, now he was finding that out. She looked pretty in spite of the pallor of death on her face. The dress suited her perfectly. 'Jyotsna, I wish you could see what a beautiful dress I got for you,' he whispered and broke into tears. The dress would go to flames with Jyotsna's body.

The moment of parting came. The body was laid down on a bamboo stretcher and tied with ropes to prevent it from falling. Anirudh and three other men shouldered the stretcher. The priest took a pot containing the burning faggots and they marched out of the house.

The sun was shining brightly. Anirudh thought that today was the last day when sun's rays would touch Jyotsna's face. He could not believe that he was shouldering the dead body of his wife, a wife, who till yesterday had been bubbling with life and enthusiasm. In two unending streams tears rained from his eyes. Passersby stopped in their way to watch the funeral procession. A madman appeared from somewhere and followed the procession, shouting shrill obscenities on the vagaries of fate.

They reached the cremation ground. Two or three funeral pyres were burning. Few people helped the priest in preparing the pyre. They placed Jyotsna's body on the pyre and covered her with fuel. Funeral pyres were not new to Anirudh. He had spent many days at cremation grounds with Jungali Baba and had witnessed enough funeral pyres. Jungali Baba had taught him to smear his body with the ash of dead bodies and meditate on Shiva for hours. He had told him that they did this to rid their minds of fear and pain that comes from the death of any loved one. But the fear was still there; the pain was still there; Anirudh was being racked by those emotions. In spite of his experiences with Jungali Baba, he could not face Jyotsna's death stoically. The time he had spent with the ascetic had been a waste; it couldn't even cure him of his fear of death.

The priest gave him a glowing faggot to set fire to Jyotsna's body. This was the last duty that he was required to perform for his wife. He wept at the cruelty of life. Friends tried to console him. 'As a person puts on new garments, giving up old ones, the soul similarly accepts new material bodies, after giving up the old ones,' he reflected and set fire to the pyre.

Flames engulfed the pyre. Anirudh watched broken hearted as the crimson flames danced around the body of his beloved. In a few minutes, the pyre was turned into a small patch of black and white ash lying on the ground and the flames were exhausted. The black and white ash was all that was left of Jyotsna – that, and the smoke, which had melted into the air. 'A part of me has burned with the pyre,' Anirudh wept. 'I will never be the same person again.' The dazed mourners began their march back to their homes.

‡

Friends and relatives departed after last words of condolence. The three people closest to Jyotsna – Anirudh, Jyotsna's mother and Kamal – were the only ones in the flat now. Someone was needed to take care of Kamal. It had been decided that Jyotsna's mother should close her room at Jai Ganesh Wadi and shift permanently to the flat.

She sat sobbing in the balcony with Kamal in her lap. Anirudh sat in the living room. The house seemed strangely silent and empty. He got up and looked around with blurred eyes. Everything in the house reminded him of Jyotsna. He could picture her nursing Kamal on the sofa, surfing TV channels, eating at the dining table, cooking food in the kitchen, brushing her teeth in the bathroom and lying down on the bed. Nostalgic memories of how they had scoured many shops to buy appliances and furniture for the house flooded his mind. He missed her arguments, the sound of her voice! Her laughter and her smile! How could he ever recover from the enormous loss that he had suffered? The rest of his life would be spent pining for her.

On a wooden stool in the bedroom was the prayer place, which Jyotsna had created. It had a triptych containing glossy photos of the Hindu trinity – Brahma, Vishnu and Mahesh. In front of the triptych was an idol of Shiva, which Anirudh had received from Jungali Baba, when he was leaving Rishikesh. Out of his mind with grief, he held the God of death directly responsible for the loss of his wife. He picked up the idol and smashed it to pieces on the ground.

He heard someone crying behind him and turned to see his mother-in-law standing with Kamal in her lap. She was sobbing. The expression on her face made it plain to him that she understood the motive behind his smashing of the statue. 'I will clean up the mess,' he said.

'I will do it,' she sobbed.

'You take care of Kamal,' he said. She returned to the balcony. He collected the fragments of the idol with a broom and threw them into the wastebasket.

At night mother-in-law slept in the bedroom with Kamal, while Anirudh made his bed on a mat in the living room. He lay awake till late in the night. Memories harried him. His traumatized state made it easy for the darkness to play tricks on his mind. Every now and then he would have a nagging feeling that he could see Jyotsna's silhouette as she went from one room to another. Any moment he expected her to come out laughing from the bedroom or the kitchen, or hear her sing a lullaby to Kamal.

First thing that woke him up in the morning was the sound of Kamal crying. He got up and went into the bedroom. Mother-in-law was rocking him in her lap.

'He woke up moments ago,' she said apologetically, as if it was her fault that he had woken up. 'I will give him the baby formula.'

'Let me handle him while you prepare the formula,' Anirudh said. He sat down on the bed and took Kamal in his lap. Mother-in-law went into the kitchen. Kamal continued to scream his heart out. Anirudh rocked the child gently. 'Are you crying for mother, Kamal?' he gently whispered. Two drops of tears fell from his eyes on Kamal's cheek.

Mother-in-law returned from the kitchen in two or three minutes holding a feeding bottle half full of baby formula. 'He is hungry. That is why he is crying.'

'You feed him,' Anirudh said, handing over the baby to her.

He went to the balcony. It was 6 AM and the soft glow of he sun had started suffusing the sky. If Jyotsna had been with him, they would now be taking a morning walk, he reflected. She would be wheeling Kamal in the pram and he would be walking beside her. They would discuss and argue about different things. Without her, he felt no desire to step out of the house. He looked at the pram lying in one corner of the balcony. Will this pram ever be used again, he wondered?

In the evening there came a letter from the village. Malti had written that she was all right and this year's rice crop had been reasonably good. She inquired when Jyotsna and Anirudh would be coming to the village with her grandson. Tears dripped from Anirudh's eyes as he went through the letter. He decided not to inform Malti about Jyotsna's death. It made no sense to torture the old woman with news of the horrific event. He would tell her what had happened whenever he went to the village. He wrote her a short letter saying that everyone was okay in Bombay and they would come to the village in a few months.

‡

The mood in the house remained melancholy in the days that followed. Anirudh spent most of his time brooding in the living room, often with tears in his eyes. He tried to pass time watching programs on TV, but none of the programs could sustain his interest and he would change channels frequently. Mother-in-law cooked food for both of them. He ate whatever she served, tastelessly, as a perfunctory duty, without paying any heed to what he was eating.

Kamal was his only relief from the monotony of grief. Whenever the child cried, he would rush into the bedroom with frantic urgency to inquire what the matter was. He feared that the child was not being cared for properly. It had gone out of his mind that the child used to cry even when Jyotsna was alive. Mother-in-law would invariably be there attending to the baby. She would say to him, 'The baby wants to be fondled and petted,' or, 'He has soiled his diapers. They need to be changed,' or, 'The baby is hungry.'

'Make him comfortable,' Anirudh would say and watch her attend to the baby. Sometimes he would take Kamal from her and, rock and pet him himself. If the baby laughed at his ministrations, he felt momentarily uplifted. The child was Jyotsna's supreme gift to him. He had a vague feeling that if he did not keep Kamal happy and cheerful, she would be unhappy wherever she was.

‡

The initial shock wore off after a fortnight. He still got a dull ache in his heart, whenever he thought of Jyotsna, but now he was able to control his emotions and no longer broke into tears. He decided that it was time to get down to the business of making a living. If he allowed himself to wither at home in endless grief, how would Jyotsna's dream of making Kamal a doctor get fulfilled? He owed it to Jyotsna to make Kamal a doctor. It was a pledge that he could not break.

Kamal was sleeping in the crib, when Anirudh got ready to leave in his taxi. He said to his mother-in-law, 'Don't leave his side, even for a moment.'

'I will take care of him, don't worry,' she said.

He found his first passenger quickly, a nattily dressed business executive, carrying a leather handbag in one hand and a cell phone in the other. The passenger sat down in the backseat and said, 'Take me to Nariman Point. I am in a hurry, so drive fast.'

These business executives are always in a hurry, thought Anirudh. Someone should tell them that the sky wouldn't fall down, if they got late by a few minutes. He started the taxi.

'You bastard, what the hell are you doing?' the passenger yelled.

Anirudh almost jumped out of his skin. His face turned red. He turned back to confront the passenger and to his relief found him talking into his cell phone.

'You are going to wreck the company. Due to your mismanagement of funds...' the passenger continued to holler into his cell phone.

Anirudh cursed his dumb luck for getting shackled with such a loud-mouthed passenger. Why can't this fool wait till he was at his destination and then expend his bile to his heart's content? He drove towards Nariman Point, while the passenger raved and ranted in the backseat.

To add to Anirudh's troubles, the road to Nariman Point, thick with vehicles, was almost like a sea of moving metal. In the bumper-to-bumper traffic, he could only maneuver his taxi at a snail's pace. The sound of running engines, screeching tires and impatient horns came from every direction. Air was choked with vehicular exhaust and dust. He cursed the traffic police for their bad traffic management. He cursed the vehicle manufacturers for making polluting vehicles. He cursed the drivers who tried to overtake him. He cursed the municipal workers for leaving garbage along the roadside. He cursed the pedestrians who crossed the road in front of his vehicle. He cursed his passenger for continuing a vile cell phone conversation. He cursed everything and everyone.

He was panting with fury, by the time he dropped his passenger at Nariman point.

‡

A hawker was selling lemon juice on a roadside stall. Anirudh thought that lemon juice would sooth his frayed temper. He stepped out of his taxi and asked the hawker to prepare a glass for him. Within moments the juice was ready and the hawker handed him the glass. Anirudh was about to bring the glass to his mouth, when he noticed a red lipstick smudge on its edge. 'Don't you wash the glasses before serving your customers?' he asked heatedly.

The hawker was a jolly fellow. He smiled at Anirudh's words and said, 'You would not have minded drinking from this glass, if you had seen the woman whose lips made that smudge. She was something to look at. Just like Madhuri Dixit.' He winked mischievously.

'Preserve this glass for your grandfather,' Anirudh said contemptuously. 'I will have my juice in another.'

'As you wish,' the hawker said and prepared another glass.

Anirudh returned to his taxi after finishing the juice. Two college girls, holding a bunch of books in their hands and provocatively dressed in flimsy tank tops and skin fitting Jeans approached the taxi. 'Will you take us to Mithibhai College?' one of them peered into the taxi and asked.

'Sit down,' he said, opening the backdoor of the taxi. The girls chatted and laughed, while he drove towards Mithibhai College. He loathed their merry conversation. It angered him to see anyone happy, when he himself was plunged in the depths of misery. Empty chatterboxes, he called them, in his mind. What do they know about life? They think life is a joyride. Let them grow older and then they will find out, what a pain in the neck life is.

When he returned home at night, he was down in the dumps. Kamal was lying in the crib, laughing and mumbling, as his grandmother jingled a plastic rattle close to his face. Anirudh picked him up from the crib and held him close to his chest. He felt soothed by the intimate contact with his baby. It comforted him to think that his baby did not have the capacity to conceive of the world's ugliness and hence was clean. Clean in the absolute sense. He kissed the baby and basked in a consciousness that was unpolluted and hence was still clean and free. Kamal gurgled with delight and his small hands explored Anirudh's face.

‡

Dusk had set in. He was walking in a street dimly lit with pale yellow streetlights. Where was he going? He didn't know. Suddenly a chasm opened where his feet were and he fell into it. The chasm was full of sewer water and garbage of every imaginable kind. The filth was more than neck deep and he could barely keep his mouth and nose out of it. He felt nauseated and crazily tried to scramble out of the chasm, but its walls were too steep for him to climb out.

He yelled for help. No one responded to his call. He knew that there were people in the street. Why aren't they helping me? He wondered. After a length of time a baby appeared at the chasm's edge. Anirudh realized that it was Kamal and he was about to fall into the chasm. 'Kamal, get back,' he shouted. Instead of stepping back, the baby only laughed and stepped into the chasm. The murky liquid swallowed him instantly. Anirudh splashed around to find Kamal. Moments later, he saw him standing at the other end of the chasm. Kamal's smile had turned into a grimace and there was malevolence on his face. Anirudh cringed with horror. The chasm had succeeded in corrupting his pure child. Slowly the chasm closed in on both of them, burying them in the muck.

He woke up with a start and found himself lying on a mat in the living room. His shirt was drenched with sweat and his breathing labored. The nightmare had left him shaken. Was it possible that someday Kamal would become as loathsome as everyone else he saw around him? God, that could not be true! Was there nothing he could do to protect Kamal? His mind didn't have any answer to these questions. The world around him was too complicated for him to comprehend. There were chasms lurking everywhere. If someone managed to avoid one chasm, then there were second, third, fourth, infinite number of other chasms waiting. In the end everyone had to fall in some chasm and get swallowed. There was no escape.

Jyotsna had been his shield against the world. Only she had the power to protect him and their son. Without her, he was defenseless. If only she had not died. He switched on the living room light and looked at the wall clock. It was only few minutes past midnight. A major part of the night lay ahead. But he wasn't sleepy anymore. This was not unusual, since Jyotsna died he had been sleeping in fits and starts. At times, he remained awake through most of the night. He walked stealthily to the bedroom door and peeped into the bedroom. In the dim light of the night lamp, he could make out Kamal sleeping soundly in the crib. His eyes remained focused on the sleeping child for a few moments and then he plodded into the kitchen for a glass of water.

Back in the living room, he switched on the TV and lounged on the sofa. He browsed through channels randomly before settling on a channel where Bombay's traffic police commissioner was being interviewed. In answer to a question the commissioner was saying, '...the traffic police department is doing all it can to reduce the occurrence of fatal road accidents. Due to our efforts, the number of fatal accidents has gone down compared to last year. 939 people died in road accidents last year, this year the figure stands at 752 only...' Before the commissioner could say anything else, Anirudh flicked at the remote and switched off the TV.

He was disgusted at the casualness with which the commissioner had declared that only 752 fatalities had occurred this year. 'Only 752?' he hissed. 'Doesn't the bastard realize that the figure cannot be only 752 for the relatives of those that died. Jyotsna died in a road accident this year. I will not be consoled by the claim that number of fatalities has gone down. Her death is not a matter of statistics for me. I am going to miss her for all my life.'

He heard rustling sound behind him and turned to see his mother-in-law standing at the door. 'I heard some sound,' she said guiltily.

Anirudh realized that he had been voicing his emotions loudly. 'I was...watching TV,' he mumbled.

Mother-in-law lingered in the room for a moment or two, looking at him with concern, and then went back into the bedroom.

‡

Anirudh reverted to his thoughts. By declaring that only 752 casualties had occurred this year, the commissioner had effectively dehumanized the victims. Wasn't that the most callous thing to do? The commissioner didn't want the viewers to reflect on the pain and anguish associated with each individual case. So he clubbed all the fatalities together and turned them into a number. 939 died last year; 752 died this year; the kill rate has gone down. Bravo! What an efficient commissioner! What an efficient traffic department! Was Jyotsna's death and that of 751 others a matter of mundane statistics? It was not, thundered Anirudh to himself.

The world knows how incompetent the traffic department is. Most perpetrators of fatal accidents never get caught. Jyotsna's killer, the driver of the Toyota, which crushed her, was yet to be apprehended. In fact such was the inefficiency of the traffic department that the Toyota involved in the accident had still not been identified. He felt sure that his wife's killer would in all probability never be caught, just as the driver of the Mercedes, which killed the two teenagers at Mud Island, was allowed to go scot-free.

The two teenagers! He gasped with horror. He had not thought of the Mud Island accident for a long time. Now he realized that the two teenagers were also among the 752 fatalities, along with Jyotsna. Because of his wrong testimony their killer was not caught. He had accepted money to lie under oath. The money that he had received from Gautam Rahi and Ved Rahi was tainted with blood of the two teenagers. It was blood of the two teenagers that had paid for this flat and everything in it. All of a sudden the house started feeling awash with blood. He thought that he could smell the nauseating smell of blood and felt sick.

The time was now ripe for macabre images to dance in his mind. Questions, chilling and extreme, popped up in his mind.

Was there a connection between the death of the two teenagers and that of Jyotsna? Was it because he had brought blood money to his house that Jyotsna died? The questions drove him to the edge of sanity. Suddenly he was convinced that Jyotsna's death was a retribution for his acceptance of blood money. Her death was a punishment for the great crime he had committed. Because he sold himself for money and gave wrong deposition in the Mud Island accident case, destiny had punished him by taking Jyotsna away from him.

O God, don't let that be true, he moaned. I cannot own the blame for Jyotsna's death and continue to live. But there was no respite for him. The implacable accuser in his mind continued to hold him responsible for Jyotsna's death. The very fact that Jyotsna was a victim of a hit-and-run accident, as the two teenagers were, made him certain that there was a connection between the two accidents. Overwhelmed with grief and self-loathing, he cursed himself for his avarice. If only he had refused to be bribed and had allowed justice to prevail in the Mud Island accident, Jyotsna might have been spared the untimely death.

His keen casuistry placed the blame for Jyotsna's death squarely on his shoulders. Casuistry sometimes leads people to commit acts of violence, especially if the mind is in an unhealthy state. That is what was happening to him. The realization that Jyotsna's death was somehow connected to his accepting the money from the Rahi's had paralyzed his mind and had left him at the mercy of random emotions, which had nothing to do with reality. His heart throbbed violently. Tears of rage and frustration filled his eyes. Is there any way by which I can make amends for my great sin? He asked himself hysterically. Goaded by a blind and irresistible force, he groped for something, anything at all, that he could do to make amends for his great mistake.

His thoughts started to center on Gautam Rahi. Not only was Gautam Rahi responsible for killing the two teenagers, but also for Jyotsna's death, albeit indirectly. It was he, who tantalized him into accepting money and changing his deposition. Had Rahi not bribed him, he would not have given wrong testimony and destiny would not have had any cause to take Jyotsna's life. Rahi was the real culprit. He was responsible for Jyotsna's death. Suddenly he was convinced that Jyotsna's death could only be avenged by punishing Rahi. The police would not be of any help against someone as rich as Rahi, who had enough money to bribe his way out of any legal problem.

'I will make him pay dearly for his crime,' Anirudh hissed to himself. 'I have to take matters into my own hands.' Instead of depending on the police, he would directly deliver the punishment. He would have justice; Jyotsna would have justice; the two teenagers would have justice. The justice of the most primeval kind: blood for blood, Jyotsna's blood and that of the two teenagers for Gautam Rahi's blood. He would kill Gautam Rahi and avenge Jyotsna and the two teenagers. He would stab Gautam Rahi to death.

Once the decision was taken, a terrible sense of urgency descended on him. He wanted to execute his mission quickly. He felt restless and his heart throbbed violently.

‡

Sitting in the room became unbearable for him. He needed to move around. His hands and legs hungered for activity. He stood up and went into the balcony. There was not a whiff of air and it felt dull and gloomy. The street below, lit by a long line of streetlights, was completely deserted. The only creatures in sight were a few stray dogs fighting for morsels of food at a garbage dump down the road. The windows in the buildings around him were dark. People were sleeping peacefully in their beds. They were not planning an act of vengeance as he was.

'If only I had a gun,' he murmured to himself, 'That would make it much easier for me to kill Gautam Rahi. But lack of a gun is not going to stop me from doing what has to be done. I will use the large kitchen knife, which Jyotsna had bought to chop mutton pieces. One stab at the right place with it and the person will surely die...'

His reverie was interrupted when he heard a cough. A beat constable was standing directly below the balcony. Where did this guy come from, Anirudh wondered. Maybe he suspects something. Was I murmuring too loudly? Did the constable hear my voice? Does he know that I plan to kill someone tomorrow?

A chill crept up Anirudh's spine. He was desperate to know what went on in the constable's mind. In a moment of reckless courage, he said, 'Hello there. Isn't it too late to be walking in the street?'

The constable looked up and smiled. 'Since thieves remain awake at night, a policeman has to do the same,' he said.

'It is because there are law-enforcers like you in the street, that people like me can feel safe in the house,' Anirudh said glibly.

The constable was visibly pleased. His smile got wider. 'That is what policemen are for – to protect honest citizens,' he said. 'You are not sleeping?'

'I woke up few minutes ago and now I am unable to go back to sleep. So I decided to pass some time in the balcony.'

'On some nights it is difficult to get sleep,' the constable said and walked away swinging his baton.

Anirudh felt amused to see the constable walking away. What a fool I made of him, he thought. I gave him no reason to suspect that I was planning to kill someone tomorrow.

Considering himself to be very smart he returned to the living room and flung himself on the sofa. He sat motionless and contemplated how he would kill Gautam Rahi. He had to plan carefully. It would be a great disaster, if he was caught and handed over to the police before he managed to do the deed.

After deliberating for sometime, he arrived at a rough plan. Tomorrow he would go to Ved Rahi's bungalow and seek an audience with the father and son. He felt sure that the Rahi's would agree to meet him. How could they refuse to meet someone, who had allowed them to get away with murder?

Based on his past experience at their house, he imagined a scenario for this time. A liveried servant would escort him to the lavishly furnished living room and make him sit on the sofa. After that the servant would leave. Few minutes later Ved Rahi and Gautam Rahi would walk into the room. They would occupy seats close to Anirudh. Some pleasantries would be exchanged and after that, Ved Rahi would ask, 'What brings you here?'

'There is something that I want to show,' Anirudh would say.

'What?' Gautam or Ved Rahi would ask.

Anirudh would make sure that there weren't any servants lingering nearby and then he would quickly pull out the large knife that he would be hiding in his clothes. Ved Rahi and Gautam Rahi would gasp with horror. Anirudh would pounce on Gautam and start stabbing repeatedly. The Rahi's would scream for help and Ved Rahi might throw himself on Anirudh to protect Gautam. Anirudh would push Ved Rahi away and continue stabbing Gautam. By the time the servants arrived, Gautam Rahi would be dead.

Anirudh felt satisfied with the plan. He felt confident that he could make it work. His mind moved on to contemplate what would happen after he killed Gautam Rahi. He realized that he could be imprisoned for life or even hanged. His own fate didn't bother him. What bothered him was his son's future.

Kamal had already lost his mother and now he was on the verge of losing his father. How would the poor boy manage to live in this world without both his parents? The thought came to his mind that for the sake of his son, he should refrain from killing Gautam Rahi. However the inclination lasted for a few moments only. The desire to get justice for Jyotsna's death was too strong to be curbed.

There was no question of his giving up the attempt to get justice for Jyotsna and the two teenagers, he told himself. Mother-in-law was there to care for Kamal. She would have at her disposal all the money there was in his bank account. There was also the well-furnished flat and the taxi. She could hand over the taxi to any trusted taxi driver for a fixed sum of monthly rent, which normally amounted to 5000 rupees. Many families in Bombay survived on less than that. There was no reason why mother-in-law and Kamal could not live on that amount. They could use the money that was deposited in the bank, whenever they faced any financial emergency. His stepmother, Malti too would not be financially affected. She had the agricultural land in the village to see her through to the end of her days.

Gradually he convinced himself that his son, mother-in-law and stepmother were not going to face any financial hardship in his absence. But he also understood that it was not just money that a son needed from his father, it was also love and care and guidance. It was too bad, that he would not be around to guide Kamal. But he felt sure that when his son grew up, he would understand why his father had to kill Gautam Rahi. He will respect me for what I have done, Anirudh told himself. After all, I am avenging his mother's death.

‡

His eyes fell on the wall clock and he shuddered. It was 5.15. He could not believe that he had spent almost the whole night in wakefulness. Well, there was nothing surprising in that. How could he waste his time in sleeping when he had to plan for his enterprise? What a momentous enterprise!

He remembered that he had to get the knife from the kitchen before his mother-in-law woke up. A tricky situation would develop, if she caught him hiding the knife in his clothes. She would want to know why he was taking the knife with him. Maybe she would guess that he planned to murder someone and then she would start pleading and beseeching him to come to his senses. A long played out melodrama was the last thing he needed in the morning. He tiptoed towards the kitchen. Not a sound came from the bedroom. Kamal and mother-in-law were still sleeping.

The knife was kept inside a drawer in the kitchen along with few other utensils. He opened the drawer and picked it up. The knife had a three-inch wooden handle and a razor sharp seven-inch blade, which tapered into a needle sharp point. There could be no doubt that when plunged, this knife would sink effortlessly into the body. It was a perfect tool to kill. Anirudh imagined with satisfaction how blood would sprout from Gautam Rahi's torn neck and chest after he finished working on him with this knife. That killer of innocents deserved nothing less than a bloody death.

But there arose a problem. The knife was too big for his trouser pockets. He had to devise a way to conceal it on his person. He decided to sew a cloth sheath for the knife in the inner lining of his trouser. That job had to be accomplished before Kamal and mother-in-law woke up.

He knew where, on a shelf in the living room, Jyotsna used to keep the box containing sewing material. He picked it up from there and sat down on the sofa to mend his trouser. He tore a handkerchief into strips and started sewing the pieces into the inner lining of the trouser. His hand shook violently, but he managed to do the job satisfactorily. He donned the mended trouser and inserted the knife into the sheath. Nothing was visible from outside.

He heard Kamal cry in the bedroom. A sigh of relief escaped his throat. He had managed to finish his job in the nick of time. Without wasting a second, he changed into his pajamas, tagged the trouser containing the knife on a hook and replaced the box containing sewing materials on the shelf. With the evidence of his activities out of the way, he marched into the bedroom to greet his son.

‡

Kamal was screaming in the crib, while mother-in-law changed his diapers.

'Why is he screaming?' Anirudh asked.

'Doesn't he always scream when I change his diapers?' mother-in-law said complacently. 'He probably does not want me to see him naked. In that case, he should stop soiling his diapers.'

'Let me change his diapers,' Anirudh said.

'You don't have to do that, when I am here,' mother-in-law said fretfully.

'I want to change his diapers. Move away.'

Mother-in-law yielded her place reluctantly, but she lingered in the room and kept an eye on how Anirudh was managing the diapers. It seemed as if she wasn't sure he was capable of changing the baby's diapers and expected him to make a mistake. Finally when she was satisfied that the job had been done to her satisfaction, she said, 'I will get the feeding bottle ready.'

'Okay,' Anirudh said. He picked up Kamal in his lap and started rocking and petting him. The baby soon ceased crying. Anirudh went into the balcony. He jingled the bells, fixed in the pram and whispered, 'Your mother used to take you for a ride in this pram. Do you remember her Kamal?'

The baby laughed. A pang arose in Anirudh's heart. He realized that today might be the last day, when he held Kamal in his arms and saw him laugh. Few hours from now, he would be in police custody, arrested for murdering Gautam Rahi. He was overwhelmed with tenderness for his child. How cruelly fate was treating this beautiful child only a few months old? First he lost his mother and now he would lose his father.

Mother-in-law came into the balcony and said, 'Feeding bottle is ready.'

Anirudh took the feeding bottle from her and came into the living room. He sat down on the sofa and started feeding Kamal. Mother-in-law went into the kitchen to do some work.

'Your mother wanted you to become a doctor,' Anirudh whispered, as Kamal sucked at the feeding bottle's nipple. 'I will not be here to help you achieve her ambition. You will have to do that on your own. I am sure you will someday be a great doctor.' He paused for few seconds and then continued, 'If only you could understand me. There is so much that I wish to tell you. Even if we never meet again, you should always remember that your father loves you. The world will tell you that your father is a murderer. You should not believe that. He is a man of justice and of respect.'

He placed the feeding bottle on the center table when the baby was fed. 'Did you like the milk?' he asked. 'Get Kamal's rattle, will you.'

Mother-in-law came out of the kitchen rinsing her hands and fetched the rattle from the bedroom. Anirudh jingled the rattle in front of Kamal's face, making the baby laugh.

‡

Few minutes later, mother-in-law emerged from the kitchen again, this time to remind him of the time. 'It is 7.30 now. Don't you have to get ready for work?'

'Good heavens!' Anirudh uttered. '7.30 already.' He handed Kamal over to mother-in-law and rushed into the bathroom taking his shirt and the trouser containing the knife with him. After sometime, he emerged from the bathroom bathed and dressed.

When he was having his breakfast, mother-in-law, who was sitting on the sofa with Kamal in her lap, asked, 'Did you see our kitchen knife?'

Anirudh was rattled by the question. Did she know that he was hiding the knife in his trousers? Instinctively his eyes went to the spot where the knife lay against his thighs. It was not visible. 'I didn't,' he said looking at her to see if she believed him.

'I can't find it anywhere,' mother-in-law said with some confusion in her voice.

'There are other knives in the kitchen, use them.'

'That is not the point. Things should not get lost from the house,' mother-in-law insisted.

'It must have got misplaced.'

'That is my guess as well.'

Her reply made him realize that he was not under suspicion for taking the knife and he felt comforted. He finished the breakfast quickly and got up to leave. When he was at the door, he turned to say, 'Take good care of my son. I don't want him to suffer for any reason.'

'You don't have to tell me all that,' mother-in-law said simply.

'Go and drive your taxi and stop worrying about my grandson. I will look after him.'

Anirudh nodded and stepped out of the house. It struck 8.30 when he stood next to his taxi. He hesitated for a moment. Should I spare Gautam Rahi? The question would not cease pursuing him. He cursed himself for his vacillation. He patted the knife that lay inside his trouser for reassurance and whispered, 'I will have justice for Jyotsna's death, at any cost.'

With that firm resolve he opened the taxi's door and sat down behind the steering wheel. His heart pounded violently as he started the taxi, but he did not waver and was soon on his way, for a tryst with the men who had tempted him with their money.

Thirteen

He had a long way to go, as the bungalow was situated at the other end of the city, in an area where only the fabulously rich could afford to reside. He avoided as much as possible dwelling on his mission, instead he reflected on the joyous experiences he had shared with Jyotsna. A stream of happy memories made him smile and laugh. Many people, who looked into the taxi, wondered how happy and carefree the taxi driver was. They had no idea what trauma lay concealed beneath the thin veneer of happiness that was reflecting on his face.

An old man dressed in a white safari suit, holding some papers in his hand was crossing the road. Anirudh noticed him from a distance, but didn't slow down, as he felt there was enough distance between them for the old man to safely reach the other side of the road. The old man, however, was not swift enough to get past the taxi in time. Within moments Anirudh realized that and his legs jammed into the brake, while his hand pressed the horn. Tyres screeching and horn screaming, the taxi came to a halt, but not before the front fender had bumped into the old man. The old man fell down. 'My God! Why did this have to happen?' Anirudh cried with horror.

Frantic with worry that the old man may be badly wounded, he jumped out of the taxi and rushed to aid him. The old man didn't require any aid. He got up on his own, beating his dress with his hands, to get rid of the dust he had caught from the street.

'Are you alright?' Anirudh asked.

'Hopefully,' the old man answered.

Anirudh bent down and started gathering the papers belonging to the old man that lay scattered on the street.

A few passersby collected. 'How did this accident happen?' asked one member of the crowd.

'Don't you watch while you are driving cabby?' another said heatedly. 'You almost killed this old man.'

Before Anirudh could speak in his defense, the old man said, 'It was my fault. I should have watched before attempting to cross the road.'

Anirudh felt relieved to see the old man take all the blame on himself. 'Thank you for saying that,' he said gratefully.

'You don't need to thank me for speaking the truth,' the old man beamed.

'Here are your papers.'

The old man received the bunch of papers from Anirudh and said, 'I hope none of my papers have been lost.'

'There is no chance of that. I am sure that I have gathered all of them. I even checked under the taxi.'

Seeing that there was not going to be any confrontation between the driver and the victim, the crowd lost interest in the case and dispersed.

'Allow me to drop you wherever you are going,' Anirudh said.

'Of course, I will let you do that,' the old man said, looking wistfully at the taxi driver. 'This is a fortuitous meeting. Isn't it, Anirudh?'

Anirudh was astonished to hear his name drop from the old man's mouth. 'Do we know each other?'

'Don't we? Have you forgotten me?'

In a sudden flash the realization dawned on Anirudh that it was Jungali Baba standing in front of him. 'Jungali Baba You, of all the people, here,' he exclaimed.

'Didn't I tell you on the day we parted that someday we will meet again?'

'But to meet like this! I almost crushed you under my taxi.'

'Why worry about something that didn't happen.'

'You have changed. What happened to your long matted hair, flowing beard, the trishul you always carried in your hand? I find it astonishing to see you dressed like a normal person.'

'I have returned to what people call normal life.'

'What do you do now?'

'Same thing that I used to do before I became a Naga Sadhu, I am a professor of physics at Bombay University.'

'I had lost all hope of ever meeting you again.'

'Let us go to my house. It is close by,' Jungali Baba said. 'We have a lot to talk about. Don't we?'

'Yes, we do,' said Anirudh. He had forgotten all about his mission to kill Gautam Rahi. They sat in the taxi and Jungali Baba gave Anirudh the directions to his home.

‡

They arrived at an upper-middle-class neighborhood. Jungali Baba's flat was located on the 7th floor of a swanky ten-storey residential building. Anirudh parked the taxi on the roadside and they entered the building. They took the elevator to the seventh floor.

The legend etched on the nameplate at the door was: Yogendra Nath Chaturvedi, Professor of Physics. Jungali Baba saw Anirudh staring at the nameplate and said, 'That is my name.'

'We lived together for so many years, but I never imagined that you could be anything but Jungali Baba.'

'I was Jungali Baba in those days. Yogendra Nath Chaturvedi had gone into hibernation while I was a Naga Sadhu.'

'Has Jungali Baba ceased to exist, since you returned to normal life?'

'Yes, now I am only Yogendra Nath Chaturvedi.'

Jungali Baba opened the door and they entered the living room. A complete wall of the living room was lined with shelves full of rows after rows of leather bound books. Anirudh felt that he had never seen so many books in all his life. In the middle of the room there was a sofa set, with maroon upholstery, and a glass center table. A study table stood in a corner, on which lay a computer. The windows were draped with thick green curtains. A painting of the Ganges emerging from snow-covered mountains was hanging on a wall.

Anirudh looked around the room with amazement.

'You look surprised,' said Jungali Baba.

'I am comparing this place with our hut at Rishikesh.'

'Do you find any similarity?'

'Not any obvious ones! This place gives me a feeling of asceticism, in spite of all the modern things you have here. I don't know why I get that feeling.'

'Asceticism means that one should not clutter up one's life with unnecessary objects and pleasures. My house contains all that I need to be a scholar and a physics professor and nothing else.'

'Just as our hut at Rishikesh contained all that we needed to be a Naga Sadhu and nothing else.'

'Now, you see the connection between the hut and this flat.'

'Yes, both are the abodes of an ascetic,' Anirudh said thoughtfully.

'Sit down, Anirudh,' Jungali Baba said. They sat down on the sofa.

'Since how long have you been in Bombay?' Anirudh asked.

'Two years.'

'Two years! Why didn't you make any attempt to contact me?'

'It's not that I didn't want to meet you. I thought about you very often. But there was a feeling inside me that I will find you when the time was right.'

'I was wondering why you gave up being a Naga Sadhu?'

'One day the truth dawned on me, that I was wasting my time by being a Naga Sadhu.'

Anirudh was taken aback by the words. 'But you were such a dedicated devotee of God.'

'There is no God, my boy,' Jungali Baba said cynically.

'That coming from you...' Anirudh began with consternation and then stopped.

'After years of penances, meditations and austerities, I finally woke up to the reality that there was no place for God in the universe. The universe is a perfect entity, in the sense that it is perfectly regulated by laws of logic, science and mathematics. A whimsical and arbitrary God, who does not care for any rules and regulations, would destroy the universe in a moment.'

'I don't get you.'

'The concept of God was invented by few people, who wanted to subjugate and rule the majority. If you look at history of the world, you will find that every major religion has founded kingdoms, in some part of the world and in some point of time. Has that happened by coincidence or by design? I will give the answer. Religions have founded empires because that was their true purpose. God has nothing to do with the supernatural or the spiritual; it has everything to do with the temporal. In precise terms it has everything to do with power. Power Anirudh, the power to rule, control, subjugate and to destroy. There is this great flaw in the human race that makes it more difficult to motivate people in the name of truth, science or reason, but quite easy to do so in the name of faith, religion and the supernatural. That is why God had to be invented. So that people could be motivated into making sacrifices for founding great empires and civilizations.'

'What a waste,' Anirudh uttered, shaking his head with despair. 'You underwent inhuman austerities for years, in your quest for God, with what result? In the end you found that God didn't exist. The years that you spent as a Naga Sadhu were a complete waste. Your quest was a fruitless journey. Doesn't your failure rankle you and make you furious? Don't you feel the need to go out and vent your anger on someone, who has wronged you somehow?'

'My quest was not fruitless. I became a Naga Sadhu in order to find God and in the end I did find him. God is the body of laws, on the basis of which the universe functions. The cold and simple laws of logic, science and mathematics form the heart, mind and soul of God. My quest was full of hardships, but it was not unsuccessful. I found the God that I quested for. I deciphered his true nature.'

‡

Suddenly Anirudh's hand brushed against the knife that lay concealed in his trouser and he remembered his mission to kill Gautam Rahi. He thought that if he had not encountered Jungali Baba, he would have become a murderer by now.

'What are you thinking?' Jungali Baba asked.

'Nothing,' Anirudh winced. Has Jungali Baba read my mind? Does he know, that I am carrying a knife? The questions asked themselves. He saw that a faint outline of the knife could be made out in his trousers, due to his sitting posture. Anirudh was alarmed, even though the outline was too faint to be deciphered, he felt that Jungali Baba, with his unusually sharp senses might be able to detect the knife. He changed his sitting posture hastily.

'I am eager to know all about you. How you live? The people who have come into your life?' Jungali Baba said.

'I am an ordinary taxi driver.'

'You make an honest living. That is something to be proud of.'

'Yeah,' Anirudh mumbled sadly as if he was not convinced that his profession was something to be proud of.

Jungali Baba gazed at Anirudh's sad face for a moment or two and then getting up from the sofa said, 'I will make tea for both of us. After that you must tell me all about yourself.'

'I will come with you. I want to see the rest of your house,' Anirudh said and got up with Jungali Baba.

There were three more rooms – the dining room, the bedroom and the study with shelves after shelves stocked with books. These rooms, like the living room carried an air of uncluttered living and were fastidiously neat.

'Do you keep a servant to help you manage the house?' Anirudh asked.

'I do everything myself. The years that I spent as Naga Ṡadhu have imparted me with enough discipline to take care of myself.'

They went to the kitchen. Jungali Baba placed a pot containing sugar, tea powder, milk and water on the gas stove to boil. Anirudh watched Jungali Baba prepare the tea. He remembered how they used to cook food, on open fire, when they lived in the hut on the banks of Ganga. They returned to the living room with two cups of tea.

'Tell me about yourself,' Jungali Baba said.

Anirudh thought for a moment and said, 'I don't know where to begin.'

'Are you happy?'

'I am passing through a rough patch. My wife died few days ago.'

'Oh! I am sorry to hear that. Do you have any children?'

'A son, about two months old.'

'What do you call him?'

'Kamal.'

'I can make out by your face that you are traumatized by your wife's death.'

'I was very close to her.'

'Tell me about your wife. How did you find her? What kind of a woman was she? Tell me about the times that you spent with her.'

A floodgate opened inside Anirudh, and the thoughts, the feelings, the memories that he had been withholding inside him since Jyotsna's death, started tumbling out one after the other. Talking about the halcyon days that he had spent with Jyotsna was like an emotional catharsis for him. His mood fluctuated between happiness and sadness, according to the nature of the incident that he was describing. His monologue lasted for a long time. Jungali Baba listened attentively and sympathetically.

When he reached the end of his narrative, he said, '...I had been on my way to kill Gautam Rahi, when my taxi struck you.'

Without batting an eyelid, Jungali Baba said, 'I was wondering why you were carrying a knife in your trouser. Now I know why.'

Anirudh was not surprised. He said mildly, 'I feared that you would have noticed the knife.'

'I could make out the knife's contour when you sat on the sofa.'

Anirudh pulled out the knife from his trouser and placed it on the center table. 'It is not comfortable, sitting with this thing in one's pant's.'

'I don't doubt it,' Jungali Baba said, looking at the long knife. 'I feel pained that I didn't get a chance to meet Jyotsna. She must have been a wonderful person.'

'Yeah, that she was,' uttered Anirudh, with a sigh. 'Do you think that she would have remained alive, had I not received money from Gautam Rahi?'

'You made a grievous mistake by accepting the bribe. You should not have allowed the lure of money to deviate you from the path of truth. However, Jyotsna didn't die because of that mistake of yours.'

Anirudh waited for Jungali Baba to explain himself.

'A human being has total control on all aspects of his life, except on two things: birth and death,' Jungali Baba said. 'Birth and death are the exclusive preserve of the capricious entity called chance. Only chance can decide when a person will be born and when he or she would die. Your wife died because she happened to be at the wrong place, at the wrong time. Had she been a few minutes early or late at the spot, where the accident took place, or if she had been standing a few feet away, then the vehicle might have missed her and she might have still been among the living. Her death was an accident or in other words sheer bad luck. Your action or Gautam Rahi's action had nothing to do with her death.'

'But I keep getting the feeling that Jyotsna died because I accepted money from Gautam Rahi and changed my deposition.'

'It is your guilty conscience which gives you this feeling. You must have seen people flagellating themselves outside places of worship? They do so to repent for their sins, real or imagined. You, too, are indulging in self-flagellation, by presuming that there is a connection between Jyotsna's death and your acceptance of money from Gautam Rahi. You are accusing yourself of Jyotsna's death to repent for your sin. You planned to kill Gautam Rahi because subconsciously you felt that by killing him, you will be able to punish yourself effectively. Such guilt complexes and self-accusations become more prominent in a person who is under stress, which you are. You are traumatized by your wife's death. Your mind is unable to accept that someone like her could perish in an ordinary accident. You want to believe that her death is an extraordinary event, a wrath of the Gods, a divine punishment for your crime.' Jungali Baba paused for one or two moments and then said, 'That is simply not the case. You have been deluding yourself.'

'Why did she die?' Anirudh's voice was a wail of pain.

'She died because she was unlucky enough to get struck by a moving car. Death is like a lottery ticket, where winning and losing depend solely on the vagaries of chance. Human beings have the power to make whatever they want of their lives, but birth and death are beyond their control. You are assuming too much on yourself, when you think that your actions may have led to Jyotsna's death. Even if you had refused the bribe and given correct deposition, you could not have forced the capricious chance into sparing her life. Human beings don't possess the power to influence chance. Chance happenings are events that just happen, without any rhyme or reason, so there is no way for anyone to do anything about them.'

Anirudh looked at the knife that lay on the center table and wondered if it was mere chance, which saved Gautam Rahi's life today.

'There is something else that I want to tell you,' Jungali Baba said. 'Even though I no longer believe in the existence of the God, I remain a firm believer in life after death. People do not fade into oblivion after they die. The soul continues to exist after the body gets destroyed. Your wife has shed her body, but her soul is still conscious. She is sitting beside you. I can feel her presence.'

'What? Where?' Anirudh panted.

'She has not left your world. Her soul has remained by your side from the day she died.'

'How is she?'

'She is very sad. Your constant grief has anguished her. When you took the decision to kill Gautam Rahi, she was frightened out of her wits. She cried and tried to reason with you, but of course you could not hear her.'

'I…I am confused. I can't understand what you are saying.'

'She is worried about Kamal's future. There will be no one left to care for her son, if you go to jail after murdering Gautam Rahi.'

'I never knew…'

'You must get hold of yourself,' Jungali Baba did not wait to hear what Anirudh had to say. 'Your wife needs you even after her death. Her soul will not attain peace, while you are languishing in grief. For the sake of your wife, you should now forget her and begin a new life.'

'I didn't know that my grief was hurting Jyotsna.'

'You must get the idea of punishing Gautam Rahi out of your mind. Gautam Rahi was not responsible for Jyotsna's death and neither were you. You don't need to punish yourself any more, for the mistake you made by accepting the bribe. The trauma you have suffered over that mistake has been punishment enough. You are a free man now.'

Some of the cobwebs shifted from Anirudh's mind and he breathed a deep sigh of relief. 'I am lucky to have met you today.'

'I think it was your wife, who brought me in front of your taxi. She wanted to stop you from reaching Gautam Rahi's house.'

'Can that be true?'

'She will do anything for you. Her love for you is unbounded.'

A cool breeze came in from the window and lapped Anirudh's face. The breeze carried the fragrance of Jyotsna's body. Anirudh knew that she was close by.

'I thought that I had lost her when she died,' he whispered. 'Now I realize that she is still with me.'

'She is happy now, as she knows that you are out of danger.'

'It was her ambition to make Kamal a doctor. Will I be able to make her dream come true? Can a taxi driver make his son a doctor?'

'Kamal will one day be a great doctor, I am sure of that. I will help him in becoming a doctor.'

'Really, will you help Kamal?'

'I don't have a family of my own. You are the person closest to me. I consider you as my son and Kamal as my grandson. I will do anything for both of you.'

Anirudh's face lit up with happiness. The wind murmured, as it moved through the window and it sounded like a woman's laughter. Was Jyotsna laughing?

... In the adjacent flat someone switched on the radio. 'Life,' said a solemn voice, 'goes on ...'